THE PILOT PULLED UP on the control stick and the heli-copter started to climb. Too fast though, lurching sideways. The helicopter spun. A treetop passed the windshield. Nicole shrieked.

The helicopter dropped. The pilot swore and reached for something—

The tail hit the tree. Metal crunched as everyone went flying.

"Seat belts!" Daniel shouted as the helicopter lurched.

I heard Corey yell, "Holy hell!" and looked back to see a hole in the tail end of the helicopter.

Daniel yanked me onto his lap, and managed to get the belt over both of us.

"Kenjii!"

She stumbed to me and I grabbed her with both arms, wrapping them around her as tight as I could.

I heard Nicole yell, "Dad!"

And then we hit.

ALSO BY KELLEY ARMSTRONG

THE DARKEST POWERS TRİLOGY
The Summoning
The Awakening
The Reckoning

THE DARKNESS RİSİNG TRİLOGY
The Gathering

DARKNESS RISING
❧BOOK TWO❧

the Calling

DISCARD

KELLEY ARMSTRONG

HARPER
An Imprint of HarperCollinsPublishers

The Calling

www.epicreads.com

Library of Congress Cataloging-in-Publication Data

Armstrong, Kelley.

The calling / Kelley Armstrong. — 1st ed.

p.   cm. — (Darkness rising ; bk. 2)

Summary: Maya and her friends—all of whom have supernatural powers—have been
kidnapped after fleeing from a forest fire they suspect was deliberately set, and after a
terrifying helicopter crash they find themselves pursued by evildoers in the Vancouver
Island wilderness.

ISBN 978-0-06-179706-4

[1. Supernatural—Fiction.   2. Shapeshifting—Fiction.   3. Survival—Fiction.
4. Wilderness areas—Fiction.   5. Vancouver Island (B.C.)—Fiction.   6. Canada—
Fiction.]   I. Title.

PZ7.A73369Cal 2012   2011024391

[Fic]—dc23   CIP

                                                                                    AC

Typography by Erin Fitzsimmons

13   14   15   16   17   LP/RRDH   10   9   8   7   6   5   4   3   2

❖

First paperback edition, 2013

For Julia

ONE

I DON'T KNOW WHO WAS more anxious—Daniel or Kenjii—but they weren't making this emergency helicopter evacuation any easier. I patted Kenjii and she shifted until her full hundred pounds of German shepherd rested squarely on my feet. When I tried to wriggle away, she moved closer and pinned my legs. I sighed and glanced at Daniel. He was staring out the window, fingers drumming.

I twisted to look at the others. Daniel and I were in the first passenger row, behind the pilot and Mayor Tillson, who was in the copilot's seat. Behind us were the mayor's daughter, Nicole, and his niece, Sam Russo, gazing out their respective windows. Hayley Morris and Corey Carling sat in the last row. Hayley was talking; Corey wasn't listening.

"We're going north." Daniel had to yell to Mayor Tillson to be heard over the helicopter noise. "We're supposed to be heading to Victoria, aren't we?"

When the mayor didn't respond, the pilot said, "Change of plans, son. Victoria's backed up with evacuees.

We're taking you to Vancouver."

"Okay, so why are we heading *north*?"

We live on Vancouver Island, near Nanaimo, which is almost directly west across the Strait of Georgia from the city of Vancouver, British Columbia.

"Wind," the pilot said. "Same one that's driving that fire is forcing us to circle north. Don't worry. I'll have you there in an hour."

I looked at Daniel. His face was drawn with worry. I couldn't blame him, under the circumstances. We'd outrun a forest fire and outwitted a mysterious fake rescue team only to be whisked from town before we had time to catch our breath.

I was worried, too, about a lot of things, but right now, mostly about Rafe Martinez, unconscious on the floor behind my seat. How much smoke had he inhaled? What was he going to do when he found out that his sister, Annie, was still missing?

I twisted the bracelet on my wrist. A cat's-eye stone on a worn leather band. Rafe's. He'd want it back when he found out that I'd told them not to wake him up because he wouldn't leave without Annie. That would be the end of anything between us. But I could live with that. Better than I could live with myself if I'd let him die in that inferno.

"Are the other helicopters going to Vancouver, too?" Daniel asked. "The ones with our parents?"

"I believe so," the pilot said. "Is that right, sir?"

When Mayor Tillson didn't answer, the pilot glanced over. "Sir?"

He bent to see the mayor's face and chuckled. "Seems someone doesn't mind the racket this bird makes. He's sound asleep. I'm sure he said the other helicopter was just a few minutes behind us."

I leaned forward. The mayor was slumped in his seat, his face toward the window, at an angle that didn't look comfortable at all. When I undid my seat belt, the pilot glanced back.

"Whoa, none of that. This isn't a 747. Belt on at all times. Maya, isn't it?"

I scooted to the edge of my seat and touched the mayor's arm. "Mr. Tillson?"

"Hey," the pilot said, voice sharp. "If you want me to check on your parents, just say so. Your mayor has had one hell of a day with this fire, and you kids running off didn't help. Let the man get some rest."

Sure, the mayor must be exhausted, but with everything that happened, I doubted he could relax enough to fall asleep.

"Mr. Tillson?" I said, shaking him harder.

Daniel undid his belt. Sam did, too, getting up and walking forward, hunched, as she stepped over Rafe.

"Okay, that's enough!" the pilot barked. "In your seats, belts on. Everyone!"

"Or what?" Sam said. "You'll pull over and make us walk the rest of the way?" She shook the mayor's shoulder. "Uncle Phil?"

Mayor Tillson's head lolled. Nicole shrieked and fumbled with her belt. I pressed my hand to the mayor's neck.

"Is he all right?" the pilot said, sounding concerned now.

"He's breathing," I said.

"Could it be a heart attack?" Sam asked.

Before I could answer, the pilot cursed and said, yes, that must be it, with the stress and all, and the mayor was, as he put it, "a big guy." He'd get a doctor on the helipad right away.

"Wh-what?" Nicole said, scrambling over Rafe. "Did he say heart attack?"

"If it is, we'll get help," I said as Corey pulled her back.

The pilot was on the radio to his dispatcher, filling him in between bouts of yelling at us to sit down.

I moved in front of the mayor to undo his jacket. When Sam tried to wedge up beside his chair, Daniel nudged her toward our seats. Anyone else, she'd have told him to go to hell, but she listened to Daniel.

"Maya can help," Nicole said when the pilot tried sending me back to my seat. "She knows first aid. She runs a hospital."

"For *animals*," Hayley said.

Corey told her to shut up, but she had a point. My dad was the local park ranger, and I had a rehabilitation shed for nursing injured animals back to health. I did know first aid, though, and the basics of dealing with a heart attack victim. Step one: call a doctor. Kind of tough, under the circumstances. Step two: give the victim an aspirin. That wouldn't work while he was unconscious. But *why* was he unconscious? I remembered fainting as one of the signs, but not sustained lack of consciousness.

We had to get him to a doctor and, until then, I could only presume it was heart failure and perform CPR if he stopped breathing.

I unbuttoned the mayor's shirt. When Nicole inched forward, the pilot snapped at her, and Corey told him to go to hell, which really didn't help matters. I glanced at Daniel.

"Nicole," Daniel said, "I know you're worried, but he's okay. He's breathing and we're looking after him." He turned to the others. "Sit down, guys. Everything's under control."

It didn't matter that Daniel barely raised his voice and the pilot's shouting and the noise of the helicopter almost drowned him out. Everyone sat. Even Kenjii, who'd been anxiously nosing the mayor's hand.

"We need to get him lying down," I said. "If it's cardiac arrest, his heart may stop. I can't perform CPR while he's sitting."

"Then you aren't performing CPR," the pilot said. "There's no room. We'll be landing soon."

I laid my palm against the mayor's bare chest. I could feel his heart. Beating, but fluttery. Was that a sign of a heart attack? As I moved back, I saw a spot of blood on the shoulder of his shirt, where we'd peeled his jacket away. I remembered the mayor putting on his Windbreaker before climbing into the helicopter.

"We need to get his jacket off," I said.

As Daniel helped me get the mayor out of it, the pilot yelled, "Whoa! Hold on! Back in your seats. We'll be landing in a few minutes."

Fortunately, as long as he was flying the helicopter, all the pilot could do was yell. And if there are teenagers who actually respond to adults shouting at them, I've never met one.

When we got the mayor's jacket off, I checked his upper arm. There was a puncture wound. A dot, slightly swollen, crusted in dried blood.

"Injection?" I mouthed to Daniel.

He frowned and leaned to my ear. "Could be an insect . . . No, wait. Before we got on, the pilot clapped Mr. Tillson on the arm. I remember the mayor rubbing the spot, like it hurt." He paused. "Like he'd been injected."

Daniel slowly turned on the pilot. I could feel the rage pulsing off him. I grabbed his arm and squeezed so tight it had to hurt. Only then did he drop his gaze.

"His heart's beating fine," I said to the pilot. "Just have someone waiting at the pad."

I refastened the mayor's seat belt, then started moving back toward my seat. I don't know exactly what happened next. My gaze was on Nicole, who looked terrified. I think the pilot grabbed for me. Or maybe he just reached out to get my attention.

Daniel yelled "No!"

That's all he did. I'm sure of it. Daniel shouted and the pilot snapped forward. His head cracked against the instrument panel, and he crumpled in his seat.

"Wake him up!" Hayley shouted. "Someone wake him up!"

Daniel and I shook the pilot. The helicopter dropped a couple of feet and we stumbled. Corey ran over.

"Help me get him out!" he shouted to Daniel as he grabbed the front of the pilot's jacket. "I can fly it."

"Based on what?" Sam appeared at his side. "Video games?"

Corey scowled. "You got a better idea?"

"Yes."

The boys pulled the pilot out of the way and dumped him in the narrow gap behind the front seats.

Sam slid into his spot, grabbed the throttle and the control stick, then planted her feet on both pedals. The helicopter stabilized and began to rise, but listed to one side.

"You have to get her level," Corey said.

"No, really?"

He reached for the control stick. Sam swatted him aside.

"Do you know helicopters? Or just planes? Because they're not the same."

The helicopter leveled for a second, then started to spin.

"Sam doesn't know what she's doing," Hayley said. "Stop her."

"She's keeping us in the air," I said.

"Everyone else?" Daniel said. "Sit down and put on your belts. Now."

Hayley and Nicole obeyed, but Corey hovered at the front, wedged between Sam and me.

I reached for the radio and put on the headset. It took some fiddling to get the radio going, but we had a shortwave at the park, so I had some idea how to operate it.

"SOS!" I said. "Helicopter out of Salmon Creek. Pilot unconscious. Repeat, helicopter pilot unconscious."

I stopped transmitting and listened. Static.

"SOS!" I said. "Emergency situation. Helicopter over Vancouver Island. Pilot unconscious. Repeat, pilot *unconscious!*"

The helicopter dropped again.

Corey bent to look at the control panel. "You need to—"

"I'm working on it!" Sam snarled.

"Here, let me—"

I didn't see what Corey did, but the helicopter pitched to the side, hard and sharp. Corey fell onto the mayor. Kenjii barked, claws scraping the floor as she slid onto the unconscious pilot.

Sam swore, her hands shaking as she reached for a lever. "Everyone sit down. Just sit down!"

The helicopter lurched again and Sam's hand hit something. A crack and a rush of air. Nicole shrieked. This time, Hayley joined her.

"The door!" Corey said. "Holy hell. The door's open!"

"Everyone hang on!" Daniel yelled. "Maya, grab Kenjii!"

I lunged for the dog's collar and, just then, I heard a gasp. Everyone was yelling and wind rushed through the half-open door and I shouldn't have heard anything. But I heard that gasp.

"Rafe!" I screamed.

As I turned, I saw a blur of motion. Rafe, his eyes opening as he sailed across the floor of the helicopter. Out the open door.

TWO

I DIDN'T THINK. I shoved Kenjii into the safe nook between the front seats and scrambled toward the door as the helicopter jolted again, righting itself.

Daniel lunged for me and missed. Wind rushed in through the open door. I could barely breathe, barely see. Then I saw Rafe's hands gripping the bottom frame.

Rafe's hands *slipping* from the bottom of the door.

I dropped and grabbed his wrists just as he lost his grip. As he fell, I shot forward. I kicked wildly, trying to hook something with my legs. Then someone caught my foot and I stopped with a jolt.

I didn't need to look back to see who had me. The same person who'd had my back since we were five. Daniel.

"Corey, get over here!" he shouted.

The helicopter lurched, and I slid again, Daniel still

holding my ankle. My hands were locked around Rafe's wrists, his around mine. Then Corey caught my other foot, and the helicopter leveled off.

I could hear them shouting inside. Their words came in fits and starts, sucked away by the wind roaring past my ears. And in those first few seconds of confusion, I didn't really even understand what had happened. I could hear the wind. Feel the wind. Taste it even. But it took a moment for me to crack my eyes open and realize I was hanging outside the helicopter.

Hanging outside the helicopter.

The earth bobbed and whirled below us, trees and rock and water spinning into a blur.

"Don't look down!" I thought it was Daniel, but then realized Rafe was staring up at me.

"I've got you!" I shouted.

He smiled, this weirdly calm smile. "I know."

"Just hold on!"

"I am."

"We'll get you down."

"It's okay, Maya."

His voice was as strangely calm as his smile. My heart was thudding so hard I could barely breathe, and he just kept smiling up at me, his gaze locked on mine. Calm washed through me, slowing my heart, as if I was feeling what he did, an oddly disconnected peacefulness.

"It's okay," Rafe said again. "They've got you."

The helicopter spun, whipping us around. Pain shot through me as Rafe's weight almost wrenched my shoulders out of their sockets, and my hold on his wrists broke. Corey lost his grip on my leg. I heard him shout and Daniel shout and the girls join in, and I kicked, trying to get my leg back up where someone could grab it.

The helicopter tilted again. I started to slide, Daniel sliding with me. And I knew we were going to fall. Rafe, me, Daniel, we were all going to fall.

"Hold on!" I shouted to Rafe.

"It's okay," he said, and I wasn't even sure he spoke aloud, didn't see his lips moving. "It's okay."

He let go.

I clawed the air, screaming.

I didn't even see him drop. The helicopter banked and I caught only a blur of treetops spinning past and when I looked around, there was no Rafe. No sign of him at all.

Corey and Daniel dragged me back into the helicopter. Someone got the door closed. I don't know who. I was crying and shaking so hard I couldn't see, couldn't hear, couldn't think.

As I huddled on the floor, I felt Daniel behind me, his arms around me. Kenjii pushed onto my lap, and I buried my face in her fur, gripping handfuls and sobbing against her.

It took a moment before anything else penetrated, but when it did, I heard Sam and Corey arguing, Nicole crying, and I felt the helicopter jerk and shudder, and I remembered where I was and what was happening. I couldn't break down now. No matter what had happened, I couldn't break down now.

I pushed my dog away, patting her head, and staggered to my feet. Daniel rose with me, his hand still on my arm.

"Maya."

"I'm . . ." *I'm what? Fine? Good? Okay? No. I'm not. I'm absolutely not.* I took a deep breath. "We need to land."

My voice shook. My whole body shook. I could hardly breathe, it hurt so much. But I squeezed up to the front of the helicopter. Sam glanced over. She opened her mouth. Nothing came out.

"He might be okay," Nicole said. "He might—"

"He's not," I said. "We all know he's not."

I couldn't even hope Rafe had survived because that would mean I'd have to think about it—about him and what just happened and if I did, I'd curl up in a ball on the floor again.

I started toward Sam. I had to talk to her. Get her to land the helicopter. But I froze. Just . . . froze.

Daniel nudged past me. "We need to land this," he said to Sam.

"That's what—"

"That's what you've been trying to do, I know." His voice was calm, reassuring. "But we need to get her down, any way we can. Before anyone else gets hurt."

She swallowed hard. Her hands trembled on the controls. Daniel crouched beside her, his hand on her shoulder.

"How much do you know about flying?"

"M-my dad had a friend who was a helicopter pilot. He showed me how. That was a couple of years ago. It's not the same as his helicopter either. I'm really trying but—"

"I know you are. How do we get her down? We're over the strait now. Does that help? Water?"

"I don't think so. I need open ground. Just a small piece, but I can't find any. It's all trees and—"

"What about that island?"

Daniel pointed to one of the many small islands dotting the strait below us. It was partially bare, as if the owner had cleared it for building.

"I—I can try," Sam said.

From most people, the hesitation would be expected. From Sam—the girl who was afraid of nothing—it meant our chances were slim. But what choice did we have? Nicole was trying to rouse her dad. Hayley was doing the same with the pilot. I took the headset and got on the radio again. No one was responding. So either we tried to land or we kept flying until Sam lost control and we plunged into the strait.

"You can do this, Sam," Daniel said. "You know you can."

He kept reassuring her as I worked on the radio. Why wasn't anyone answering? The pilot had been talking to someone just before he collapsed.

Or had he? Even if he had, I realized it was probably whoever he worked for. Whoever told him to drug the mayor and fly us off course.

And who was that? Who *would* do that? The same people who'd chased us through the blazing woods?

"You're doing great," Daniel said to Sam as treetops came into view. "Hell, I could jump out from here."

"You might want to do that," she said shakily.

"Tell you what," Daniel said. "Take her lower, and if you don't think you can set her down, everyone will jump. Everyone except you and me. Okay?"

She nodded.

"And it's not like landing a plane, right?" he continued. "You just set her down, nice and—"

A yelp from Hayley cut him short. I wheeled to see the pilot shoving her aside as he started for us.

Hayley screamed, then said, "He burned me! Oh my God."

I could actually smell burned fabric, and there was a brown patch on her shirt. As the pilot lurched forward, I swore his eyes glowed.

"Hey!" Daniel said. "Hold on!"

The pilot yanked Sam out of the seat and slid in.

"Just put her down here," Daniel said. "We lost—"

The pilot pulled up on the control stick and the helicopter started to climb. Too fast though, lurching sideways. The helicopter spun. A treetop passed the windshield. Nicole shrieked.

The helicopter dropped. The pilot swore and reached for something—

The tail hit the tree. Metal crunched as everyone went flying.

"Seat belts!" Daniel shouted as the helicopter lurched.

I heard Corey yell, "Holy hell!" and looked back to see a hole in the tail end of the helicopter.

Daniel yanked me onto his lap, and managed to get the belt over both of us.

"Kenjii!"

She stumbled to me and I grabbed her with both arms, wrapping them around her as tight as I could.

I heard Nicole yell, "Dad!"

And then we hit.

THREE

THE HELICOPTER LANDED NOSE down and tilted onto its side. My head cracked against Daniel's and I must have lost consciousness for a moment, because next thing I knew, water was flooding in.

The helicopter creaked as it teetered, and I knew we must be perched on an underwater ledge . . . over what could be a very deep body of water.

I twisted to tell Daniel, but he was already pushing me toward the other side, saying, "I know." Then, "Everyone! Get over there!"

I glanced back to see Nicole and Sam sitting there, just staring. Corey bent over Hayley, then picked her up. She lay like a rag doll in his arms.

"She's okay," he said. "Just unconscious."

"Dad!" Nicole shrieked.

I turned toward the front seat. The pilot was dead. He'd gone out the windshield, and was now draped over the crumpled front of the helicopter. Tendrils of blood snaked through the water all around him.

Mayor Tillson still wore his seat belt, but he was wedged in, the crushed dashboard pinning his big chest. Blood dribbled from his mouth.

I pressed my fingers to his neck. No pulse.

"He's—" I began.

"No, he's not!" Nicole shoved me so hard the helicopter rocked.

"Let's get him out of there." Daniel looked for Corey, who was still holding Hayley. "Sam? Give me a hand? Nic and Maya, stay over by the door with Kenjii and keep that side weighed down."

Sam and Daniel grabbed the mayor under his armpits and pulled, but he wasn't budging, and with every wrench, the helicopter rocked. Daniel bent to peer under the crushed cockpit, and Sam checked her uncle for a pulse. When Daniel came back up, shaking his head, she shook hers, too, biting her lip and blinking hard.

Daniel turned to Nicole. "He's gone, Nic. There's nothing—"

"No, he's not!" she shouted. "You're only saying that because Maya did. You always listen to her."

Everyone stopped and stared. Sweet, quiet Nicole stood there, her face twisted with rage, hair coming loose from her ponytail, spiking around her face, her mascara running.

I moved up to Daniel and Sam and whispered, "She's in shock. Let me see if I can get his legs free."

"There's no use," Sam said. "He's—"

My look shushed her. I squeezed in as far as I could to get a better look, but the slightest movement made the helicopter rock.

"You need to get off," Daniel said as he crouched beside me.

"Of course she does," Nicole said. "You're always worried about Maya. Why? She doesn't deserve—"

Sam spun on her. "Shut the hell up!"

Daniel and I stared at both of them. It was Corey who murmured, "Nic didn't mean it, guys. She just lost her dad."

"And I just lost my uncle," Sam said.

"Take Nicole out," Daniel said. "Please. Before—"

The helicopter groaned again and began to tilt.

"Off!" Daniel shouted. "Everyone off!"

He grabbed the door handle. Sam and I helped, all three of us yanking until it finally opened. Water poured in, but it only came up to midcalf. Land was a few meters away.

Corey went first, carrying Hayley. Sam, Nicole, and I followed. The helicopter jerked. I lost my footing and plunged backward into the icy water that filled the cockpit. Daniel grabbed my arm and Kenjii swam to me, taking my shirt in her teeth and hauling me until Sam could pull me out, Daniel right behind us.

The helicopter gave one final wail, metal scraping on rock, then rolled off the ridge into the deep water.

"Kenjii!" I shouted.

Sam and Corey had to hold me back as I fought and screamed for my dog. Daniel jumped in. He'd barely gone under when Kenjii surfaced. I ripped free from the others and waded to the edge as Daniel climbed back onto the ledge. Kenjii's nails kept slipping on the underwater rocks, but with me pulling on her collar and Daniel pushing from behind, we managed to heave her up.

We waded through the knee-deep water toward the tiny island. As soon as I was on land, I let myself collapse and would have stayed there if Daniel hadn't caught me under the arms and propelled me to higher ground. I was about to drop on the grassy bank when Corey shouted, "It's Hayley! She's not breathing!"

I stumbled to where he crouched beside her.

"I was sure she was breathing before," he said. "I should have let you check. *Damn* it."

Hayley lay on her back in the long grass. Her skin was tinged blue.

Daniel steered Corey away as I ripped open Hayley's shirt and started chest compressions. He sat Corey down and told him to stay there, then returned, and took over the compressions while I breathed into her ice-cold lips.

On my third breath, I felt her chest move. On the fourth, she coughed. We got her sitting up and breathing.

"Wh-what happened?" she said, looking around. "Where's the helicopter?"

I told her. She just sat there, nodding, like it wasn't sinking in, but when I asked if she understood, she snapped that she wasn't stupid, and I backed off.

I kept backing off until I found a flat place to sit. Daniel slid in behind, arms around me, letting me lean back against him. Kenjii came over and put her head on my lap and I cried then. Just cried.

When I could finally speak, I twisted to face Daniel and said, "It's my fault Rafe's dead."

"No, it isn't," he said fiercely. "I'm the one who knocked out the pilot."

"How? You never touched him?"

"I—I don't know. I startled him or something."

I shook my head. "You didn't. I don't know what happened, but it wasn't your fault. I'm not talking about the crash anyway. I mean that if it wasn't for me, Rafe wouldn't have fallen."

"No, Maya. He let go. I saw it. He made a choice and there was nothing you could do about that."

"I—"

"He did the right thing. If he'd held on, you'd have fallen, and maybe me, too. I know it doesn't make this any easier, but he did the right thing."

"That's not what I mean. He should never have been on that helicopter. If I'd let them wake him up, he'd have insisted on staying to find Annie."

Daniel shook his head. "They'd have put him on that helicopter whether he wanted to go or not."

"But he'd have been awake. He wouldn't have fallen—"

"If he resisted getting on, they'd have sedated him, just like they did with the mayor. You know he'd have resisted. Nothing would have changed."

When I tried to look away, he caught my chin and turned me to face him.

"Nothing," he said.

My eyes filled with tears again. "It doesn't seem real. The fire. The people in the forest. The helicopter crash. Mayor Tillson. Rafe." I looked up at him again. "It can't be real. I'm asleep. It's a nightmare. Tell me it is."

He hugged me so tight my ribs protested. "I wish I could."

His voice cracked and I hugged him back, as hard as I could.

Someone cleared his throat behind us. It was Corey. He crouched and said, in a low voice, "I know this is a bad time, guys. I'm really sorry. But the girls— They're freaked out and they need someone to tell them what to do and . . . that's not me. They want one of you two. Daniel, I'll stay here with Maya if you can talk to them."

I wiped my sleeve over my eyes. "No. Sitting here isn't going to help." It just gave me a deep, dark pit to lose myself in when I really couldn't afford to be lost.

We both got up and followed Corey.

Nicole and Hayley were huddled in the long grass, staring out at the island to the west. Vancouver Island. Our island. Shrouded in fog.

The girls were shivering. Even Sam, leaning against a tree, twisting the bar in her ear, was trembling, though she kept giving herself an abrupt shake, as if annoyed by her weakness.

I had to give myself a shake, too—a mental one—as I took stock of our surroundings.

With the fog rolling in, I couldn't tell how big our island was. But it had looked small from the air. The ground was rocky, with patches of long grass and scrubby trees.

The sky was overcast, so dark I thought night was coming until I checked my watch and realized it wasn't even six.

Mom had been in Victoria when the forest fire broke out. Was Dad with her now? Were they waiting for our helicopter to land? Planning what we'd have for dinner to take my mind off the forest fire?

Had Dad's helicopter gone to Victoria? Was it only our helicopter that had been diverted or . . . ?

"Maya?" Daniel said.

Don't think about that. Can't think about that. We needed to get some place warm and dry before dark.

I whispered that to Daniel. He gestured for me to walk with him.

"We're going to scout the island," he told the others.

No one offered to come along. No one said a word. They just nodded, their gazes as empty as I felt.

"We need to tell them everything," Daniel whispered as we walked away. "Otherwise, they'll want to wait for rescue. Which we know we can't do."

"Because we don't know who'll come for us. Real rescuers or fake ones."

He nodded.

"I'll . . ." I struggled to get my brain in gear, but I felt like I was still out in the water, fighting to keep my head above the surface and wishing I could just sink into peaceful oblivion. I blinked hard. "Sorry. I'll talk to them."

"No, I will. You just need to back me up. Can you do that?"

I nodded.

Tell them what was going on. God, that sounded so easy. But where to start?

It began less than a week ago. No, that's not true. It began a year ago. When Serena died. My best friend. Daniel's girlfriend.

Serena had drowned. It shouldn't have happened, not to the captain of the school swim team, swimming in a calm lake.

Then Mina Lee came to town. She called herself a reporter, but everyone figured she was a corporate spy. We live in Salmon Creek, a town of two hundred people that was built and owned by the St. Cloud Corporation, so they could conduct drug research. Mina came to Salmon Creek pretending to be writing an article on the local teens—what it was like growing up in a tiny corporate town. She'd really wanted to talk to us—and she was especially curious about Serena's death, and Daniel and I began to think that she suspected the medical research was responsible.

A few days later we'd found Mina Lee's body in a cougar cache. Had she been killed by the big cats? Or died of misadventure in the woods? Or had she been murdered and dumped?

We broke into her cabin and found files on all the teens in our class. Only two were missing. Mine and Sam's. Sam had stolen hers. When confronted she said it was because she didn't want others knowing her parents had been murdered. But we'd started wondering if there was more to it, if she might have had something to do with those murders, something to do with Serena's death, too.

Then there was the note Daniel had found in Mina's cabin. Four strange words in it, including *benandanti*. Italian witch-hunters. We knew the word because of Mina. She'd left him a note to call her, on a library book page about benandanti.

I'd recognized other words on that list. *Yee naaldlooshii*. Skin-walker. A few days before, I'd been called that by an old woman who'd said that's what my paw-print birthmark meant. That I was a skin-walker. A shape-shifting witch. Crazy, huh? Except . . . I was. So were Rafe and Annie, who'd come to

Salmon Creek looking for the girl who'd been another subject in an experiment to resurrect the latent skin-walker genes. That girl, apparently, was me.

So all that happens, and I'm trying to figure out how to tell Daniel I'm a skin-walker when the forest fire struck. Daniel, Rafe, and I got caught in it. We'd seen a fire-and-rescue truck, and Daniel got a bad feeling—he gets them; I've learned to trust them. Turned out it wasn't fire and rescue. Who was it? I don't know, but they'd been after us, and one man knew my name and had my eyes, and I was pretty sure I knew what that meant, but I refused to process it. Too much else waiting in the queue.

So how much should we tell the others? I trusted Daniel would know. Normally, we'd hash it out together. But today, I needed him to take charge and he did that.

As we walked, Daniel and I scouted the island to be sure there wasn't any shelter. In order to get off it, we'd need to swim, which carried the risk of hypothermia. Not something we cared to do if there was an alternative. There wasn't. The island didn't have so much as a rock pile big enough to hide behind.

So we returned and Daniel explained to the others what had happened in the woods as we'd been fleeing the fire.

"It sounded like these people deliberately set the blaze," he said as he finished. "Maya and I thought they were trying to clear Salmon Creek to get into the lab and steal the drug research. But if the pilot drugged the mayor, then that doesn't make sense. We were already leaving town."

"How do you know he was knocked out?" Sam asked.

"I saw the pilot grab the mayor's arm," Daniel said. "Right before we got on the helicopter. Mr. Tillson rubbed the place, like it hurt. Then Maya found the injection spot."

"So they wanted Mr. Tillson?" Hayley asked.

Daniel shook his head. "We think whoever set the fire either bought off the pilot or planted one of their own guys. I heard Mr. Tillson say that the first helicopter had already landed in Victoria. That means whoever is behind this wanted ours. In the evacuation plans, we're all supposed to be on that helicopter. Not Mr. Tillson specifically, though. Just an adult to chaperone us."

"So in sedating him, they were getting rid of our chaperone," I said. "They wanted one of us."

I thought of the list Daniel had found, with the word *skinwalker* on it, and I thought of the man in the woods, who'd called me by name. So I seemed to be the one they wanted. But when I glanced up, Sam looked like a cartoon character with a "Who me?" bubble over her head.

"It doesn't matter who or what was the target," I said. "We need to figure out what we're going to do now."

"Why do we need to do anything?" Hayley said. "They'll come looking for us."

"Um, yeah," Sam said. "That's Maya's point. The people who tried to kidnap us will come looking for us to finish the job."

"You don't know that."

"Sam's right," Daniel said. "The first people who come for us will likely be the kidnappers. It'd be safer to get to a phone and call our parents."

Everyone looked around. The mainland was a dark blob on the eastern horizon. To the west was Vancouver Island. About a kilometer of water separated the two.

"Umm . . ." Corey began. "Not to question your judgment, buddy, but that's a bit of a swim. The water's damned cold. I bashed my knee good in the crash, and I'm not the only one who's hurting. I get what you're saying, but the pilot's radio seemed to be out, so they won't know where we are. If we light a fire, someone out boating might see us."

"That's a good idea," Sam said. "Or it would be. If we had matches to light a fire. Or if anyone was actually out boating."

"Why don't we just find a place to hide?" Hayley said. "That way, when someone does come, we can see if it's a real rescue or not."

"How the hell are you going to tell the difference?" Sam said. "Ask them? And no one's going to find the crash site. You know why? There *is* no crash site."

She pointed out over the empty water. When the helicopter had dropped over the ledge, it had disappeared. Only a few small pieces of debris floated, already being dispersed by the tide.

"And we don't know that the radio equipment wasn't working," Daniel said. "Whoever wanted that helicopter may know exactly where it went down."

That didn't keep Corey and Hayley from arguing that we should stay put, and Nicole from quietly agreeing. Which only pissed off Sam all the more. To us, the danger was obvious. We should be in the water already, swimming for Vancouver Island. To the others, it was too much to believe, too much to take in. Easier to think this was all a tragic mistake and that a rescue team would find us at any moment.

Eventually, Daniel and I managed to persuade them that no one was going to come for us. There was no shelter on this island, and there could be cottages just past the shoreline on the mainland.

Finally, they all agreed to swim for it.

FOUR

SWIMMING FOR THE SHORE was not a simple matter. Daniel and I were soaked, but the others were dry from the knees up, and in October, they'd need that dry clothing. The problem was how to get it across.

There weren't any backpacks in the debris floating from the wreck, but Daniel rescued a piece of plastic. The others stripped to their undergarments, wrapped up their clothing as best they could, and put it in the plastic. Daniel made sure Corey put his headache medication in, too. Corey got migraines. Bad ones. Unfortunately, all he had on him was a couple of tablets he carried loose in his pocket.

By the time we got to the water's edge, we were all shivering so hard I could hear teeth chattering.

A layer of marine fog covered the surface. As I stood there with my toes in the icy water, tendrils of fog slipped around my ankles and I remembered a line about fog coming in on little cat's feet.

Cats. Cougars. Skin-walkers. Rafe.

My stomach clenched and my toes clenched, too. I closed my eyes and struggled to ground myself.

"Can you see the land?" Nicole whispered beside me.

I pointed. "See the treetops above the fog?"

She nodded, then rubbed down goose bumps on her arms. "About earlier. I—I don't know why I blew up like that."

"Your dad just died."

"I know . . ." She nudged a submerged rock. "I'm still sorry."

"It's okay."

"Are you sure we should do this?" Hayley called from a few feet away. "It's so cold. Is it safe?"

I looked over at her and Corey and Sam, standing along the shoreline, arms wrapped around themselves, their faces as gray as the fog. Fear and confusion on every face. Terror on Sam's, as she stared wide-eyed into the fog.

Daniel and I went first. Kenjii circled me as I eased into the water. When she realized I wasn't just taking a walk into the surf, she leaped in front of me, barking, ordering me to dry land. I continued on, up to my waist now. She snapped at my fingers and tried to herd me back to shore.

"Maybe there's something out there," Nicole called. "Didn't someone catch a great white shark a few years ago? And we have plenty of killer whales."

"Great whites don't come this far inland," I called back. "And I doubt this stretch of water is deep enough for orcas, but even if it is, they don't attack in the wild. You're only at risk if you're jumping into their aquarium tank."

"Kenjii just knows Maya doesn't like to swim," Daniel said. "Here, I'll take her—"

He reached for her collar. She growled and he pulled back.

"Or maybe not . . ."

Kenjii lowered her head and whined, as if in apology.

"She's scared and confused," I said. *No, we are, and she's sensing it.* "Just give me a sec to calm her down."

I petted her and promised her it was okay. Once she'd relaxed, I told Daniel to go on ahead with her, so she couldn't see me. She glanced back a couple of times, but when I seemed to be staying put, she let Daniel take her for a swim.

Corey went in behind Hayley, herding her. She was on the swim team, so she should be fine, but she was still disoriented from her near-drowning experience. Sam went next, her chin up, expression unreadable. Daniel had asked Nicole—who was also on the swim team—to go last and help anyone who fell behind, namely me.

I'd estimated the strip of water to be about a kilometer. That's just over three thousand feet. Not a short distance. Not an incredibly long one either, or so I kept telling myself as I paddled through the frigid water. It was half of the distance from my house to the park gates. One sixth the distance of the

Run for the Mountain event I did in Nanaimo every year. One twentieth the distance of the Harbour City Half Marathon I ran last fall.

Easy. Except for the fact that I loved to walk and run, but hated swimming. Part of my skin-walker heritage, I guess. When I get in water deeper than a bathtub, there's this part of my brain that screams at me to get out, and no amount of self-talk ever silences it.

But maybe this time that part of my brain realized, as a cougar would, that there was a difference between swimming for pleasure and swimming for survival. While I was cold and uncomfortable, I stayed relatively calm. Even managed something close to an actual breaststroke, which I'm sure made Nicole happy, stuck at my snail's pace as the others pulled away.

Every now and then I could make out Daniel's dark shape as he glanced back to check on us. No one said a word. Only the splash of hands and feet hitting water broke the eerie silence. I couldn't see how much farther we had to go. Couldn't see how far we'd come. Just fog everywhere, my friends dark blotches in the gray.

Sam was huffing off to the side. She liked to scrap, but she wasn't an athlete, and she sounded winded. I was about to veer her way when she stopped puffing, as if she'd gotten her second wind. Or stopped swimming. I opened my mouth to call to Daniel to check on her.

Before I could speak, my foot brushed something. A fish I

presumed, but then it wrapped around my ankle and yanked me down.

I didn't fight at first. Something had my foot. Something was pulling me under. Just like a year ago, when Serena drowned. For a second, I thought, *That's it—I'm having a nightmare.* Everything that had happened today—the fire, the crash, Rafe—was clearly just part of a bad dream. It had to be.

Then I began to choke and the survival instinct took over. I kicked. I flailed. But something kept dragging me under.

No, not something—*someone.*

When Serena drowned, I'd been so worried about her that I'd paid no attention to *what* had me. This time, I could feel warm fingers wrapped around my icy-cold ankle, and when I kicked, my toes brushed what was unmistakably hair.

I tried to grab whoever was holding me, but every time I moved, my attacker moved. I couldn't see anything. My eyes stung and my lungs ached. But I knew it was a person holding me down. Just a person. I could fight that.

Only I couldn't. I kicked and I writhed, but those fingers weren't letting me go and I couldn't breathe, and when nails dug into my ankle, I shrieked and my mouth and throat filled with more water, and I realized I was drowning.

Then the toes of my free foot touched rock. The bottom. I pushed myself down even as my brain screamed that I was going the wrong way. I bent in half and reached to feel not fingers, but vegetation wrapped around my ankle. Seaweed. I ripped it off, then shot toward the surface.

After a few strokes, I wasn't sure I was still going up. All I could see was darkness. Then a scream sounded above me.

They were looking for me, yelling for me. I was going the right way. I was going to be fine, just fine. I put everything I had left into a few last strokes, propelling myself toward the surface, breaking through, then gasping for air too soon, water rushing in, choking me.

I went under again. I gave a tremendous kick, arms and legs flailing so hard that a cramp shot through my stomach and I screamed, swallowing more water.

I could hear Daniel shouting, then Corey. But no one was coming. Why wasn't anyone coming?

I broke the surface again, and this time managed to get a breath. Then I heard Nicole screaming for help—that something had her, was pulling *her* down.

A fresh cramp shot through me and I went under again.

My muscles pleaded for relief, but I managed to break the surface again.

"Maya!" Daniel yelled. "Where's Maya?"

Nicole shrieked and I wanted to shout to Daniel to forget me, save her before she drowned like Serena. That's all I could think of. How he'd saved me when Serena drowned. I wouldn't let that happen again. I couldn't.

Nails scraped my arm and I panicked, then felt wet fur.

Kenjii. I wrapped my arms around her neck and lay my

face against her back, flutter-kicking as best I could. Daniel reached me then.

"Nicole," I said. "Get Nicole."

He hesitated. I pushed him toward Nicole, getting more and more frantic until Corey called that he and Hayley had Nicole and she was fine.

"Sam?" I croaked.

"Sam!" Daniel yelled. "Where are you?"

"She's—" Corey started. "Here she is. She's fine."

Daniel made me get on his back and we headed to shore, Kenjii swimming beside us.

FİVE

WHEN WE MADE IT to shore, Daniel didn't insist on getting to dry ground this time, just let us all collapse where we could, panting and shivering, Nicole crying softly, Hayley trying to comfort her, Sam hovering awkwardly.

We emptied the makeshift pack. It'd been on Corey, and he'd gone under in the search. We'd tied it as best we could, but there were openings. The clothing was wet. His pills had disintegrated. He said that was fine—he wasn't likely to get a migraine soon and if he did, he could tough it out. Which was a lie, but there was nothing we could do about it.

Daniel made the others put on their clothing, coaxing gently but insistently. Theirs were almost as soaked as Daniel's and mine, and they huddled there, shivering and sniffling.

The sky was so dark now it looked like night already.

It smelled like rain, too. None for weeks and now it came and there was a small part of me that thought, *It'll put out the fires*, but I couldn't bring myself to care. My forest might be saved, and all I could think was that night was coming and the temperature was dropping and if it did rain and we couldn't find shelter, get dry, and try to light a fire, hypothermia would kill us by morning.

We'd all be dead. Just like Rafe.

I pulled my legs up, wrapped my arms around them and shivered as I tried to get myself under control. Just beyond this rocky beach was the forest. I'd seen it earlier. I knew the forest. It was my home more than any house ever could be. I'd survive this. We'd all survive it.

But no matter how hard I stared to the west, I couldn't see the trees. Just fog and shadows everywhere, the six of us lost in it, as if we'd already died, stumbled into the afterlife and—

"What happened out there?" Corey asked.

I looked up. He was pivoting slowly, shoulders tight, on guard against . . . Against anything. Everything. Whatever could be lurking in that rolling field of gray.

"Something pulled me under," Nicole said. "It wrapped around my foot and I couldn't get away."

"That's what happened to you, too, Maya, isn't it?" Corey said.

I nodded. "It pulled me to the bottom, then let go."

Nicole and I compared stories. She didn't have much to tell. Something grabbed her leg and pulled her down. Did it feel like a bite? Seaweed? She didn't know.

Finally Daniel turned to me. "Was it like what happened with Serena?"

I nodded.

"Serena?" Hayley said. "How would she know that? No offense, Maya. I mean, I know you were there and it was awful but—"

"Something dragged Maya under that time, too," Corey said. "Daniel pulled her to safety."

Silence. I knew what they were all thinking. *Daniel pulled Maya to safety. And Serena died.*

"It was my fault," I said. "He didn't know Serena had gone under, too."

"Maya tried to tell me," Daniel said. "I didn't understand. It was my fault."

"It was *no one's* fault," Sam said. "Neither was this. Maybe there's something out there. Giant eels or whatever."

"Giant eels?" Corey let out a whoop of a laugh, too loud and too long. Desperate to cast off the fear and unease and find his old self again.

"Hey, I'm not the moron who was worried about great white sharks," said Sam.

"Um, that was Nic."

"It doesn't matter what happened," Daniel said, "only that no one was hurt." He looked at me, then Nicole. "You're both okay, right? Well, I mean . . . I know you're not okay, but—"

"I'm fine," I said.

Nicole nodded.

"Me, too." Hayley straightened, as if not to be outdone. Getting her footing, like me searching for my forest and Corey for a joke. We were all stressed out. We'd deal with it our own way. At least we *were* dealing with it, not curled up on the beach in fetal positions. Right now, that was the best we could hope for.

It was night by the time we'd gotten ourselves together enough to head out. There were no lights anywhere to break the fog and the darkness. We walked along the shore for a bit, but couldn't find any docks or boat moorings. So no cottages just across the water, as we'd hoped. We needed to head inland.

As we walked in silence, Kenjii whimpered, reacting to the tension. I could feel it myself, bristling through the air like electricity. Every time she made noise, the others would jump, and look around as if they expected grizzly bears to lumber out of the fog. Only Daniel stayed steady, assuring everyone that Kenjii was just nervous because they were.

I was, too. I think that's what got her going the most. I kept telling myself I was fine, that the forest was right there. I could smell the sharp tang of evergreens. But when the wind whined around us, I jumped with everyone else.

Finally, I saw trees and my heart stopped pounding. I walked faster, needles crunching under my feet, the sound, the smell so familiar that my throat ached, and I had to reach out, fingers brushing the boughs as we passed. The fog disappeared, as if kept at bay by the trees. Safe. I was in the forest, Daniel was beside me and I was safe.

"Uh, Maya?" Corey said behind me. "Maybe . . . this isn't such a good idea."

I turned. The others were ten feet back, barely inside the tree line. Nicole and Hayley had moved closer to Corey. Sam hung back, looking into the woods as if I was asking her to jump off a cliff.

"The fog's gone in here," I said. "It was marine fog. It doesn't penetrate the forest."

"Yeah," Corey said. "I'm thinking the fog's not such a problem. It's very . . . dark. We don't know what's in there."

"Yeah, we do," Sam said. "Bears, cougars, wolves . . ."

"None of which are nocturnal," I said. Actually, they were crepuscular, which meant they were most active at twilight—both dawn and dusk. In other words, right about now. But I wasn't telling these guys that. "They'll stay out of our way if we stay out of theirs."

"But how can we stay out of their way if we can't see them?" Hayley asked.

I turned and looked into the forest. I could see fine, but I was part cat. To them it would be dark. Very dark.

"I'll lead," I said. "Kenjii and I spend so much time in the woods that our eyes adjust quickly."

"I don't know," Hayley said. "It's really dark. And really spooky."

I turned again and saw a scene worthy of a tourist bro-chure—a rocky, natural path dotted with unfurled ferns and soaring, vine-ribboned redwoods. Somewhere to our left, a nighthawk trilled. Even the leftover fog was like fine lace drifting past on a cedar-perfumed breeze.

"I'm not seeing spooky," I said. "Dark, yes, but what's spooky about it?"

"What's *not* spooky?" Sam muttered.

Hayley pointed. "You can't tell me that isn't creepy."

I followed her finger to see branches draped in elegant, pale-green Spanish moss.

"That? Seriously? It's moss, Hayley, not an alien life-form. We just escaped a helicopter crash and a death brush with something in the water. *That* was scary. This is the for-est. This is where we're going to find shelter and water."

"Shelter? I don't want a damned cave, Maya. I want a house, and we're not going to find that in the middle of—"

Daniel stepped between us. "All right. This isn't helping. We have to get through these woods in order to find help. That could mean holing up for the night, but we'll be okay. Maya knows her way around the woods and so do I. You need to trust us to look after you."

He spoke to them, but it was for my benefit, too. A reminder that they didn't have our experience and they were not going to see the forest the way I did.

I led everyone for a while without any sign of light or noise from a road, then I veered south. Instinct, I guess. On

Vancouver Island, like anywhere in Canada, the population tends to shift south. Most times that's for warmer weather. The island, though, is temperate rain forest, meaning we rarely see the white stuff. We gravitate south because it's simply more hospitable land. While my sense of "where" we'd crashed was vague, I knew it was north. Probably a long way north. The pilot's goal, I suspected, had been someplace more remote.

It wasn't a stretch to think that the people responsible for this—and for setting the fire that got us out of town—were the scientists my birth mother had escaped sixteen years ago. Yes, Sam seemed to think they might be after her, but I was sure I was the target. That meant I had to rescue myself. Get to a phone, call my parents—my adoptive parents—and tell them everything. Yet my escape couldn't jeopardize my friends. If it came down to it, I'd need to get away, separate them from the danger I posed.

For now, they needed me to navigate the forests and find help. Heading south was easy so far—I could hear the crash of waves and smell the ocean to my left, meaning we were going the right way. We hadn't walked very far, though, before Corey stopped as we were circling around an outcropping of rock.

"Is anyone seeing lights anywhere?" Corey said. "Because all I see is bushes. We need to get higher."

He started scrambling up the rock pile. The stones were dark. Covered in lichen. Slippery lichen.

"Stop!" I said.

His foot slid and the leg he'd hurt in the crash buckled. We jumped to grab him, but his knee cracked against rock as he fell. He let out a yowl and a string of curses. His jeans had split and underneath, his knee was bleeding. When I tried to touch it, he grabbed my hand.

"I need to check it out," I said.

The skin had been scraped from his kneecap. It felt whole underneath, but he gritted his teeth at my touch, meaning it was probably badly wrenched.

"We're going to need to wrap it," I said. "Or you won't be able to walk."

The only thing we could spare for wrapping was socks. Daniel gave his and I tied them together. When the socks were wrapped around Corey's leg, he could stand, with effort and Daniel's arm for support.

"Figures," Corey muttered. "Survive a forest fire, helicopter crash, and killer eels, only to slip on a rock."

"That's what you get for trying to take charge," Hayley said.

"No kidding."

We made it to a grassy clearing, but Corey was in a lot of pain. Walking was only making it worse.

"Getting to a higher spot to look around is a good idea," I said after we sat him down. "We'll find a tree while you rest—"

"Whoa, wait." Corey started struggling to his feet. "I'm okay. I'll be slow, but I can move."

"He doesn't want to be alone," Hayley said. "You know how he is. Leave him alone and he discovers he's not as much fun as he thinks he is."

Corey shot her the finger. She was right, though—Corey really wasn't one for enjoying his own company. People seemed to feed his bottomless well of energy.

"I'll stay with him," Nicole said.

Daniel nodded. "Hayley and Sam, you guys should stay, too. Maya's going to be the one scaling a tree. Kenjii and I will stand point, but everyone else should rest. We won't go far. Plenty of trees nearby."

Hayley agreed to stay behind. Sam did not. Daniel seemed annoyed, but she didn't get the hint. In the end, it was easiest to let her come.

"There's something I need to talk to you guys about," Sam said once we were out of earshot of the others. "About what happened on the helicopter."

"You did an amazing job," Daniel said. "If it wasn't for you . . ."

"None of us would be here," I said.

She went scarlet at that, and trudged along for a few minutes before she continued, "It's not that. It's about . . . when the pilot was knocked out. What you did, Daniel."

"Daniel didn't get within three feet of him," I said.

"That's what I mean. All he did was yell."

"I must have startled him," Daniel said.

Except that Daniel had done the same thing when we

were escaping the fire. Whatever it was, he hadn't just yelled loud enough to startle the men. Not when it happened twice. But Daniel stared at us with honest confusion.

"It's not important right now," I said.

"Actually, it might . . ." Sam shook her head. "You're right. It can wait."

SIX

WE DIDN'T GO FAR from the others. My sense of direction in the forest was uncanny, as my dad always said—along with my ability to find my way back to a spot—but I wasn't relying on that now.

I stopped under a huge tree and said, "I'm going up. I'll look for lights."

Daniel boosted me to the nearest branch. Tree climbing here isn't easy. Many redwoods are like telephone poles vaulting to a canopy of greener limbs way over our heads. It's a matter of finding the right tree to shimmy up.

What made this climb difficult wasn't the tree itself. I'd spent the last couple of hours trying to forget what happened on the helicopter. What happened to Rafe.

That'd been easy when we had to keep everyone moving forward. But when I went up the tree, it reminded me of our climbs together. I could hear his laughter, feel that strange pulse, as if I could sense his heart beating. He seemed to be right beside me, and if I just looked over, I'd see him there, grinning and—

More than once, I almost gave up and slid back down. Told them I couldn't do it. I was too tired. The tree was too difficult.

I let a few tears fall. I caught my breath. And I kept going. Rafe had died to save me, and now I had to help save everyone else.

I climbed as high as I could, past the point where I heard Sam say to Daniel, "Should she be going that high?"

Near the tree's crown, I looked out and my heart plummeted into my soaked sneakers. Trees. That's what I saw. An endless expanse of inky black trees.

I stayed up there for about ten minutes, straining for any sign of light, even the flicker of headlights on a distant road. Then I climbed back down.

"It's dark," I said, after I leaped to the ground.

"Um, yeah," Sam said. "It's night. How the hell you expected to see anything—" She stopped as she realized what I was really saying. "Oh."

"I'll try again in the morning."

But we all knew that if there'd been any houses or inhabited cabins nearby, I should have been able to spot light.

We trudged back to the others and told them.

"There must be people out there somewhere," I said when

we finished. "We're not in the middle of Alaska. The nearest house can't be more than ten, fifteen kilometers away."

"Which Corey can't walk with his busted knee," Hayley said.

"I know. That's why we'll split up in the morning. I can move fast—fifteen kilometers isn't even a half-marathon."

"I'll go with you," Daniel said. "I can keep up. For tonight, though, we need to get someplace more sheltered."

I nodded. "We'll need to find a stream, too. Fresh water."

"You mean we have to go *farther* into the forest?" Corey said. "We got off that island for you, but I'm not sure we should be hiding so far away that we won't see a real rescue team if they come."

And so it began. Round two of the great debate. Once again, we split along the same lines—Sam, Daniel, and I wanted to push on, while Corey, Nicole, and Hayley wanted to stay. Daniel could have swayed Corey. But he was injured and we couldn't bring ourselves to insist he tramp through the forest in agony.

We finally agreed to head closer to the beach, where they could spend the night. We'd return for them in the morning.

Splitting up felt wrong, like we were just being stubborn. Yet as wrong as it felt to separate, it felt even more wrong to stay so close to the crash site. Also, Daniel and I were soaked. We needed to try starting a fire to dry out. We couldn't do that within sight of the crash.

So Sam, Daniel, and I left Corey, Hayley, and Nicole and continued on with Kenjii. We located a stream and followed it until we found a cave where we could spend the night. Well, not so much a cave as a sheltered spot under an outcropping of rock. But sheltered was the key word. Plenty of dead vegetation had blown in and dried out, and Daniel managed to knock rocks together, get a spark, and light a tiny blaze. Considering I'd escaped a raging forest fire earlier that day, I was good with tiny.

We huddled around that small campfire and tried not to think about how cold it was or how hungry we were. Kenjii was dry now, and she felt like a furry hot water bottle between Daniel and me. I should be able to find nuts in the morning, maybe even some late berries. For now, there was nothing we could do about it. We'd drunk from the stream and it was indeed fresh water and that was all we needed, however much our stomachs disagreed.

I looked at Sam, huddled with us by the blaze, and I figured now was a good time to ask her some tough questions. No way was she going to stomp off into the night, away from the heat.

"You know why those people took us," I said. "Or you think you do. It has something to do with you. With why you were searching Mina Lee's cottage, why you took her file on you, and why you flipped out when I grabbed it."

She said nothing.

Daniel had stretched out on his side, cheek propped on

his hand. He lifted his head now. "This isn't the time to keep secrets. If you think you know why they're after us, you need to—"

"Benandanti."

Daniel sat up. "What?"

"Benandanti," Sam said. "It's—"

"We know what it is. A cult of Italian witch-hunters killed during the Inquisition."

She stared at us. "Where did you hear that?"

"Mina sent Daniel to a book at the Nanaimo library," I said. "She gave him a reference and page number. It led to an article on the benandanti."

"Oh." She paused, then nodded, her expression . . . satisfied. Pleased even. "Well, the book didn't get it right. They never do. Benandanti weren't witch-hunters. They were demon-hunters, who evolved into general-purpose evil hunters. Supernatural evil, that is. So sure, witches would be a target, if witches were hurting anyone with their powers. So would sorcerers, werewolves, vampires, half-demons. Especially half-demons, because they have demon blood and demons were the benandanti's original target."

"You're saying this like . . . you believe in it," Daniel said slowly.

Rafe had said skin-walkers had gone extinct, but other races hadn't. He hadn't said what those races were, but I figured it was all those paranormal types Sam just mentioned, ones we still saw in movies and books, continuing to play a role in folklore after others faded. Because they had continued to exist while others, like benandanti, had not.

"You know why Mina sent you to that page, right?" Sam said.

"I figured she picked some random entry in a book no one ever checked out."

"Really?" She met his gaze. "Is that honestly what you think?"

He shifted position, his expression lost in the shadows from the flickering fire. When he didn't answer, Sam continued.

"The book probably told you the main power of the benandanti was dream-walking. They leave their bodies to hunt evil at night. People believed that because it explained how benandanti seemed to strike without anyone seeing them, without leaving a trace on the bodies, without their victims fighting back. The truth is that benandanti do have powers, but dream-walking isn't one of them. They can sense trouble. They can repel trouble. And they can charm and persuade people to do things they might not want to. Does any of that sound familiar, Daniel?"

He didn't answer.

Sam carried on. "Everyone knows you get bad feelings about people, and you're usually right. I bet you got really strong vibes from Mina Lee. She was a half-demon. You might have gotten weaker ones from the pilot, too. He was a minor half-demon, I think. With the power of fire, judging by those burns on Hayley. Mina's power was teleportation."

Daniel had his hand near his mouth, his eyes half closed, expression deliberately hidden. I could see the pulse throbbing in his neck as his heart beat faster. I remembered what he'd said about Mina the first time we met. *There's something wrong with her.* I remembered how she'd seemed to vanish, not once but twice. Teleportation. And the pilot. Fire.

"You also have the power of persuasion," Sam continued. "I've seen you flip it on like a light switch. It's been getting stronger. Maybe you're telling yourself that you just have a knack for leadership, but deep down, you know it's more than that. And the power to repel evil? I saw you do it on the helicopter. That's how it works. Like a sonic boom. You didn't even need to touch him. It's not a perfect power, though, which is why benandanti are also naturally skilled fighters." She met Daniel's gaze again. "You're seriously going to tell me none of this sounds familiar?"

"If you're saying I'm one of these benandanti—"

"Um, yeah. That's my point."

He shook his head. "No. It's . . ."

"Crazy?"

"I know something happened on that helicopter," Daniel said. "And it happened earlier today, in the forest with Maya. Whatever it was, it wasn't normal. So if you tell me I have some kind of psychic power that throws people when I get mad, I might believe you. But witches and werewolves and demon-hunters? I don't know where you got all that stuff from but—"

"I'm a benandanti, too," Sam said. "Only my parents didn't hide it from me like yours did."

"You're . . . ?" I couldn't finish.

"Couldn't you tell from my awesome charisma?" Sam gave a twisted smile, almost sad. "My parents said it would develop, along with my other powers, but I kinda think I'm missing that part of the equation. Missing the control part, too, as you may have noticed. I got the fighting bug, and it bites whether I want it to or not. I could sense that Mina was a half-demon, but I missed it with the pilot until he grabbed Hayley. I don't have the repelling part yet, either."

"So that's why you thought Mina was investigating you?" I said.

Daniel looked at me sharply, as if to say, *You're buying this?*

Before I could speak, a figure burst from the trees, breathing so hard she doubled over. It was Hayley. "They came," she panted.

I crawled out of the cave and stood. "Rescuers?"

She shook her head. "At first, that's what we thought. They pulled up to the island in a boat and they sent a diver into the water. Corey said we had to be careful, just sit tight and watch, but Nicole wouldn't listen. She went down to the shore, waving her arms and yelling, and they saw her and they started coming toward her on the boat. When they got about halfway, she turned and started running back to us, and they . . . they shot her."

She fell against me, shaking, and I put my arms around her.

"What?" Sam said, scrambling up. "Who shot Nicole?"

When Hayley didn't answer, Sam tried to wrench her from me, but I shook my head and motioned for her to wait.

When she quieted a little, I asked, "Could you tell if she was okay?"

"Sh-she wasn't. Oh God." Hayley hiccupped a sob. "They shot her in the back, and she fell. She fell and she didn't get up. Corey wanted to go after her, but I wouldn't let him. I know that sounds awful, but there was no way we could get to her without getting shot ourselves. All we could do was watch. They came on shore and they picked her up and carried her to the boat and put her in, and she never moved, and we knew she was . . ."

Hayley caught on the word, tried again, choked, shook her head. "Gone. We knew she was gone. Then they started shining lights at the forest and we heard them say that we all must be in there. I wanted to run, but Corey couldn't, so he told me to come find you. I didn't want to leave him, but I made sure he was hidden under some bushes, then I snuck away."

We quickly decided Sam should stay behind with Hayley.

Daniel and I had just left when Sam came running after us.

"How much do you guys trust Hayley?" she said.

Hayley and I were not friends. I'd been doped at my sixteenth birthday party—hard to believe it had only been a few days ago—and everyone was sure it had been Hayley.

"Since when do you trust her?" Sam continued. "You know she doesn't like you. Think about it. Shooting Nic? Does that make any sense? Not unless you want a story that'll make us come running back . . . straight into a trap. What if these people grabbed Nicole, Corey, and Hayley? They'd want one of them to lure us out of hiding. Who would do it?"

I looked at Daniel. He rubbed his mouth, thinking. Then he said, "Hayley seemed really upset. I don't think she's that good an actor. If it played out the way you said, Hayley would have used the opportunity to escape. She'd tell us Nicole and Corey were both dead so we could all run."

As usual, Daniel's argument worked for Sam, and she agreed to go back and wait with Hayley. If he did have some magical power of persuasion, he didn't need to use it with her.

Had she always sensed what he was? Is that why she liked him?

Were they really both benandanti? Was it a coincidence I'd ended up in the same town as another supposedly extinct supernatural? That Sam ended up in the same town as both of us?

When Rafe had said we were part of an experiment, I'd wondered if it was connected to Salmon Creek—a medical research town. But they did drug research, not genetic work. Besides, I'd been adopted at birth and my parents had moved to Salmon Creek for a job. That had seemed to rule out the possibility of a connection.

But now . . .

I glanced at Daniel. Since Sam left he'd been walking in silence, following me on autopilot.

I should tell him what I was, let him know there might be a connection.

"How are you doing?" I said.

"Okay."

"I—" I began.

"I don't know what to think," he interrupted. "What happened in the forest, when I yelled at that guy . . . I thought I'd hit him without realizing it. I was mad enough, seeing him pointing that gun at you. But when it happened again on the helicopter, with the pilot, I knew I'd done something. I just didn't know what."

After a few more steps, I opened my mouth, but again he got there first.

"I think . . . I think Sam might be onto something. Everything she says is true. Even about the pilot. I had a bad feeling, when we got on the helicopter, but only a slight one, and with everything that happened, I figured I was just stressing out. I don't believe the parts about demons and all that, but I can

57

see maybe having some power to sense bad vibes in people. I mean, it's not like she's saying I'm a vampire or a werewolf. That would be crazy. This is just a little weird."

No, it wasn't like she'd said he was a werewolf. It wasn't like she'd said he could change into an animal. That would be crazy.

I shut my mouth and carried on in silence.

SEVEN

W HEN WE DREW NEAR the place we'd left Corey, we realized going straight to him wasn't wise. We decided to take a look from farther down the shore.

We could hear a boat motor, but the running lights were off. There were people on board with flashlights, though, so we could see where it was.

Did that mean everyone was back in the boat? Did they have Corey?

A distant splash told us someone had gone in the water. Retrieving the bodies? Removing identifying parts from the helicopter? It sounded far-fetched, but if you kidnapped kids in a helicopter that crashed, you didn't want local fishermen finding the wreckage.

Daniel tapped my arm. I followed his outstretched finger

and saw two more flashlight beams strafing the forest right around where we'd left Corey.

I gripped Kenjii's collar as we crept closer. Another flashlight beam flickered through trees farther down. Three searchers. At least two more on the boat plus the diver.

So how would we get to Corey? Was he even still there? If they'd found him, had they—?

My brain stuttered over the thought.

Shot him? That was the easy way of saying it, like it didn't mean what I knew it meant. Killed him.

Nicole was dead.

"Nic," I whispered. "Nic's—"

"We don't know that," Daniel whispered harshly, and I knew that's what he'd been telling himself. It's what I'd been thinking, too. Shot. Just shot. Hayley hadn't seen exactly, so we could keep telling ourselves Nicole was only injured.

Kenjii whined and brushed my hand, and I patted her head.

"Corey," Daniel whispered.

He meant we couldn't think about Nicole. Just like we couldn't think about Rafe. We had to focus on saving everyone else.

Oh God. How had it come to this? Where I had to concentrate on saving the friends I could. Forget the ones I couldn't. The ones I'd lost. The ones who were already . . .

Daniel clutched my arm.

"Maya," he whispered. "I need you."

I nodded and took a deep breath to steady myself. Then I got us as close to the searchers as I dared, picking my way through shadows too dark for Daniel to see. I stopped, and we hunkered down. I wrapped both arms around Kenjii, whispering for her to stay quiet.

After a moment, a radio crackled.

"No, we haven't found them," a male voice said. "And we're not going to. Even if they stuck around, they'd see us coming from a mile away. Especially after you shot the girl."

I couldn't make out the voice on the other end.

"Yeah, well, by that time, they'll be long gone. If they aren't fifty feet underwater."

More unintelligible murmuring as the person on the other end responded.

"Just because you only found Jason and the mayor doesn't mean they were the only ones who died. The others could have fallen out or floated from the wreck or—"

"Shut the hell up." Another man's voice. One that didn't come from the radio. One that made the hair on my neck stand up. The man in the forest. The man who'd pointed a gun at me. The man who had my eyes and my cheekbones.

"The kids are fine," the man continued. "They're in excellent shape. Athletes, all of them. Champion swimmers and runners and fighters. Whatever else the St. Clouds screwed up, they did that right. They made them survivors."

"I'm sor—"

"You want to keep your job? Then don't apologize. Just

find these kids. Find my daughter."

Blood pounded in my ears and I grabbed a tree for support, nails digging into the bark.

Find my daughter.

He meant me. I'd known that. From that moment in the woods, I'd known it. I just hadn't wanted it to be true.

Daniel gripped my shoulder, squeezing until I looked at him.

"It's okay," he murmured. "We can do this."

I could tell by his expression that he hadn't heard what the man said. He didn't have my enhanced hearing.

I had to forget what the man said. I'd always known I was adopted. Rick Delaney was still my real dad. He raised me. Nothing else—*no one* else—mattered.

I whispered to Daniel, telling him the other things that the men had said.

"They're after all of us," Daniel said.

"I think so."

"I don't get it."

I think I do. I think it wasn't any coincidence that my family wound up in Salmon Creek. It wasn't any coincidence that Sam came here, either. They found me and they found her, and they brought us back to Salmon Creek, with the rest of you. I don't know what it all means, but I'm starting to understand. I can't tell you any of that, though. I wish I could. God, I wish I could.

"Maya?"

I wanted to throw my arms around his neck and apologize.

I'm sorry, Daniel. I should have told you earlier. I screwed up and I think I'm still screwing up.

He hugged me and whispered, "It's okay. We'll figure it out."

I pulled away. "I . . . I think I might have figured it out already. This isn't the time to explain but . . . I think Sam might be right about you and her, and I think there's more to it, and that's why they're after us, so you need to be careful."

"We'll both be careful," he said. "We'll have each other's back. As always."

As always.

"We'll find Corey, then we'll get out of here," Daniel continued. "Get to a phone. Call our parents. Go home."

I'm not sure we can do that. I'm not sure Salmon Creek is still there, and if it is, I'm not sure it's safe. I'm not sure we can get Corey. I'm not sure he's still—

"Corey's fine," Daniel said, as if reading my thoughts.

"I'm sorry," I said. "I'm not holding up very well."

"Yes, you are. We just need to get this done, then you can have a breakdown. I'll join you."

I smiled. "Thanks."

"Anytime. Now, let's go."

ఴ   ఴ   ఴ

63 ఴ

Like a cougar with a cache, I knew where we'd left Corey. Hayley said they'd moved a little, but he'd be close enough for me to find him.

The three searchers were still at work, but they seemed to be employing a grid pattern, like when a little boy in a neighboring town had gone missing and we'd all joined the hunt, systematically scouring the forest until we found him, scared and exhausted. Once we realized that these searchers were walking a grid, it was a simple matter of waiting until they'd passed the area where we'd left Corey so we could sneak in.

Still they'd abandon the grid if they heard something. So Daniel stood guard with Kenjii, and I got down on all fours and crawled.

When I saw a white shoe peeking from under a bush, I crept closer and whispered, "It's me." Corey started at the sound of my voice, then caught himself.

"You guys shouldn't have come back."

"We did. Now, *shhh*, before I regret it."

I crawled under the branches and gave him a quick, one-armed hug. I whispered that we'd wait a minute to make sure all was clear. Then I said, "We're going to crawl out of here until we get to Daniel, so he can help you walk."

"I can walk—"

"Don't play the hero or you'll get us captured."

"That's so sweet. Makes me feel all warm and fuzzy inside."

"Hey, I hugged you, didn't I? Now follow me and try not

to make any noise."

"Yes, ma'am." He leaned down toward my ear. "I like it when you order me around. It's really hot."

I stifled a laugh, and for the first time since we'd gotten in that helicopter, I felt a little more like myself.

With his wounded knee, crawling wasn't easy for Corey. It was more of a half-crawl, half-drag. When we reached Daniel and Kenjii, Corey shakily got to his feet, tested his knee, then slung an arm over each of us. We made our way through the forest, avoiding the flashlights. It was slow. Excruciatingly slow.

When we finally got back to Hayley and Sam, we sat Corey down and I took another look at his knee. It had scabbed over and was bruising. I touched it, gently, pretending to check it out, as I closed my eyes and concentrated on fixing it.

That was supposed to be one of my powers—healing. It worked with animals, but I didn't know *how* it worked or if it would work on people at all. I tried anyway, focusing and brushing my fingertips over his knee, willing it to heal.

There was no way of telling whether it helped. With animals, it was never an instantaneous cure. They just seemed to get better strangely fast. I hoped for the same with Corey.

When I finished rewrapping Corey's knee, Daniel said, "I know we're all ready to drop. But if there's any chance we can put a little more distance between us and them . . ."

"We should," I finished.

Sam and Hayley struggled to their feet. I could tell they

were exhausted, but they didn't complain. Maybe they were beyond that.

Daniel put Corey's arm over his shoulders and we set off again.

EİGHT

W E HEADED FARTHER INLAND, not really going any-where, just going. No one talked. No one even asked what was going on, why were these people after us, why had they shot Nicole. Reasons weren't impor-tant.

We trudged through the woods, Kenjii and I in the lead. After a while, I let her go ahead and pick the clearest path. The shock of Nicole's death had dulled my senses. I didn't see the beautifully gnarled old trees and the delicate new ones. I just saw trees. Endless trees. When I heard the mournful hoot of owls or the staccato patter of paws, I didn't stop to listen. Even the smell of cedar seemed too sharp, acidic, as I strained to pick up every smell I usually hated on my forest walks—the stink of gas or diesel fumes, the acrid scent of smoke. Signs of life. Human life. There were none.

Even when I managed to pull my thoughts away from Nicole's and Rafe's deaths, I still found plenty to dwell on. I thought about Annie and wondered where she was, if she was alive, if she was safe. Could she take care of herself? She was nineteen, but since she began shape-shifting, she'd started regressing intellectually. Reverting to a more animal-like state. That's why Rafe had been so determined to find the scientists who'd reactivated our skin-walker gene. Because he hoped they could help Annie. Would the same thing happen to me?

I thought about the man on the shore, too. My biological father. I tried not to dwell on that—didn't matter, wouldn't let it matter—but those thoughts only led to ones of my biological mother, who'd abandoned me as an infant. I used to say she was giving me a better chance at life, but Rafe told me she'd had two babies. Twins. She gave me up and kept my brother. My twin brother. Were they still out there? Was *he* still out there? Again, it wasn't the time to dwell on that. But I did anyway. At least until I started thinking about my parents—my real parents—and worrying about them took over everything else.

I finally snapped out of it when I realized we'd started walking uphill. I blinked and looked around. Fewer trees. More rocks. Ahead? Pitch black. I had to crane my neck way back to see stars dotting the night sky.

"A mountain."

"Hmm?" Daniel said.

I jumped, and realized he was right beside me. Probably had been for a while. He put his hand on my back to steady me and said, "What'd you say?"

"I know why I couldn't see lights from the treetop. There's a mountain in the way."

"Damn." Daniel lowered his voice. "Corey's not going to be able to make it up that. Not tonight."

"I don't think any of us could make it up that tonight. Except maybe the two-time island wrestling champ." I struggled for a smile.

"Don't count on it. I'm running on fumes here."

"Let's find a spot for the night then. We should be far enough from the crash site by now."

We headed off the deer trail we'd been following and found a clearing next to a dead tree that acted as a windbreak. Once Daniel and I pronounced it suitable, everyone pretty much just collapsed where they stood.

Daniel and I were the last ones standing. When I started to lower myself to the ground, he tapped my elbow and pointed to a spot a few feet away.

"Looks more comfortable," he said.

There was a slight hollow there, where dried vegetation had collected. As I lay down, I could smell it, sharp and earthy, and the smell comforted me as much as the soft bedding. Kenjii curled up in front of me. Daniel stretched out behind me, close enough that I could feel the warmth radiating from him, and that relaxed me, too. If anyone had asked me five minutes ago if I could sleep, I'd have thought the question was insane, but my head had barely touched the ground before I was gone.

"Maya . . ."

I rolled over. Dead needles crackled under me. My foot bumped Daniel's, and he mumbled in his sleep.

"Maya . . ."

Another restless toss. A branch jabbed me this time, hard enough to make me open my eyes. I could make out the faint gray of dawn to the east.

I blinked and looked around. Corey, Sam, and Hayley were about five feet away, sound asleep.

I yawned and curled up again.

"Maya . . . Help . . ."

I bolted upright. A breeze wafted past, and I caught a smell I recognized.

Rafe.

I got to my feet, careful not to wake the others. Kenjii snorted, but she was too exhausted to stir. Once away from camp, I lurched blindly through the forest, following that teasing scent on the breeze, pushing the branches aside, not slowing down to look for a path or even a clear route.

I stumbled into a stream. Icy water filled my shoes, and I

slipped and fell to my knees.

"Maya . . ."

"Where are you?" I called.

"Over here. I'm . . ." A sharp intake of breath. "Hurt."

"Okay, stay where you are. I'm coming."

I broke into a jog. Only no matter how fast I ran, his scent and his voice didn't get any stronger. I kept going until I tripped over a root and hit the ground hard.

"Maya . . ."

"Just—"

"Maya? Is that you?"

I pushed to my feet, wincing as I flexed my stinging hands. "I'm—"

"Maya! I need you."

His voice seemed to come from all around me. I spun, trying to pinpoint it, but he kept yelling, more panicked with every shout, my own panic rising until I flung myself forward—

Hands grabbed me and yanked me back. For a moment, all I saw was the darkness of night. Then it fell away, dawn light filtering through the trees, and I was standing in front of Daniel, his fingers wrapped around my wrist. Kenjii was beside me, whimpering.

"Maya—"

"I have to go," I said, wrenching from his grasp. "It's Rafe. He's out here. He's hurt and . . ."

I turned and saw Sam and Hayley, then heard a crashing

in the undergrowth. Corey lurched through, using a branch for a cane.

I blinked. Sam and Hayley hadn't been there a second ago. I hadn't heard Corey crashing through the bush. It hadn't been this light out.

I looked up to see the sun now above the horizon. My eyes filled with tears.

"I—" I swallowed. "I—"

Daniel took both my wrists and turned me to face him. "You were sleepwalking, Maya."

"It just . . . I could hear Rafe and he was hurt and I was trying to get to him and—" My breath hitched. "It seemed real."

Daniel pulled me into a hug and I let myself collapse against his shoulder. I kept thinking about how real it had seemed and how I'd never sleepwalked before and . . .

And what if I hadn't been sleepwalking? What if I'd been having a vision?

Not that Rafe would really be calling for me. As that cold dawn light hit, I realized how silly it seemed, Rafe just lying there, yelling for me. If he could move, he'd be moving.

But if it had been a vision, that could mean Rafe really was out there. Really hurt. Really trying to find me.

I pulled away from Daniel and turned to Sam.

"Do you know where Rafe fell?" I asked. "Where the helicopter was?"

Her lips parted as if to ask why. Then she gave a soft, "Oh."

"I don't mean exactly," I said. "Obviously, you can't tell that. But do you have any idea? We were over the island, right? To the south of here? West? Southwest? Did you notice any landmarks?"

"Maya . . ." Daniel said.

I turned to meet his gaze. "I know I was sleepwalking, but it might have meant something." I lowered my voice so the others wouldn't hear. "A vision. Like the one I had with the marten." I'd had a vision of one of my recuperating animals, telling me how it had been injured.

"That wasn't—"

Daniel stopped himself. I knew he'd been about to say that it wasn't the same. He was right. It wasn't. But when he saw my expression, he couldn't finish, and when I saw his, I wished I hadn't said anything.

He looked as if he was in pain. Real pain. Wanting to give me hope. Knowing he couldn't, and that it wasn't right to try, wasn't fair.

"We were too high," Corey said, his voice uncharacteristically soft. "He . . ."

"He couldn't have survived," Sam finished.

A normal person couldn't have survived. But Rafe was a skin-walker. Part cat.

When I looked at Daniel, though, I knew I couldn't say that.

The more I clung to impossible hopes, the more I hurt him.

And we *had* been too high. I could argue and bluster and tell myself maybe, just maybe he'd survived, but I knew better.

Rafe was dead and if I was dreaming of him, that was my guilt talking. He was dead and I felt responsible.

"I—I'm sorry," I said. "Just . . . I need to sit down."

Daniel took a tentative step toward me.

"I'm okay," I said. "Just give me a minute on my own. Then we'll go."

I found a quiet spot where I could sit on a log and recover. Kenjii followed and sat with her head on my lap, dark eyes troubled.

A few minutes later, I heard someone looking for me, and I knew it wouldn't be Daniel. If I said I needed to be alone, he'd give me that space. When Hayley stepped around a tree, I stood.

"Sorry," I said. "You guys want to get going, right?"

She shook her head and came to sit beside me on the log. I hesitated, then lowered myself to it again.

"I think we should try to find Rafe," she said.

I took a deep breath. "I know he didn't make it."

"But you'll feel better if we look. We might as well go in the direction the helicopter came from. Just in case."

She had a point. We had to walk. Why not walk that way?

I shook my head. "If we're going back for anyone, it should be Nicole. If there's a chance she's alive—"

"There isn't. Not from what I saw. And if she did survive, that means they want her alive, which means she's safe enough for now. I think we should try to find Rafe."

I turned to her. "I know you liked him. Everyone's focusing on me, but you lost him, too."

"No, I didn't. He was yours."

"He didn't belong to any—"

"I only started flirting with him to make Corey jealous. Then I guess I did kind of fall for him. But the guy I was crushing on wasn't Rafe Martinez. Not the real one, anyway. I get that now. He was showing me someone else. He was showing us all someone else. Everyone except you."

"That's not—"

"Corey told me what Rafe did on the helicopter. How he let go so he wouldn't pull you and Daniel out. The Rafe I knew wouldn't have done that. Wouldn't even have thought of it."

"He didn't mean to trick you," I said. "He was looking for something in Salmon Creek. Something he really needed to find, to help his sister. He didn't mean to hurt anyone."

He didn't mean to hurt anyone. Not Hayley and the other girls he'd chased and cut loose. Not me, the one he'd finally caught, only to admit he'd pursued me for a reason.

I understood that now. I wished I could have understood

it then. I wished I could have said something in that last moment, before he let go.

He'd told me it was okay. His last words to me.

Why couldn't they have been my last words to him?

NINE

I T WASN'T EASY SETTING out again. We were tired and aching from sleeping on the cold ground. Even Sam complained. Everyone's jeans were still damp. My sneakers squirted water with every step from sleepwalking into the creek. The clothing that had dried stunk of mildew and felt stiff and scratchy. And we were hungry. I took them back to the creek for washing and drinking. It would keep us alive until we found food. We drank enough to fill our stomachs temporarily, and we headed out.

Once we were walking, I started feeling more myself. I seemed to be establishing a pattern here. Muster my strength and charge forward. Collapse in a puddle of grief and guilt. Charge forward. Collapse again.

I said as much to Daniel and the others chimed in, making mock bets on who would spend the most time in therapy after this, and whether we could get group discounts. The joking was strained, though, and the more we walked, the less we talked.

Eventually we were tramping through the forest in silence. That didn't really help, because the quiet meant every time we startled an animal and it took off, brush crackling, Corey or Hayley or Sam—sometimes all three—would jump and spin around, their backs to ours, like bison fending off a pack of wolves.

"It's a rabbit," I'd say.

"It's a grouse," Daniel would say.

We'd both add, "If anything bigger comes near, Kenjii will let us know."

But it didn't help. For our friends, the forest—with its sun-dappled groves and majestic, soaring redwoods—was no less terrifying in daylight that it had been last night.

We'd camped near the base of the mountain. Whether it actually qualified as a mountain, I had no idea. But it was tall and it was wide, and it was on our way—which explained why we hadn't been able to see any lights—so I thought of it as "the mountain." Seeing it had come as a relief to all, the thought that we might get to the top, look down, and see civilization. Or it did come as a relief, until we realized how long a hike it would be—all of it uphill.

Still, it was our best option. We just needed to go up the side. Which would be fine, if we'd had anything to eat. And if Corey had miraculously healed overnight. He was doing better, but it was a tough haul for him. For all of us.

One good thing about the mountain? It gave us a reference point. If everything was quiet, I could still pick up the distant crash of waves to my left, but the mountain was an even better compass point to keep us going in the right direction.

We slogged uphill for at least two hours. I was guessing at the time. My watch had survived the first dunk after the helicopter crash but not the second one, when I'd been pulled right under. Daniel's still worked and I think Corey's did, too, but no one was asking them for the time—no one cared.

When I heard the burble of a stream, I picked my way through a patch of bramble to get to it. Hayley was right behind me, fighting through the branches instead of ducking them. Sam got poked in the eye. When she cursed, Hayley jumped and slipped on a muddy patch. Corey ripped his shirt on thorns helping her up. All three complained, loudly and bitterly.

"We need more water," Daniel said. "Which means you need to get to it, because we can't bring it back for you."

"Well, maybe if Hayley was more careful," Sam said. "Not letting the branches fling back."

"Well, maybe if you weren't walking right behind me," Hayley said. "Why do we need water anyway? We drank before we set out."

"We need to drink from every stream I can find," I said. "As I've said, dehydration is the biggest risk we face out here."

"Okay," Corey said. "But could you find a path without mud and thorns?"

"I'll make sure the next one's paved."

Daniel leaned toward me as we walked. "I bet if we bolted, we could lose them in ten seconds."

"Don't tempt me," I muttered.

He grinned and put out his hand to help me over a muddy patch. I crossed, then called back a warning to the others. Daniel seconded the warning and pointed out the mud. Hayley still slid and fell.

At the stream—a little cascade splashing over a rock ledge—we got a drink. As we were leaving, Hayley said, "I can't do this," dropped, pulled up her knees, and buried her face against her legs.

"I'm sorry, guys," she said, her voice tight. "I just can't. I'm cold and I'm tired and I'm hungry."

I crouched beside her. "I know you're uncomfortable, but we're okay. Our clothing is dry now and it's not cold enough for hypothermia. We can survive without food as long as we don't dehydrate—"

"You don't get it, do you?" Corey snapped. "We're tired and hungry, and you blather on about hypothermia and dehydration—"

"Hey!" Daniel bore down on Corey. "She keeps talking

about hypothermia and dehydration because you guys won't shut up about being cold and hungry."

"Well, maybe we don't need to hear how this isn't going to kill us," Corey said. "Maybe we need more than a pep talk."

"Like what? Sympathy? Right. Because that's going to get us out of these woods. Maybe you can show a little sympathy yourself under the circumstances and—"

"Enough," I said. "You're right, Corey. I'm sorry. I know your knee is hurting. I know everyone's cold. I know everyone's tired. I know everyone's hungry. I know everyone's worrying about their parents and what's going on back in Salmon Creek. And we're thinking about Nic and Rafe and—"

Oh God. My parents. Nicole. Rafe.

I tried to finish, but I couldn't remember what I'd been saying, and I just stood there with everyone staring at me. Then Daniel was beside me, rubbing away the goose bumps on my arms and Corey was hobbling over, looking like a kicked puppy. He put an arm around my shoulder.

"I'm sorry," he said.

Hayley echoed him, on her feet again, standing there awkwardly.

I wiped my eyes, and gave Corey a quick embrace before nudging him back. "I should look at your knee."

"Nah, it's—"

"I should check it." I glanced up at him. "Please."

He nodded, and limped to a boulder to sit.

"I'll go see if I can find some berries," Daniel said.

"You won't and even if you do, eating a little . . ." I looked around at the others, then back to Daniel. "Sure, that'd be good."

"No," Hayley said. "Eating a little will just remind us how hungry we are. There has to be a summer cabin around here somewhere. Everyone leaves food behind. I'd settle for cold beans from a rusted can."

Corey's knee looked the same as it had that morning— scabbed over, bruised and tender to the touch. It had to be killing him to walk, but when I asked if he wanted to stay behind, his response was an emphatic no with an edge of panic.

"Can I apologize again for snapping?" he said.

"No." I sat back on my haunches. "We need to slow down for you. You're in pain and you're not going to remind us of that."

"It isn't that bad. Really. I—"

"See? Gotta be a tough guy." I lowered my voice so the others wouldn't hear. "How's your head?"

"I didn't hit my head. Not yet anyway."

"You know what I mean. Your headaches."

"I'm fine." When I opened my mouth to protest, he clapped his hand over it. "I'm not pulling any macho crap, Maya. My head is fine. I'm getting twinges, but it's nothing

I don't get everyday, even with the meds. I'll be okay." He looked around him. "And as soon as we get out of this place, I'll be even better. So let's hit the trail."

The ascent was getting steep, so I decided to hike ahead. The others would follow slowly—we all had to get over this mountain, one way or another.

Someone needed to come with me, for safety's sake. Daniel would be my first choice, but when Sam volunteered, I took her up on it. I wanted to talk to her. Alone.

I left Kenjii with Daniel, using a length of vine as a leash. She didn't like that. He didn't like it much either, until I explained that by keeping her, he could find me as they followed along behind at their own pace.

We picked a landmark, then Sam and I hiked off toward it. It was rough going. Daniel would find an easier route for the others, but I was taking the most direct one, which meant rock climbing. Soon Sam was puffing, red-faced. I found a stream—not much more than a trickle over the rocks—and we drank our fill, then I made her sit on the rocks so we could rest.

"You'd never met your aunt and uncle before your parents died, had you?" I said as we rested.

She shook her head. "Never even heard of them. At the funeral, my parents' lawyer introduced us. I knew my dad had a couple of sisters, but it freaked me out, no matter how

nice the Tillsons were. I tried to run away. Told the lawyer they weren't really my relatives. Everyone thought I was
having a breakdown. The doctor gave me something. The
rest was a blur. I expected to wake up locked in a laboratory."

"Instead you woke up in Salmon Creek. Did you think the
Tillsons were really your aunt and uncle?"

"I tried to." She stood and stretched, then we started walking again, hiking up a steep incline. "Most days I believed it.
Even when I didn't, I figured it was a mix-up and I didn't
want to argue. Mr. and Mrs. Tillson are"—she swallowed—
"were great. Really nice to me, no matter how much of a brat
I was. Salmon Creek wouldn't have been my choice of a place
to grow up in, but it seemed safe. If I had to be somewhere,
I might as well have been in some nowhere Canadian town
where the bad guys wouldn't find me."

"Only they did. That's what you thought when Mina Lee
started asking questions. That they'd found you. Until you
figured out what Daniel is. And by then it was too late to run.
You were on the helicopter with us."

She nodded. Didn't add anything.

"The book Daniel and I read said there aren't any more
benandanti," I continued. "It said they were wiped out during
the Inquisition. Only they weren't. They just hid their powers
and intermarried with regular people until future generations
didn't have any powers. The benandanti went extinct. Then
they were resurrected in an experiment."

She looked over at me so sharply she bumped into a tree.

"Mina Lee hinted at something like that," I lied. "With Salmon Creek being a medical research town, I figured any resurrection must be science, not magic. Daniel was born there. You were brought there. They say the town was created to do medical research but . . ." I shrugged, then continued, "You thought you'd wake up in a laboratory. You did. Just not the kind you expected. I think Salmon Creek is one big petri dish, designed to protect and nurture the first members of an extinct supernatural type." *More than one type.* I glanced over at her. "I'm right, aren't I?"

She paused, and I realized she hadn't figured all that out.

"You do think there are more in town, right?" I said. "More benandanti?"

"Maybe Corey," she said. "His parents aren't Italian, but that doesn't mean anything. We're a long way from the Inquisition. There's been a lot of intermarrying."

Like my birth mother, who apparently carried the skin-walker gene, but looked Caucasian. I didn't. I'd inherited my looks from my . . . I thought of the man in the forest and squeezed my eyes shut. Enough of that.

"Daniel and I thought that the people who started the fire were after the research," I said. "And we were right. We just didn't know *kids* were the research."

"I guess so."

"You said your parents were hiding from someone. The researchers? Or someone else?"

She shrugged.

"Did they warn you?"

Shrug.

"They were murdered. Do you think these people were responsible?"

Shrug.

"So that's how it's going to be? I share and you don't?"

"You didn't share anything. You made connections that might be totally wrong."

"Maybe I've got more."

She shook her head. "You think you're smart. Well, maybe you are, but you're still just a kid who got caught up in something. Daniel and I, we're the ones they want. I know you're used to being special, Maya, but for once, you aren't."

I'd been about to tell her the truth. As much as I wanted Daniel to be the first to know, it had seemed wiser first to share with someone who'd believe me.

But if I said something now, I'd sound like I was just trying to be "special." Sam's about-face, from ally to antagonist, reminded me of my suspicions about her involvement in Serena's death.

I played back her earlier words. "Mr. and Mrs. Tillson were great." No mention of Nicole, when I knew Nicole had gone out of her way to make Sam feel welcome.

Someone had pulled Serena under the water and drowned her. Someone had pulled me under, then and now. Someone had pulled Nicole under, too.

Sam hadn't liked Serena. She hadn't liked Nicole. Apparently, she didn't like me much either, no matter how hard she tried to pretend otherwise.

Who did Sam like? Daniel. Who had been pulled under the water? His girlfriend, his best friend, and a girl who wanted to be his next girlfriend.

"I think you should go back with the others," I said. "You're slowing me down."

A look crossed her face, so fast I couldn't quite catch it. Then her features hardened.

"Oh, so that's how it's going to be? Invite me along because I might tell you something useful? Send me away when I don't?"

"Sound familiar?"

"What?"

I stepped toward her. "Last night, in the water, I didn't notice you going to your cousin's rescue. Or to mine. In fact, when we nearly drowned, I didn't see you anywhere at all. You popped up afterward."

Her mouth went slack, before she managed a strangled, "What? Are you—? Wait a minute. I didn't—"

"You said it yourself. You're special. You have powers." I met her gaze. "And we have no idea exactly what those powers are, do we?"

I turned and loped uphill.

It took Sam a moment. Then she shouted, "Maya! Wait! Hold on!"

Brush crackled as she ran after me. "I'm sorry, okay? Just wait and listen to me. I didn't have anything to do with pulling you under the water. Or Serena, if that's what you think. I can barely swim. But I might know—"

I heard a crash and a yelp as she tripped. I picked up my pace. By the time she recovered, I was too far away for her to catch me.

TEN

I MADE IT TO the crest in about an hour. Then I had to climb a tree to get a better look. Any other time, this would have been the gift at the end of a long hike, and I'd have found a last spurt of energy to grab the bottom branch and swing up.

Now I stood at the base of a tree and thought, "I can't do this." I remembered last night's climb, the grief and the loneliness. Here on the ground, I could keep that at bay. But up there . . .

Rafe was up there. Maybe he always would be.

Or maybe he wouldn't. Next year, I might be climbing trees, remembering him only when a certain scent wafted past. Like with Serena. For months after her death, I'd go out of my way to avoid passing any lakes. That changed. I still couldn't go swimming in the one where she'd drowned.

I probably never would. But just this summer, I'd gone with Daniel and a bunch of summer kids to another lake, and I'd been there at least an hour before someone shrieked, and I thought of Serena and had to leave.

Remembering. Forgetting. I'm not sure which is worse.

I gripped the tree trunk and closed my eyes, focusing on the rough bark under my fingers. Then I opened my eyes and stared at it. Rubbed my fingers over it. See, feel, smell the tree. Just a tree. Not a reminder of him.

I circled it. No branch low enough for me to swing onto. I embraced the trunk and shimmied up ten feet to the first branch. From there it was an easy climb.

My energy ebbed fast and before I was high enough, I had to stop and rest. I sat on a branch and looked out. There was little to see from here. Just endless emerald needles perfuming the air.

I let my feet dangle and took a deep breath. The wind whispered past.

Maya . . .

I rubbed the back of my neck and closed my eyes. Don't do that. It's just the wind.

A branch overhead creaked.

Help . . . Maya.

I swung up to the next branch so fast I almost lost my grip, and I sat there, trembling, looking down and thinking of what would have happened if I'd fallen. Then I thought about what Rafe's fall must have been like. The terror of those few minutes. The despair of knowing there was nothing he could do to stop it.

Had he regretted letting go? Had he thought *Maybe, just maybe, I would have been okay if I held on?* Did he blame me for not holding on to *him*?

Up again. Climbing, climbing, climbing until I was so high my empty stomach made me light-headed and I had to stop, eyes squeezed shut, until the feeling passed.

Then I looked out, and when I did, I wasn't looking for a road. Wasn't looking for a house. I was looking for him.

I told myself I was looking for his body. That if I could find it, I could mark the spot, make sure he got a proper burial. But that was a lie.

I was looking for Rafe. In spite of every bit of logic that told me he was dead, I could not stop myself from looking. From feeling he was out there.

Of course there was no sign of him and so, finally, I began scouring the landscape in earnest.

I made out the brown ribbon of a dirt road and a distant clearing that could be a town. However, if we were at the north end of the island, a clearing was just as likely to indicate a past forest fire or logging operation.

I was about to decide the road was our best bet when I spotted a thin line of smoke rising near the foot of the mountain. I found a better vantage point, and could make out the faint outline of a roof, smoke swirling above it. The sight was so incredible that I didn't quite believe it at first, climbing yet another evergreen, until I was certain I wasn't imagining things. There was a house or a cottage down there. And someone was home.

I scrambled down the tree and took off to find the others.

When I glimpsed the white of Daniel's T-shirt, I started to run, grinning for the first time in days. Kenjii hit me in a full-on tackle, her vine-leash dangling behind her, as she knocked me down and licked me like we'd been separated for months.

"I saw a road," I blurted as Daniel rounded a bend in the path, Sam right behind him. "There's a road down there. I think there's a cabin, too."

"What?" Corey brushed past Daniel and Sam. "A house? You saw a house?"

Hayley barreled forward. "There's a house? Where?"

I took a deep breath. "I *think* I saw a *cabin*. Whether there's anyone in it or not—"

"Who cares?" Corey said. "It's civilization. Let's go."

He broke into a jog, and his knee gave way. I managed to catch him before he fell.

"The only place you're going is flat on your ass," Daniel said. "Slow down. Even if it is a cabin, it's not going anywhere." He turned to me and I could tell he was struggling to play it cool. "You said there's a road?"

"I did. That part I'm sure of. And where there's a road, there are people. In theory."

The grin burst through. "In theory." He threw an arm around me, a half-embrace, whispering, "Good work," and I started to shake a little. It was over. Our ordeal was almost over.

Except it wasn't. Our real problems—being subjects in a supernatural experiment—had only begun.

I took a deep breath and hugged Daniel back. We'd worry about that later. For now, we needed to get to civilization.

Before we continued, I insisted on checking Corey's knee.

"Looking good, huh?" Corey said as I cleaned the scrapes. "You've got the touch."

Apparently, I did. The bruises were fading already.

When we set out again, I motioned for Daniel to walk up front with me. No one tried to join us. They figured we were discussing the situation and planning our next move, and they were happy to leave that to us.

"You want to talk about Sam?" he said. "I take it you guys had a falling out."

I gave him part of the story—that I'd told her my theory about Salmon Creek and the people chasing us, and she'd reciprocated by insulting me.

"She blows hot and cold, and it makes me nervous," I said. "I feel like when she is being chummy, she's putting it on to get what she wants. It's almost . . ."

"Sociopathic?"

I lifted my brows.

"Someone who can be charming to achieve their own ends,

but ultimately doesn't care about others. And, no, I'm not study-ing crazy people. I've read case studies in my uncle's texts."

Criminal law texts. Daniel wanted to be a lawyer, and although he was still two years from university—and even more from law school—he was already preparing.

"Do you get that vibe from her?" I asked.

He shook his head. "I'm not sure I would, if she's the same thing I am. But I agree about the hot and cold part. I don't think she's a sociopath, but it is—"

"Troubling. I shouldn't take off alone with her anymore. None of us should."

"Agreed."

It was a quiet walk, but the silence became peaceful, happy even. We weren't lost any longer. We were walking through wilderness just like the one surrounding Salmon Creek. A wooded playground. Lakes to swim in. Streams to fish in. Cliffs to climb. Hollows to fill with bonfires and beer bottles. Nothing scary about that.

No one trudged now. No one bitched when I led them through thick brush to get a drink. We were still a long hike from the cabin, and everyone was thirsty.

When we found the stream, tumbling over rocks into a pool below, you'd think it was the first time we'd seen a water-fall. Shoes and socks came off. Shirts followed. Or Corey's and Daniel's did, then mine, Hayley gaping like I'd stripped naked, though I was wearing a bra. She kept her shirt on.

Sam didn't take off anything, but she sat on a rock, looking almost content, as the rest of us splashed in the water, washing off the filth.

As we got out, I imagined lounging out on the flat rocks surrounding the pool, dozing in the sun, letting my aching muscles relax. But there was no time for that kind of break. We'd had our drink. Time to hit the trail. The end was near.

We'd reached the bottom of the mountain when Kenjii stopped. Her ears swiveled forward and she glanced up into the trees.

"Cat," I said to the others.

Corey looked at Kenjii, who was silently scanning the treetops. "Yeah, you can tell by the way she's going crazy, barking and racing around to drive off the despicable feline. Your dog is weird, Maya."

"No, she's just accustomed to Fitz," Daniel said.

True, but Kenjii hadn't minded felines even before Fitz—a three-legged bobcat—adopted us. She'd grown up with a wild cat—a partial one, at least.

A sudden yowl made Hayley jump and Kenjii stiffened, her expression not nearly as friendly now.

"Cougar," I said, motioning the others back.

A flash of tawny flank ten meters overhead confirmed it. I continued to back everyone up slowly. The cat was high in the tree, stretched out on a sturdy branch. A female. I could tell by the size, and the first thing I thought was *It's Annie. She's come looking for Rafe.*

But it wasn't. Like me, Annie had a paw-print birthmark on her hip. There was no mark on this cat's flank.

The cat peered down at us, her black-tipped ears swiveling, long, thick tail flicking. When I kept moving the others back, Corey said, "I get that cougars are dangerous, Maya, but this one doesn't look that big."

"Because she's way up there," Daniel said.

I nodded. "It's a female. She's smaller than a male, but she's still bigger than Kenjii. One chomp of those fangs would be the last thing you felt. And she wouldn't hesitate to do it if you got in her way. So let's just give her some room. Please."

The cat yowled again, then got up and stood on the branch, lowering her head to peer down at us.

"I think she's hungry," Sam said.

I shook my head. "It's not winter yet. She isn't starving, and she wouldn't attack five of us even if she was. Something's wrong."

It wasn't odd that the cat had let us get so close. Cougars are masters of camouflage. We might have passed right under her if it wasn't for that yowl. Which is how I knew something was bothering her. No way should she have let out that cry and given herself away.

Something was bothering me, too. A black pit of anxiety swirled in my gut. I found my gaze drawn up to the cougar. As I met her eyes, I felt a fresh jolt of fear. The cat paced along the branch, and I knew it wasn't my own anxiety I was feeling.

"Uh, Maya?" Corey called. "You said she was dangerous, so can we leave the kitty alone now?"

"Something's *really* bothering her."

Daniel walked over. "Is she hurt?"

"I don't think so. Just . . . upset. Anxious."

"Um, yeah," Corey said. "Because there are a bunch of teenagers and a very big dog blocking her way down."

"That's not it," I said. "She—"

The cat's ears swiveled and she looked sharply to the east. I caught a high-pitched whine.

"An ATV."

The others glanced about until the sound got louder. Corey heard it first and grinned.

"Hallelujah," he said. "I never thought I'd be happy to hear one of those damned things."

I flashed back to the last ATV I'd seen—driven by the people who'd set the fire. Daniel caught my eye, obviously thinking the same thing.

Corey hobbled forward. "It's just over there. Heading this—"

The ATV headlight bobbed into view. Daniel shoved Corey to the ground, yelling "Down!" to the rest of us. Sam and I obeyed. Hayley looked around, confused, until I grabbed her hand and yanked her.

"What the hell?" Corey whispered.

"Have you forgotten the last time someone ran toward rescuers?" Sam hissed. "Nicole?"

Hayley paled and flattened herself against the ground.

"That was on the other side of the hill," Corey said. "How would they even know to look for us here?"

"They had ATVs before," Daniel said. "If they're the same guys, they've had plenty of time to load those ATVs on a truck and bring them up. We should back into those bushes and watch."

The bushes were about ten meters away. As we crawled into them, we startled a couple of deer on the other side. They bolted, heading straight for the ATV.

There was a thud and a shout. The ATV motor died.

"Son-of-a-bitch!" A man's voice rang through the forest.

A radio squawked. He answered it.

"Yeah, that was me. Just hit a deer. Remind me who had the bright idea to use these damn things? Some project manager sitting in his fancy L.A. office, I'll bet. Never seen a forest, much less tried to search one. I could have hit one of the kids for all I would have noticed, whipping around like this. I can barely see through these woods. Can't hear anything. But you can bet your ass those kids can hear us."

"And a good thing, too," Corey muttered.

A voice tried to interrupt the man's tirade, but he cut it off, saying, "Calvin's got the right idea, searching on foot. I'm leaving this piece of crap here. If the Nasts want it, they can come get it. Tell Calvin I'll meet him at the bend in ten."

We heard the man stalk off, branches crackling in his wake.

"Now that's sweet," Corey said when he was gone. "An ATV, just sitting there, ours for the taking. The ride goes to the handicapped guy."

"I thought you were doing fine," Hayley said.

"My knee's acting up again." He stretched his leg and mock-winced.

"No one's taking the ride," Daniel said. "Even if it's still running after hitting a deer, it's too noisy."

"Let's wait for them to finish searching this area and move on, like they did last night," I said. "Then we'll check out that building I saw. If we can't get help there, we'll see if the ATV still runs."

After lying low for about twenty minutes, Daniel and I decided we should start for the cabin. We left Kenjii behind with Corey.

The cottage was a hunting lodge—a cabin lacking a single flourish that turned it from a functional building into a vacation residence. It was off-season, but these places often did double-duty as a "getaway from the kids and the missus" refuge for men. I have to admit, I don't get that. Shouldn't you be able to take some time to yourself without lying about "going hunting" for the weekend? Maybe my expectations for honesty are too high. I've been told that before.

It seemed as if the cabin owner was on such a break from domesticity, because while no smoke came from the chimney now, a massive pickup sat in the drive.

I started forward, but Daniel caught my arm and word-lessly pointed. I followed his finger to see the elongated shadow of an ATV that was parked on the other side of the cabin.

I swore.

"Ditto," he whispered.

We backed up into the forest.

After a harder look at the pickup, I kicked myself for not making the connection. It was big and it was gleaming new, out of place beside the rundown cabin.

The truck was transportation for the ATVs. There was another vehicle on the other side of it. Transportation for the rest of the search party.

"They're squatting in the cabin," I said. "Using it as a base of operations. We should still get in there if we can. Not just to search for phones or radios, but to get food. Without it, we won't be in any shape to run or fight back if we're caught."

Daniel looked at me.

"Yes, I know, it's a ballsy move," I said.

He smiled. "All right. Let's check it out."

ELEVEN

D ANIEL STOOD GUARD WHILE I checked out the cabin. The terrain here was rocky grassland—sparse trees, lots of bushes, sections of tall grass. So I crawled through the grassy sections to the cabin. Then, I stood and slid along the back wall until I could peek through the window.

There was a woman inside. She was drinking from a juice box and munching peanuts. Even the sight of it made my stomach growl. As she ate, she leafed through a file.

I crawled back and told Daniel that I thought the woman had just stopped for a snack before resuming her search. We found a good place to sit it out and watch the cabin.

After a few minutes, Daniel said, in a low voice, "So you think Sam's right. About me."

"I do."

He studied my expression, then nodded. "Okay."

"You don't?"

"My head says it's crazy, but my gut . . . It feels like when I spend all night struggling with a math problem and finally the answer comes. There's this click, and I know it's right even before I check my work. Lately, there's been a bunch of things that just seem . . . wrong. With me. About me. When Sam explained, I felt that click."

"Good."

He nodded, but he didn't look convinced that it was "good." It would have been easier for him if Sam had explained that he was suffering from a hormonal imbalance or even mild mental illness. That he could believe. This was a lot harder.

"Guess now we know why my dad hates me."

"He doesn't hate you," I said.

"Maybe. He doesn't like me much, though. He knows what I am. I think he didn't find out until my mom left and now he suspects I'm not his kid."

"You are. I think pretending otherwise is just . . . easier for him. Your mom drops this bomb before she leaves, and he doesn't know what to make of it. He's confused. Maybe even a little scared of you. He doesn't like feeling that way about his son, so he tells himself you *aren't* his son." I caught his gaze. "Whatever it is, it has nothing to do with you. Not your mom leaving. Not your dad being angry. She made choices she couldn't deal with, so she dumped them on him. He couldn't deal with them, so he dumped them on you. They aren't your problems. But you're handling them just fine."

"Thanks."

His lips curved in a faint smile. It wasn't enough. I wanted to make him really smile. Make him happy.

"So now do we get to talk about your problem?" he said.

"Hmm?"

"Whatever you've been wanting to tell me and haven't."

"I—"

"You've had a lot on your mind, and you can't seem to find the right time or the right way to say it."

I nodded.

"It's about these people," he continued, waving at the cabin. "You've found out something else. Something about you, not me."

"Does your new bag of tricks include mind reading?"

He laughed. "Only when it comes to you, Maya. So, do I get the story now?"

I nodded. "It's . . . It's about Rafe. Kind of. Why he came to Salmon Creek. He was looking for something. Someone. We . . ."

I struggled to think of a way to finish that line. Daniel waited patiently.

"It . . . It's about his sister," I said. "Or it starts there. Kind of. Do you remember the tattoo artist? Her—"

The bang of a screen door made us both jump. Footsteps thumped on wood. Then the woman stepped off the front porch and strode to the ATV.

"I guess I have to wait a little longer to hear the rest," Daniel said.

When the woman disappeared on the ATV, we headed for the cabin.

The interior looked like I expected. Two rooms—a main one and a tiny bedroom. Dusty stuffed fish and moth-eaten elk heads on bare walls. A wood plank floor that seemed as if it hadn't been swept in years. Cobwebs decorating the ceiling. Furniture that would have been rejected by Goodwill. Mouse droppings everywhere. A few dark furry bat forms hung from the upper eaves. In the city, the place would have been condemned as a public health hazard. Here, it was just a typical hunting shack.

As we searched for food, I found the file the woman had been reading. It was tucked in a cupboard. When I picked it up, Daniel shook his head.

"We can't take anything like that. Risky enough stealing food. They'll definitely notice if their papers are missing." He walked over. "Are they . . . about us?"

I showed him the top one, a topographical map of the island. Beneath it was a list with all our names on it.

"Okay, read fast," he said. "I'll find food."

I skimmed the document. More than once I had to slow down, not sure I was understanding. I forced myself to keep going, assimilating as much as I could while jotting down names and phrases on a pad of paper left on the table.

Daniel came back. "Got nuts and granola bars, drink boxes, and two bottles of water. We can refill the bottles at streams. I could take more, but then it'd definitely be noticed."

"That's good. Just give me a sec to finish—"

Footsteps thumped on the front porch. Daniel grabbed the papers from my hand. As he put them back, I dashed into the bedroom. There wasn't a closet. I dove under the bed.

I doubt anyone had cleaned under there since it was moved into the room, and maybe not even before that. The inch-thick dust I could live with. It was the mouse droppings and used tissues that would have sent me scurrying for another place. But there wasn't time. Daniel dove in behind me, and we lay with our heads near the foot of the bed, so we could peer out the doorway.

I watched boots walk in—expensive hiking boots and a few inches of denim pant legs. One person. Male. He let the door swing shut behind him, and headed straight for the cooler. He popped open what sounded like a beer bottle, and chugged the contents.

As he drank, he wandered, the thump of his boots punctuated by the tap-tap of texting. Then he grunted.

"Damned hellhole," he muttered. "Oh, sure, there'll be cell service. Right. The only thing this island has is mosquitoes."

Our mosquitoes weren't bad at all—I only had a bite or two after a day in the woods. He was just being cranky. It sounded like the same man who'd hit the deer, and obviously, his mood hadn't improved. He muttered some more as he tried to text again, then picked up the radio, hit a button, and complained to someone on the other end.

"If it's an urgent message, I can relay it to headquarters," said the man on the other end. "But I have a feeling it's not urgent, Moreno."

"No? You don't know Sheila. If I don't call her by tonight, she'll be throwing my things out of the apartment window, sure I'm shacking up with some girl in Vancouver."

"I'll let you call her on the satellite phone later, okay? *If* you get your ass back out here."

"Yeah, yeah. I was just grabbing some water."

He disconnected. We waited for him to go. And waited. Apparently, he wasn't done drinking his "water." At least five minutes passed before he finally made his way toward the door.

He got the door open, then came back and rustled around in the pantry. A pause. Then "huh." I knew Daniel had been careful about putting everything back the way he found it. Daniel was always careful.

The guy grabbed a granola bar, wrapper crinkling as he ripped it open. He munched it on the way to the door. We watched his boots as he hesitated. He turned, as if looking around the cottage. Then he took another bite, and chewing loudly, headed out.

"He made us," Daniel whispered as he shot from under the bed.

I scrambled after him. "What?"

"He knows we're here."

"Are you sure?"

Daniel was already at the door, throwing it open and charging through.

TWELVE

B Y THE TIME I caught up, the man was facedown with Daniel on his back, as if he'd knocked him flying clear off the porch. Knocked the radio from his hand, too. It lay a few feet from the man's outstretched fingers.

"Moreno?" The other man's voice came over the radio. "What's up now?"

The man—Moreno—lifted his head to answer. Daniel slammed his face into the ground so hard I winced.

A moment of silence, then the other man sighed and disconnected.

"Guess you made one too many unnecessary calls," Daniel said.

"No," Moreno said. "He realized I'm in trouble. He's coming."

I glanced at Daniel, but he shook his head. The man was

bluffing. He motioned for me to stand watch, though, just in case.

"We need to get him away from here," I said, "so we can interrogate him."

"Interrogate me?" Moreno sputtered a laugh. "You kids are cute, you know that? You escape from a helicopter crash and suddenly you're outlaws. Let me tell you how this is going to work—"

Daniel heaved Moreno to his feet. The man swung at him, but Daniel ducked easily and returned a one-two punch that left Moreno reeling.

"Island wrestling champ," I said. "Only third place in boxing, though, so you're getting off easy."

Moreno steadied himself, then charged. I stuck out my foot and tripped him.

"Ouch," I said as he hit the ground. "That's kind of embarrassing."

Daniel hauled him up again and led him toward the forest. I ran back inside and grabbed rope and a towel to gag him if we needed to. But Moreno didn't try to scream for help. He just let Daniel lead him along, smirking, as if humoring us.

"You taking me to the other kids?" he asked.

"There aren't any others," Daniel said. "We're the only ones who made it."

Moreno laughed. "Right. That's sweet, protecting your buddies. Did you forget we have a source now? Little Nicky?"

"Ni-Nicole?" I said.

Daniel glanced back at me, his look warning me not to fall for it so fast.

"We saw her get shot," I said.

"Um, yeah, tranquilizer dart. I'd have thought you would know about those, Miss Maya the animal doctor."

"You expect us to believe you?"

"Ah, getting cynical. Can't blame you, under the circumstances, finding out your entire life is a lie. Not going to trust anyone now, are you? Nicole is fine. She told us what happened on the helicopter. How things went wrong. You thought the mayor had been sedated. Daniel sent the pilot flying and knocked him out. Samantha tried to fly the bird, but Rafe fell out. Then it crashed and now the pilot and the mayor are dead." He paused. "I can't imagine how bad you must feel, Maya. All those people dead because you made a mistake about the mayor."

Daniel clenched his free hand, as if he was going to deck the guy. When I shook my head, he shoved Moreno hard and said, "She didn't make a mistake. The pilot dosed Mr. Tillson before we got on that helicopter. I saw it happen and I saw the injection spot."

Moreno shrugged. "If he did, it was to prevent exactly that sort of scenario. Panic and tragedy."

Daniel kept pushing him forward until we were deep in the woods. Then he kicked him in the back of the legs, knocking him to his knees.

"Tough guy, huh?" Moreno said. "I'm not the one you're

supposed to be using those skills on."

"Oh, I think you are . . . demon."

Daniel's voice was steady, but I saw the hesitation in his eyes as he said the word. Moreno didn't and, for the first time, he looked genuinely surprised. With that, Daniel knew Sam had been telling the truth, and his chin dipped.

"Yes, Daniel knows he's a benandanti," I said.

"Suppose the Russo girl told him. We thought she might know." He looked at me. "And what about you? Figured out your superpowers yet?"

Daniel looked over at me, but there was no shock in his eyes. Just the same look as when Moreno confirmed he was part-demon, one that said he'd already suspected as much.

"I know something's happening to me," I said.

"Already? Calvin will be pleased. So, Maya, do you want to know the big secret? What you really are?"

"Of course she does," Daniel said.

"Good." Moreno flashed a smile. "Then this is where we begin negotiations. You two lead me back to that cabin and let me call my associates. We'll take you someplace safe and tell you everything you need to know."

"Um, right," I said. "We've escaped a helicopter crash, trekked through the forest all night, and captured you. But that was just for fun. Time to stop goofing off and turn ourselves in."

"Do your parents let you get away with talking to adults like that?"

"Only when those adults treat me like an idiot."

"We have the upper hand here," Daniel said. "If you're going to give us some crap about turning ourselves in because we're a danger to society? Don't bother."

"Danger to society?" Moreno pursed his lips as if considering it. "Not really. A danger to yourselves? Absolutely. You're going through a lot right now, but it's nothing compared to what's coming. You need help." He looked at me. "Have you met Annie?"

My mouth went dry and my heart started to thud.

"I take it that's a yes. I don't know how much you know about your 'condition,' Maya, but unless you want to end up like Annie, I'd suggest you take me back to that cabin. Turn yourselves in. Get the help you need. The kind of help the St. Clouds and the Edison Group can't provide."

"Edison Group?" Daniel said.

"Don't know as much as you think, do you? I'm betting, in the larger scheme of things, you barely know anything."

"Tell us, then," I said. "Otherwise, how can we understand how much danger we're in?"

"You're a clever one, aren't you? Nope. Sorry. You want more, you need to take me back to the cabin and call the others—your friends and mine."

He wasn't budging. Although we could pretend we held the power here, he knew better because he knew we weren't going to hurt him. He'd laughed at the thought of us interrogating him, and as much as that pissed me off, he had a point.

We were teenagers who'd grown up in a tiny town where we'd been treated like precious gems, which I guess, in a way, we were. We'd had an easy life. While we were tough enough to survive in the woods, we wouldn't hurt Moreno in order to make him talk. It went against every value that had been instilled in us. Daniel's power of persuasion was apparently on the fritz, so we were stuck.

For a moment during our attempted interrogation, I considered getting Sam. I suspected she could have handled this. But I honestly didn't think it would do any good. Moreno wasn't telling us anything else.

We patted him down and confiscated his cell phone. It needed a code, and he wasn't giving it up.

Finally, we did the closest thing to torturing him we could come up with. We gagged him with the towel and tied him to a tree a couple hundred meters from the cabin.

"Your friends aren't going to find you," Daniel said. "And the nights are getting cold. It'll be a race between hypothermia and dehydration, see which kills you first."

We paused a moment, letting that sink in, then I said, "Are you sure you don't want to talk to us?"

Moreno rolled his eyes, still looking amused.

"He'll think it's a lot less funny by morning," I said to Daniel. "We'll come back then, see if he's changed his mind."

We'd hoped that threat would be enough to get him talking. It wasn't. As we walked away, we looked back a couple of times to see if he was straining at his bonds, wildly trying to tell us he'd talk. He just sat there. Which meant we were screwed. No way we were hanging around until morning and then coming back. I suppose he knew that. Maybe he also knew we wouldn't really walk away and leave him to die— that his bonds weren't tight enough to bind him there forever. Just long enough to let us get far away as his friends searched for him.

THIRTEEN

"WE DIDN'T GET MUCH out of him," Daniel said when we were away from Moreno.

"It fit with what I read in the cabin, though. It's starting to come together but—"

Barking erupted in the forest. A very deep, very familiar, very *loud* bark.

"Kenjii!" Daniel said.

I broke into a run. Daniel kept pace behind me. As I ran, I mentally cursed the others for not quieting my dog. That bark would carry for miles.

When I was close enough for Kenjii to hear me, I gave a soft whistle. She came crashing through the bushes.

"No!" Hayley yelled. "Kenjii!"

"It's okay," I said. "It's me."

Kenjii barreled into me. I managed to avoid being bowled

over, but when I tried to get past her, she bumped my legs, prodding me back the way I'd come.

"Maya?" Hayley called, loud enough to make me wince. "Daniel?"

I pushed Kenjii aside. She growled and leaped into my path, then bumped me with her head. Telling me to stay back. Don't come this way. When Daniel tried to pass her, she blocked him, too.

I shoved her aside with a firm "no." I saw Hayley and Sam, standing near the abandoned ATV and dead deer. I tried to brush past Daniel. His arm shot out to stop me. And then I saw why. Corey was crouched beside the ATV, as if he'd been working on it. On the other side of the dead deer was a snarling, spitting cougar.

"She came for the deer," I whispered. Seeing the cougar from another angle, I noticed her hanging teats. "She's lactating, which means she has cubs close by. The ATVs have probably been scaring away the game. She's getting desperate."

"I appreciate the Nature Channel commentary," Corey said. "But it's really not helping, Maya."

"Sorry."

"Think you could use some of that animal whisperer mojo? Tell her the deer looks tasty, but she can have it. In fact, I insist."

"You've forgotten everything my dad taught us all about dealing with big cats, haven't you?"

"Oddly, it's slipped my mind. Something to do with seeing six-inch fangs a foot from my throat."

"They're two inches, tops, and she's a meter away."

"Maya . . ."

"Step one, maintain eye contact. Step two, stand up. Never crouch around a cat—it makes you look like prey."

He shot to his feet so fast the cougar started, then snarled.

"Um, move slowly," I said.

"Thanks."

"Don't worry. She wants the deer, not you. Dead prey is easier to catch. Let her know you're surrendering it by backing away, slowly, while keeping eye contact."

He did that. The cat stood her ground, crouched, but her ears were forward, head raised, rear legs still. In other words, considering attack, but not yet sure it was necessary.

Once Corey had retreated a few meters, the cougar slunk forward, going for the deer. She grabbed it by the neck. Then, hauling it with her, she swung around, her back to the ATV as she looked over at us, checking out the remaining competition.

I tightened my grip on Kenjii's collar, but she was staying calm.

"Don't move," I murmured to the others. "Keep eye contact, but don't move."

As I spoke, the cat met my gaze. Her eyes widened and her rounded pupils dilated. She lifted her head and sampled the air. Then she growled.

I tried to step back. I knew I should, but my legs wouldn't obey. I stood my ground and I held her gaze, and when I did, everything else seemed to disappear. I felt the rush of wind. Heard my feet pounding against the earth. Smelled grass and pine needles and blood. Smelled the blood of the deer and felt the birthmark on my hip begin to throb. The throbbing pulsed outward, an ache that ran down my legs and up into my arms and—

A wrench on my arm yanked me back to reality as I saw the cougar leap. Saw her fangs flash in a snarl, gaze still locked on mine. Saw Kenjii running at her.

I screamed and lurched forward. Beside me, I dimly heard Daniel yell. Felt his fingers brush my arm. Heard my father's voice. *If Kenjii ever goes after a bear or a cat, you can't interfere, Maya. No matter how hard it is to stand there and let her protect you, you cannot interfere.*

He was right. I knew he was right. And it didn't matter. I looked into that cat's eyes, and saw her change target, hitting my dog instead, and rage filled me, an indescribable primal rage, like when a cougar had attacked Daniel. There was no way in hell I was letting her hurt Kenjii.

The cat took my dog down and they rolled, snarling and hissing. I kicked the cat. Kicked her with everything I had, and she fell to the side. I kicked her again, aiming for her wide skull. My foot made contact. The cougar went down hard. Kenjii leaped on her and pinned her by the throat.

"No," I said before Kenjii could bite down. "No."

The word sounded strange, harsh and guttural, but it stopped Kenjii and she settled for pinning the cat.

Daniel caught my arm. I shook him off and walked over until I was right in front of the cat. Then I bent by her head and looked into her panic-filled, rolling eyes.

Go. Take the deer and go. I don't want to hurt you.

I meant to say the words aloud. I didn't hear them, though. Not outside my head. I looked the cat in the eyes and I thought them again, and she went still, gaze fixed on mine as her eyes stopped rolling.

Go on. Take the deer. Feed your cubs. Leave us alone.

She snorted as if she understood. I caught Kenjii by the collar and gently pulled her back. When Daniel moved up behind me, I reached back and took his hand. He hesitated for a second, then squeezed it, and stood beside me as the cougar picked up the deer by the throat again and dragged it off into the woods.

"Situation averted," I said. My voice still sounded strange.

Daniel squeezed my hand again, reassuring me. But the others said nothing. I looked back to tell them it was okay, she was gone, and we were safe, only they weren't staring after the cougar. They were staring at me.

I released Kenjii and started to speak, then coughed to clear away whatever was making my voice sound so odd. I reached up to rub my throat. When my fingers brushed my skin, they felt strange, rough.

I looked down at my hand. It was . . . wrong. Misshapen.

My fingers were thick, my nails almost like claws. There was hair on the back of my hand. Thick tawny hairs. As I stared at it, my hip started to throb again.

I looked over at my other hand, the one Daniel was holding. It was the same way. He squeezed it again and leaned toward me, whispering, "It's okay."

I wrenched away and ran.

FOURTEEN

I RACED PAST THE others, who stared at me like I was a sideshow freak. Kenjii tore after me. Daniel did too, calling my name. I stumbled into the forest, branches scraping me from all sides. I didn't look for a clear path, just barreled through the dense trees until I tripped over a log and went flying. Then I lay there, facedown. Kenjii caught up, licked my face and nudged me.

"Maya?"

I pushed up and scrambled into a patch of dead brush, burrowing into it, Kenjii tunneling after me. When I was sure I was hidden, I stopped and pressed my rough palms to my eyes, heaving deep breaths as my heart thudded.

I stretched my hands out. Were they going back to normal? I touched my face, running my fingers along the familiar planes and contours. They felt . . . off. Not completely different, just off, like the lines had shifted, cheekbones lower, chin less sharp, nose flattening.

I rubbed my face hard.

"Maya?"

Kenjii lifted her head from my lap. When I still didn't answer Daniel, she whined as if to say *Are we hiding on Daniel? It's been a long time since we played this game.*

"Maya?"

"I—I'll be out in a minute."

I heard him come closer. He didn't try to peer at me, just grunted as he lowered himself to the ground.

"How about we back up?" he said.

"What?"

"Back up to before we went in the cabin. I was going to tell you what I thought was going on. With you. It starts with that old woman at the tattoo studio. The one who said you were a skin-walker."

"I—"

"Not yet. This is my chance to look brilliant. So she said you're a skin-walker. You've always had a way with animals. Especially cougars. Lately they won't leave you alone. We looked up skin-walkers, and saw that they change shape and have healing powers. Now, we could've made the leap and said that proves she was right, but we didn't, because that would be crazy."

"Uh-huh."

"Like getting sent to a book about Italian witch-hunters—when I'm Italian and I'm good at fighting—and deciding that's what I must be. Crazy. But then I found that note at Mina Lee's place. A list of four terms, including *skinwalker* and *benandanti*. That made me think some more about your healing powers and the big cats and the visions and the old woman at the tattoo place and your birthmark. I thought about me, too, the weird vibes, how they keep getting stronger, and about what my dad says, and dreams I've been having, and some other stuff—just small stuff, but it's been bugging me. At that point, it was starting to look a little more odd, but it was still too big a leap."

"So when did you make it?"

"I came close to a conclusion when I sent that helicopter pilot flying, but I wasn't really ready to commit until Sam's story sank in. With you? I wasn't sure until that Moreno guy mentioned Annie. Rafe's sister. I remembered the signs of a cougar around their cabin. I was worried. You brushed it off. Then Rafe freaked out about her going missing, and you two were whispering. When Moreno mentioned her, I flashed back to the cougar who appeared at your party. The young female with a mark on her flank. Annie's a skin-walker, isn't she? She changes into a cougar."

"Yes."

"That's what the mark means. Her mark and yours."

"Yes."

I told him the story. About Annie. About Rafe. About why Rafe came to Salmon Creek. About what he found there:

me. What he told me about us, about my mother, about the experiment.

Then, slowly, I crawled out of the dead brush until I could see him sitting there, arms wrapped around his knees, listening. Just listening.

"So that's why Rafe came to Salmon Creek," I said. "He was looking for the skin-walker. That's why he was going through the girls. That's why he focused on me. He figured it out."

Daniel shifted over until he was kneeling, his face a foot from mine.

"He did like you," he said softly. "That wasn't an act. I'm sure of it."

And I'd liked him. Really liked him. I realized that now. Too late, I realized that.

When I'd first felt an attraction to Rafe, I told myself it was just that. Attraction. Then I discovered we were both skin-walkers and that seemed to explain it. I'd probably have felt the same for any skin-walker guy who showed up, and he'd have felt the same for any skin-walker girl.

That made it easier. Easier than admitting I'd fallen for a guy who'd conned me. For a guy who might not really like me back. But now I realized how wrong I'd been.

When I thought of Rafe, I did remember his touch, his kiss. But what I thought about most of all was him. Just him. His laugh. His eyes. His serious side. His fears for his sister. His worries for her, for himself, for me. His honesty that night on the roof, when he'd opened up. Wanting me to get to know him better.

Now I never would get to know him better, and that's what really hurt. Too much pride. Too few opportunities.

I rubbed my face.

"It's back to normal," Daniel said.

"What?" I peered at him through my fingers.

"Your face. It looks normal, so you can stop rubbing. It wasn't bad before anyway. Just a little . . . different."

He reached to pull one hand from my face. "I know you're worried about what happened to Annie and whether it will happen to you. You're probably worried about the whole 'changing into a cat' part, too. But it's going to be okay. We'll figure this out and we'll find help and it'll be okay. I promise."

I nodded.

"I'm sorry," he said.

"About what?"

"Yesterday. I made that bone-headed comment about werewolves, and you decided not to tell me yet."

"No, that's not—"

"Liar. It was a dumb thing to say."

"Um, no, I'm pretty sure that changing into an animal does qualify as a crazy idea."

"Sure, but in a crazy cool way. I'm jealous. What do I get? Some kind of sonic boom shout? As superpowers go, very lame." He settled in beside me. "So tell me everything else. Have you ever started changing like that before?"

I smiled. "Later. Let's start with you. You mentioned dreams and other things. Tell me what's been happening."

He leaned back. I looked over at him, his face turned up to catch a few rays of sun streaming through the treetops.

"The dreams started a few months ago," he said. "Dreams of fields. Fields of grapes and olives, which is weird enough. I'm not even sure if I knew how olives grow, but in the dream, I knew that's what they were. I—"

"Daniel?" Sam's voice.

We could hear all three of them tramping through the bushes. Kenjii got up, growling.

"You tell them, girl," Daniel muttered. "No rest for the weary."

"No," I said. "No rest for the endangered. We have to—" I stopped. "Nicole. Oh my God, I forgot about Nicole."

"What about Nicole?" Sam asked as they came into view.

They were still eyeing me warily, but I ignored it. Explanations later. Right now, I had to tell them what Moreno had said about Nicole. And, admittedly, I was happy for the diversion.

"So Nicole's alive," Sam said after I finished talking.

"Somewhere." Daniel's look said he knew exactly where this was headed. "They won't be holding her around here."

"Why not?" I said. "She's their best source of information about us. And she'd be the perfect lure."

"Which is exactly why we can't try to rescue her. It's a setup."

As Daniel and I argued, the others were quiet, still assimilating the news.

Corey spoke first. "Okay, it's freaking amazing that Nic is alive. I have no idea whether we should look for her or not, but I'm pretty sure we need to discuss a few other things. Like what the hell happened to Maya back there."

"She's a shape-shifter," Daniel said. "Eventually she's going to be able to turn into a cougar. Sam and I? We're demon-hunters."

Corey studied Daniel's face, then mine.

"This is going to be a long talk, isn't it?" he said at last.

"Yep. Better sit down." Daniel pointed at the bag in Corey's hand. "And break out the granola bars and drink boxes."

FIFTEEN

WE TOLD THEM EVERYTHING—WELL, almost everything. I was saving the stuff I'd found out at
the cabin. This was enough for now. Too much
actually. Despite having seen our powers in action—my near-
transformation and Daniel knocking out the pilot—Corey
and Hayley couldn't seem to process it.

Corey kept saying, "Are you sure?" tentatively, as if he
didn't want to insult our intelligence, but he couldn't help
thinking there had to be a logical explanation. Hayley just
stared at me.

When I finally stopped talking, she said, "Are you crazy?"

"Hey!" Sam said.

"No, seriously. You think you're going to change into a
cougar? Maybe in thirty years you'll start thinking college
boys are kinda hot, but that's the only sort of cougar you can

turn into, Maya. Anything else is nuts."

"Right," Sam said. "So you weren't here an hour ago? When her face started changing?"

"Yes, something did happen to her face. I don't know what it was, but I'll bet it has to do with those vitamins and drugs they were feeding us back in Salmon Creek. That's what all this is about. They were doing medical experiments on us. It explains what Daniel did on the helicopter and what happened with Maya's face."

"And Rafe?" Sam said. "Does medical research explain why Rafe thought he was a skin-walker, too, when he'd never even been to the clinic?"

"I . . . I don't know." Hayley squared her shoulders. "No one ever saw Rafe do anything magical. He just *thought* he was one of these skin-walkers. That's from your religion or whatever, right?"

"My religion?" I said.

"The stuff you people believe in."

"You people?" Corey said. "Holy hell, Hayley. Did you really just say that?"

She went beet red. "I—I didn't mean—"

"We know exactly what you meant," Sam said. "Got a racist streak there, huh? Surprise, surprise."

"I—I didn't mean it like that," Hayley stammered. "I just meant their, you know, heritage. Indian. Um, Native. Or—or—"

"It's okay," I said. "I'm sure you didn't mean it like

that. Yes, I'm Navajo. Mostly anyway. Rafe's mother was Hopi. Both have skin-walkers as part of their belief systems, but I hadn't even heard the word until a few days ago. My mom—my adopted one—is Haida. That's what I know. No skin-walkers there."

I tried to keep my tone even. Explaining, not lecturing. Whatever problems I'd had with Hayley in the past, she'd never showed any prejudice. It still pissed me off, though.

"I'm sorry," she said. "I'm really sorry. I'm just . . . I'm going to take a walk, okay?"

"You can't wander off," Sam said. "We're being chased by—"

"She's fine," Daniel said. "I think we should all take a walk. Were you done looking at the ATV, Corey?"

Corey hesitated. "Um, no. You want me to see if I can get it running?"

Daniel nodded.

"What?" Sam said. "We don't have time—"

"Yes, we do." Daniel's voice took on that low, soothing tone. "We're going to walk back to the ATV. Hayley's going to follow us. Corey's going to try to fix the machine. And we'll all relax. Just take twenty minutes to relax. If he can't get it going, we'll set out again."

I suspected Daniel's skill wouldn't work on a fellow ben-andanti, but Sam would do as he said anyway. And it did calm Hayley and Corey. They nodded, and we made our way back to the ATV.

The ATV still sat there, keys in the ignition. Sam stalked off to sit on a fallen log and glower at us. Hayley murmured that she was going to walk a bit and promised to stay close. Daniel and I stood watch, leaving Corey to the ATV. He was good mechanically—without him, Daniel's truck would have been relegated to a scrap heap long ago. Right now, it gave him some time to think. Same with Hayley and her quiet moment in the woods.

We couldn't force them to accept that we had supernatural powers. Maybe they'd decide that these people were after us for another reason. Either way they'd keep running and that was all that mattered.

After a while, Corey turned on his haunches and said, "Too much damage. I'd need tools and even then I doubt I'd get her started."

"It was worth a shot," Daniel said. "Thanks."

Corey nodded and wiped a spot of grease from the red ATV's paint. "I don't have the same symptoms as you guys," he finally said. "But I know you think I'm something, too. Something supernatural."

"There were two other terms on that list," Daniel said. "*Xana* and *sileni*."

"Which are . . . ?"

"I have no idea. I tried a Web search on all the terms. I couldn't get results for any, including benandanti and skinwalkers, which makes no sense, because we *know* they're part of folklore."

"We think the St. Clouds were blocking those terms," I said. "In case something like this happened and we tried looking them up. If we want clues, we need to look at the extracurricular activities they pushed at us. Clearly, with Daniel and me, they were trying to boost our natural talents: fighting for him and running for me. Serena, Hayley, and Nicole were all in the choir and on the swim team. Plus they're all blonde and pretty."

"Um, thanks," Hayley said as she came over. "But what . . ." Her brow furrowed. "You think we're mermaids?"

"Isn't that sirens?" Corey said. "Those chicks we studied in Greek mythology. Lured guys to their deaths by singing."

Hayley glared at him. "I thought you liked my singing."

"Yeah, because apparently it's magical. That's how you seduce guys."

"Seduce them? Or kill them?"

"Same thing, kind of, if you think about it. Like that other guy in mythology. The one who got his hair cut and lost all his power. Mr. Parks said it symbolized men losing their power by falling for women."

"No," I said. "Mr. Parks said it symbolizes men's *irrational* fear of losing their power to women. And unless I'm remembering it wrong, mermaids don't sing and sirens don't swim."

"Ariel sang in *The Little Mermaid*," Corey said.

Sam came over to join us. "Do I even want to know why you remember her name?"

"Mermaids and sirens weren't on the list," Daniel said. "Maya's point is that Hayley, Nicole, and Serena shared common characteristics, which probably means they're the same type, and it has something to do with singing and swimming."

"And being pretty," Hayley said.

"That's not a superpower," Sam muttered.

Hayley turned to her. "No? How many times have you gotten into movies for free because you're a tough warrior chick?"

"What about me?" Corey said. "What's my superpower?"

Silence fell.

"Oh, come on. I'm good at a lot of stuff. Right?"

More silence.

"You're cute," Hayley said. "Well, cute enough."

"Fun to be around," I offered.

"So I'm . . . a clown?"

"At least you're a cute clown," Hayley said. "Not a scary one."

"You're a good fighter," Daniel said.

"And you're a good drinker," Hayley added. "You can hold your liquor better than anyone I know."

"Uh-huh," Corey said. "So Maya will grow up to be an amazing healer who can change into a killer cat. Daniel and Sam will roam the country hunting criminals and demons. Hayley and Nicole will divide their time between recording platinum albums and winning gold medals in swimming. And me? I'll be the cute, funny guy sitting at the bar, hoping for a good brawl to break out."

"In other words, exactly where you were already headed," Hayley said.

We all laughed at that, even Corey. We had to. For now, this was the best way to deal with it. Tease. Poke fun. As if we were comparing Halloween costumes. *Look, I'm a superhero. Yeah? Well, so am I.*

"I'm sure you have powers," I said. "You're just a late bloomer."

"Thanks . . . I think."

"Your headaches might be related to it," Daniel said. "They began a year ago, right?"

"And Dr. Inglis was very interested in them," I said. "She started looking after you personally and giving you special medicine."

Corey nodded. "She asked about them a lot, too. Whether anything was happening when I got them."

"Happening?"

"Like whether I was seeing things or hearing things. I thought she meant like my dad, who always smelled burned toast before he had a seizure. I figured she thought it was a sign I was getting epilepsy."

"More like a sign you're getting your powers," I said.

"And the headaches went away with the pills, right?" Sam said.

Corey nodded.

"That was the point," I said. "Suppress whatever was

happening to you until they were ready to tell us all the truth."

"Or suppress it because it's dangerous," Sam said.

"We don't know it is," I said.

"And we don't know it isn't."

"Ultimately, it doesn't matter," Daniel cut in. "Because we're doing our damnedest to get to safety before anyone needs to worry about a superpower meltdown."

"Where's safety?" Sam said. "With the people who apparently want to help us . . . by burning down our homes, killing Uncle Phil, and shooting us with tranq guns? Or with the people who did this to us in the first place?"

"Obviously you have some third option," I said. "So let's hear it."

"I can contact people my parents knew. One of them must have known why they were on the run. Maybe they can help. I was going to do that after my parents died, only I got shipped to Salmon Creek and for a while everything seemed to be okay."

"Until you discovered your fake aunt and uncle were evil," I said.

"What? No. I never said—"

"Because they *aren't* evil. I don't know whether my folks knew anything about this, but I know one thing. They're amazing parents. So were your aunt and uncle."

"My dad's not Father of the Year material," Daniel said. "But he isn't evil. If our parents did know, then it's like Rafe said about his mom—they agreed to this experiment because they honestly thought it was a good thing. Right or wrong, they didn't mean to hurt us. I'm not as sure about the St. Clouds, but I still believe we can trust our parents."

"So let's go back to Salmon Creek," I said. "Check it out. See if it's safe to return. Agreed?"

They all nodded.

There was, however, one question still to be resolved. Should we try to find Nicole?

Daniel and Hayley voted no. I wanted to look for her. Corey wavered, and I could have swayed him, but Sam locked it up by voting to keep going. I think that surprised the others—voting *against* finding her cousin. It didn't shock me, though. It fit pretty well with the image I had of Samantha Russo.

So I was outvoted, and we pushed on, hoping to find the road I'd seen from the ridge.

I wasn't angry with Daniel for opposing me. I saw his point, too. We had no idea *where* to look for Nicole. She wasn't at the cabin. We didn't have the energy to go back over the mountain, to see if she'd still be there. I really doubted she was. Leaving her behind was just a really, really tough decision to make, and I admired him for having the courage to make it.

SIXTEEN

"CAN WE WALK ON ahead?" Daniel whispered after we'd set out.

I nodded and told the others we were going to scout a little and to just keep us in sight.

He moved to the side to let Kenjii take the lead. "So what did you read in that cabin?"

I told him what I'd deciphered from the handful of memos I'd found. And "deciphered" was the right word. While they weren't written in secret code, they were intended to be read by people who already knew what was going on. There was no overt mention of benandanti or skin-walkers or supernatural powers of any kind. That meant I had to combine what I already knew with lots of guesswork.

The St. Clouds were a real corporation—I'd seen its subsidiary names on products and heard their corporation mentioned in the news. The same seemed to be true for the company that was after us—the Nasts. Piecing that together with the cryptic messages we'd found on Mina Lee's answering machine, I deduced that these were two rival corporations: the Nasts and the St. Clouds.

It seemed that these companies were both staffed by supernaturals. A progress memo had said things like "Working on getting the Enwrights flown up. Their unique skills could be helpful in this search" and "A scent tracker would be a huge benefit. Would love to hire a ww on contract but company policy forbids. Meeting with Josef Nast today to discuss."

Call me crazy, but I was going to bet the Enwrights' unique skills weren't an astounding ability to read wilderness signs. As for a supernatural scent tracker, I suspected "ww" meant werewolf—Sam had said such things really existed.

When Daniel and I had hacked onto his mother's old computer, we'd found references to an experiment in Buffalo that had gone wrong. We'd thought it was another drug-testing venture. From another memo I'd read in the cabin, I now suspected something very different.

"Project Genesis," Daniel said. "There was a Delaney on that list, too. And an Enwright, I think. Was it another branch of our experiment?"

"No, ours was referred to as Project Phoenix. Meaning they're resurrecting extinct supernatural types, like Rafe said. It looked like the Nasts were concentrating on our group. The memo said they were leaving cleanup on Project

Genesis to the St. Clouds, and they'd get involved later if it looked 'profitable.'"

"Cleanup?" Daniel swore. "Not liking the sound of that."

"Apparently the St. Clouds 'lost control' of some 'assets' and were searching for them."

"In other words, the subjects took off."

I nodded. "I think so. The only other thing I got from the memo was the name of the guy in charge of the Edison Group. Dr. Davidoff."

"Davidoff . . . ?" He swore again. Dr. Davidoff was the guy the St. Clouds sent for our annual checkup.

"He's dead," I said. "Like a bunch of other members of this Edison Group. Killed in an 'incident' last spring."

"So I guess we know why he skipped the summer teleconference."

I nodded. We walked in silence for a few minutes, then fell back in with the group.

We'd been walking for about thirty minutes when Daniel asked me to do another treetop check. I'd been avoiding it— really couldn't afford to stumble into another pit of grief and regret right now—but that bird's-eye view of the region was invaluable. Also, while I could gauge our direction by the sun and the foliage the others felt better if I climbed to "check."

So I found a tree and scaled it. Yes, I thought about Rafe, but after that cabin visit there was so much else swirling around my head that I could push it aside.

Kenjii took up position at the bottom. A few minutes later,

she stood and gave a chuff, meaning someone was coming. I peered down to see Sam approaching Kenjii warily, looking around for me. I considered ignoring her, but when Kenjii glanced up, Sam spotted me.

I climbed down to the lowest branch. She waited for me to jump to the ground. I didn't, just said, "What's up?"

"I wanted to talk to you."

"Okay, talk."

I settled on the branch, feet dangling. She stood there, looking up at my feet, then pointed at my legs. I'd taken off my socks after the crash—they'd been soaked—and hadn't replaced them. When I sat, a few inches of bare shin were exposed.

"Those scratches," she said. "They're from when you got dragged underwater, aren't they?"

"Yep."

"They're fingernail gouges. You didn't get caught on anything. You were pulled down. By a person." She held up her hands, nails bitten to the quick. "It wasn't me. And if that's not enough proof, you can ask Corey. I was in front of him when Nicole went under. I wanted to help, but he told me to stay put. I did until he had her."

"Okay."

"You're speculating that Hayley, Nicole, and Serena are the same supernatural type, right? Something to do with water. Which explains how they can swim so well and hold their breath so long. You think someone drowned Serena, someone who could stay under even longer than her. Someone who also tried to drown you."

I slid from the tree. "Where's Hayley?"

"She's not the one who drugged you."

"What?"

"At your party. Hayley didn't dose your drink. It was the person who accused her. The one who worked with her at the clinic and had access to the drugs, too."

"Nicole?"

Sam nodded. "I found the pills in her room afterward. She tried to say Hayley had planted them. I didn't believe her. She finally broke down, sobbing, saying she hadn't meant for anyone to get hurt, just that it was her big chance with Daniel and she knew you kind of liked Rafe, and he was coming to the party. She just wanted to give you and Rafe a push, so you wouldn't interfere with her and Daniel."

"I've never interfered—"

"Yeah, I know. But when it comes to Daniel, Nicole is . . ." She took a deep breath. "Anyway, I told her that she screwed up and if she ever went after you again, she'd be dealing with me."

"And you didn't think to tell us?"

She met my gaze. "The wrong decision. I see that now."

"So Nicole dosed my drink." I tried to process that, but my brain refused. Sam was lying. Covering up something when Nicole wasn't here to defend herself.

Then I realized where this was heading. "You think

Nic . . . *Nicole* drowned Serena? Tried to drown me? No, that's not— She was almost drowned herself this time."

"Was she? Or was that a diversion? She pulls you down, thinks she's drowned you, then pops up, screaming for help and no one notices you're gone until it's too late."

"No. Not Nicole. Why would she—?"

"Daniel. She's obsessed with him. She didn't think Serena treated him right and—"

"So she *killed* her for it?" I said.

"I don't think she meant to. Or maybe she did. I don't know."

"Nicole *never* had a problem with Serena and Daniel. From what I heard, you did, though."

"What?"

"Serena told me you caught her flirting with summer boys. At the diner, just before she died. You told her off."

"Sure, I told her off. She was being disrespectful. If you've got a boyfriend, you don't flirt with other guys. Daniel didn't deserve that."

"What did Daniel deserve?"

"Huh?"

I gave her a hard look, but she didn't seem to get it.

"You like Daniel," I said.

"Um, yeah. He's a great guy. Which is why he didn't deserve to be treated—" She stopped and stared at me, then choked on a laugh. "You mean— Are you asking—? You think *I've* got a crush on Daniel?"

"Don't you?"

She laughed harder. "Oh my God, you guys really are as naive as you seem." She looked at me. "I don't like guys, Maya. As friends, yes. As dating material? Wrong gender."

"Wrong—? Oh."

She shook her head. "I kept telling myself you guys had figured it out. I mean, come on. I'm a walking stereotype. I even use a guy's nickname. I was twelve when the kids at my old school figured it out, so I stopped trying to be girlie. Then I come here, and no one says anything, so I figure you all know and you're just pretending otherwise, which pisses me off, but it's better than getting *Playboy* stuffed in my locker. Apparently, I was wrong. It's not an option in your cozy little world."

"Right. So the kids who are out at Salmon Creek are only figments of my imagination?"

"Huh?"

"Maybe if you paid a little more attention to your classmates, you'd have realized that we don't care. But we don't jump to conclusions either. We figure if someone wants to be open about it, she'll tell us."

Now it was her turn to say "Oh." Then, "Well, anyway, I don't like Daniel. Not that way. I just think he's a really good guy. I didn't like seeing him disrespected, but not because I wanted him for myself. If I gave off that vibe, I sure as hell didn't mean it."

She hadn't. Daniel didn't think she had a crush on him.

Even I'd always felt it was platonic, until Rafe suggested it wasn't. But Rafe hadn't known Sam well.

"Okay," I said. "I guess I can believe that Nicole doped me, if she just thought it would 'encourage' me to get with Rafe. But killing Serena? Trying to kill me? Over a guy?"

"Have you forgotten how she acted after the crash? How she ranted about you and Daniel?"

"Her *father* had just died."

"So it *did* seem out of character to you. Right? Not a side of Nicole you've ever seen? Well, I've seen it. I saw it when I first moved in with the Tillsons. She was used to being an only child and all of a sudden, she wasn't. She started stealing things and blaming me. Spiked my orange juice once, hoping I'd go to school drunk. I couldn't prove any of it until I found her planting clinic meds in my room. I caught her off guard and she lashed out and it was just the kind of paranoid talk you heard after the crash—how I was stealing her parents, how I'd probably killed mine. Ugly, crazy talk. Then, a couple of hours later, she came into my room crying, saying she was stressed out over exams and she'd been taking cold medicine and she didn't know what happened to make her act like that, but she was really, really sorry."

"And you believed her."

"Of course I did. She was totally freaked out. I started thinking she wasn't responsible for the missing stuff, that I'd made a mistake about vodka in my OJ. Sure, she'd planted the drugs, but you know how stressed she got over exams.

Add cold medicine and it could push her over the edge. So I let it go. But I've caught glimpses of that Nicole a few times since. I don't know what's wrong with her, Maya. Maybe it's mental illness. Maybe it's whatever drugs they have her on. Maybe it's a side effect of the experimental stuff. But she's not stable. That's why . . ."

She took a deep breath. "That's why I didn't want to go back for her. I feel bad about it, but . . . we can't. She's dangerous."

Kenjii perked up. She looked to the left, then tore off.

"Daniel's coming," I said. I thought fast. "We can't tell him."

"He should know."

"What? That we suspect Nicole killed Serena? That she tried to kill me? Over him? She's gone, so I'm safe. He's safe. And if he thinks Serena died because of an accidental drug side effect, then I'm going to let him keep thinking that as long as possible."

She paused, then nodded. "Okay, you're right."

Daniel appeared, Kenjii at his side. He looked from me to Sam.

"All clear," I said. "Sam and I were just discussing what her parents told her. About everything."

I looked at Sam. She hesitated, then nodded. "Right. You should know, too. It's not much but . . . you should know."

Daniel nodded, then said to me, "Did you see anything?"

I shook my head. "I could see a lot better from the hilltop.

We're still heading in the right direction, but I couldn't spot the road."

"Let's keep going then. Sam? Talk and walk."

Sam's story was similar to Rafe's. Like his mother, her parents had left the experiment. In her case, though, that had always been the plan. Many of the parents hadn't been real couples. To ensure the best results, the scientists had performed in vitro fertilization using men and women who both carried the latent genes. But Sam's parents met during the initial screening process, and fell in love. Neither of them had any interest in living as experimental subjects—they just wanted their child to be a benandanti. So they played along up to the point where Sam was conceived and her DNA was modified to reactivate the gene. Then they bailed.

As Rafe's mom and mine found out, though, the St. Clouds weren't willing to let them go.

"Resurrecting extinct supernatural types isn't a public service," Sam said. "The St. Clouds run a business. They hire supernaturals and that's how they get the advantage on human corporations, though they still have to compete with the other Cabals."

Daniel nodded. "The guy who left a message on Mina Lee's answering machine said something about double-crossing a Cabal and paying the price. So that's what these corporations are called?"

Sam didn't respond.

"Right," I said. "So it's a big secret and you're not going to confirm. Now move on."

"There's no secret, I guess," Sam said slowly. "Only . . ." She turned to face us. "You guys probably feel like you got ripped off. Lied to. Betrayed. But I'm not sure that's such a bad thing. Imagine being four years old and moving to a new town, being told that now you have a new last name and you can't tell anyone the old one. Then you're five and you're moving again, and you have *another* name, and the other kids go to school, but you can't. Then you're six and you move, and you're talking to a nice lady at the park and she calls you by your old name and you forget you aren't supposed to answer to it. She tries to take you, but your parents stop her, then your dad goes after her, and you aren't sure what he did to her, but you're pretty sure it was bad. And that night you're in a hotel, with all your toys left behind, and you hear your mom crying about how they almost lost you, and you know you can't ever, *ever* slip up again."

She surveyed our faces. "Try living like that, and I bet you'd become really careful about everything you say, too. I bet you'll think that maybe, just maybe, growing up in a nice town, with everything you ever wanted, isn't such a terrible thing. Maybe you'll think the lies weren't so bad."

She stalked off ahead. Daniel shrugged at me, then went back to collect Corey and Hayley. I caught up to Sam.

"Don't," she said. "Just don't, okay?"

"I was only going to say that we need to head that way." I pointed.

"Right." A soft, choked laugh. "Kind of ruins the dramatic effect if I'm storming off in the wrong direction, doesn't it?" She shook her head, then waited with me for the others to reach us.

SEVENTEEN

DARKNESS WAS FALLING. THERE'D been no sign of our pursuers, so we finally surrendered to exhaustion and found a sheltered grove of trees for the night.

We couldn't risk building a fire, but our clothing was long dried, and the night was warm, with the trees blocking the wind. Kenjii stretched out against my back, which was as good as a fire, and I should have dropped into an exhausted sleep. I didn't.

About a half hour passed before I heard Daniel get up. He tried to pad silently across our sleeping area, until he stopped by my head and hunkered down.

"Yes, I can't sleep either," I whispered.

He motioned me up. Kenjii rolled to her feet and silently followed us. He didn't need me to take the lead. It was a three-quarter moon in a cloudless sky.

He kept checking over his shoulder, making sure I was still there. Every time he looked ahead, again I'd watch him and remember what Sam said about Nicole. I imagined how he'd react and that crushed any concern I had about not telling him the truth.

He'd blame himself, wonder what he'd done to encourage Nicole, when the truth was that he hadn't encouraged her. Just being himself was enough. Nicole fell for Daniel for the same reasons almost every girl at Salmon Creek had, at one time or another. He wasn't hard to look at—wavy blond hair, blue eyes, broad shoulders, gorgeous smile . . . It was the smile that did it the most, because it wasn't calculated or flirtatious—it was open and it was friendly and it told you this was, as Sam said, a good guy. A really good guy. That's why girls fell for Daniel. He could no more stop that than he could stop the sun from coming up.

So what did he get for being a decent guy? An obsessed classmate who'd apparently killed his girlfriend, and was trying to do the same to his best friend because now she'd decided I was the one keeping them apart.

Well, unless we encountered Nicole again, he wasn't going to find out about that. The obsessed classmate would remain a tragically kidnapped friend. The dead girlfriend would remain the victim of a freak accident no one could have foreseen. And the best friend had just panicked or been attacked by some underwater creature.

We reached an outcropping of rock far enough from

the others that we could talk without disturbing them. We stretched out on our backs. Kenjii nestled down by our feet.

For a few minutes we lay in comfortable silence, enjoying the warm fall night and the star-dotted sky.

"I'm sorry about Nicole," he said finally.

That startled me so much I pushed up onto my elbows. "Were you drifting off?"

"No. Just— You mean about leaving her behind? Don't be sorry."

Really, don't be sorry.

"You were right," I continued. "I was acting on emotion; you were using your head. I'm sure she's on the mainland by now. A long way from here." *At least, I hope she is.*

"I feel awful about leaving her behind."

"Of course you do. But it was the right choice."

"I'm really glad she's alive." He looked over. "That was great news. I was worried about you. Losing Rafe, and then Nicole, after you guys started being friends, and I know you weren't over losing Serena yet." He paused and cleared his throat. "Well, obviously. I just mean . . ."

"I know." I tried to see his expression in the moonlight, but he was looking at the sky again. Thinking about Serena. After a moment, I slid my hand over his. "I know you're not over her either."

"Right."

The word came out thick and he turned his face a little farther to the other side. I sat up, cross-legged. When he didn't move, I touched his shoulder.

"Anytime you want to talk—"

He sat up so fast I nearly toppled off the rock. He didn't seem to notice. He sat down again on the other side, looking the other way, feet dangling over the edge, his shoulders set.

"I'm sorry," I said. "I just never know whether you want to talk or don't want to—"

"I was going to break up with her."

He blurted it so fast, I wasn't sure I understood. I lowered myself to sit cross-legged beside him.

"You were . . ."

"I was going to break up with Serena. End it. Dump her. Right before she died."

"Oh."

"Yeah, *oh*." A sardonic twist of his lips. He went to stand. "Forget it. I shouldn't have—"

I caught his hand. "Don't. You want to talk about this, right?"

He hesitated. Then another humorless smile. "I'm not sure *talk* is the right word. More like confess."

"So what happened?" I asked. "She hadn't mentioned a fight or anything."

"Because there wasn't one. Because nothing happened. Nothing went wrong. It just—" He took a deep breath, then let it out, cheeks puffing. He rubbed the back of his neck and shifted, then took another breath. "We were doing fine. But it wasn't . . . going anywhere. When she first asked me to that dance, I didn't feel right saying no. She was a friend and—"

He swallowed. Rubbed his neck again. Looked around. Then he motioned at the rock. "Can we lie down again? I think I'll do this better . . ."

"If you're talking to the sky?"

A half laugh, half snort. "Yeah. Lame, I know, but—"

I stretched out on my back. He did the same.

"So you went to the dance . . ." I prompted.

"Right. And it was fine. I liked Serena. She was fun to be around, and easy to get along with and . . . well, you know. There was no reason *not* to go out with her, since that's what she wanted and . . ." He paused. "But that's not really a good enough reason to go out with someone either. I started figuring that out. Mostly because of the summer boys."

"Her flirting with them? She—"

"She didn't mean anything by it, I know. And I wasn't upset. I wasn't the least bit jealous or insulted and I started to realize that I should be. Even if I trusted her, I should have felt something when she flirted with other guys. Instead, I'd almost hope . . ."

He rubbed his mouth. Blurted the words again. "I almost hoped she'd meet someone else. I played the whole thing out in my head. I'd tell her it was okay, and we could still be friends. That's when I realized I wasn't being fair, letting her think things were fine and keeping her from finding someone else. I had to end it."

I nodded.

"Only doing it wasn't easy. I was close, really close when . . ."

"She drowned."

He nodded.

"I'm sorry," I said. "That must have been—"

"Hell." He spat the word. "It was hell. I felt like the biggest phony ever. The grieving boyfriend who hadn't even wanted to be her boyfriend anymore."

He sat up then. After a moment, he looked at me.

"I did grieve. I missed her. I really did."

"Like me. A grieving friend."

He nodded. "Only no one would let me be that. It felt like everyone wanted me to be heartbroken, and when I wasn't . . ."

"You felt guilty."

"It was like they went back and rewrote our history. Sure, we'd been going out for almost a year, but it . . . it wasn't serious, you know? Not like Brooke and Alan, crazy about each other, can't keep their hands off each other, and everyone knows they're going to get married and grow old together. With Seri and me, it was more like you and your summer boys. Just fun. No one expected it to be a forever thing. Then she died, and it was as if . . . as if people wanted it to be more. More tragic. More romantic."

"I don't think they meant that," I said. "If I ever made you feel—"

"You didn't. With you, I could just be the guy who lost a good friend. Until . . ."

"Until I started worrying about you not dating. Started thinking you and Serena had been more serious than I realized."

"All I had to do was tell you the truth. Only I couldn't. At first, it felt like I'd be dumping on you for no reason. By the time you started worrying about me, it was too late. I couldn't figure out how to say it."

"Kind of like me and this skin-walker business?"

A faint smile. "I guess so."

"I wish you'd told me."

He met my gaze then. "So do I."

I paused, then said, "She was happy. Serena. If you had broken it off, she'd have understood. She was—" *Crazy about you.* I couldn't say that, of course. It wouldn't make this easier. "That last year . . . She was really happy."

"Good."

More silence. Less comfortable now. I glanced over at him. Time to change the subject.

"So, you were going to tell me about your powers. Still up for it?"

"If you are."

"Definitely."

Daniel said he first noticed changes in the boxing ring—getting faster and sharper, sensing blows before he even saw them coming. The persuasion, too. He'd always found it easy to persuade people to listen to him. Simple skills like paying attention, looking them in the eye and being firm when he spoke. Lately, though, it seemed . . . too easy. Like with the tattoo artist's aunt—he'd been able to get her to talk after she refused to.

"You gotta admit, that's one sweet power," I said.

"You think so?"

"Um, yeah. Duh."

He glanced over. "Well, I think being able to change into a cougar is cool, which you obviously aren't so sure of. Maybe we can switch."

I laughed. "I wish. Shape-shifting will probably be cool, eventually, but changing from human to cat? I don't think that's going to tickle. Persuasion, though? I don't see the downside."

"No? So if I have this power, how do I know why people agree with me? Was I right when I persuaded the others not to go back for Nicole? Or did Hayley and Sam just agree because of my power?"

"No, you were right. And even if you did use your mojo, it obviously didn't work on me."

"That's good." He looked at me. "If I do have this power, I hope it never works on you. I wouldn't want that."

"Don't worry. You can count on me to keep telling you you're full of crap. And in this case, I'm not sure it was work-ing on anyone. Corey stayed undecided. I think you have to switch it on, like you do sometimes."

He nodded.

Another quiet moment. Then, "So you can tell when I switch it on?"

"I can."

"Good. If I ever do it with you, accidentally, stop me, okay?"

"You think I wouldn't?" I knocked his shoulder. "Believe me, you are not using any of that mojo on me. Ever. You want to convince me of anything, you gotta be you."

"Good." He caught my gaze and held it for a moment, then looked away quickly and said again, "Good. Still up for talking about your powers? What you've been feeling?"

"Absolutely."

Unfortunately, any discussion of my powers led to thoughts of shape-shifting, which led to thoughts of Annie, which led to worry. Worry? Hell, no. Let's call it what it really was. Outright panic. If I even started thinking of it, my heart pounded and my mouth went dry.

When I tried to skate over the subject, Daniel brought me back, and we hashed it out. Turning out like Annie wasn't a certainty—she was the only subject we knew who'd begun to shift. Growing up in a medical research town meant we knew all about side effects and outliers. Her case might be a one-off.

And if it wasn't? Then we knew where to find the scientists

157

who'd done this to us. We didn't trust them. We didn't want anything to do with them. Still . . .

"If that happens to you, we're getting their help," Daniel said.

"But—"

He put his hand over my mouth. "No buts. If it happens to you, we go to them. We'll force them to fix you on our terms." A wry smile. "I can make people do things, remember?"

I was sure it wouldn't be that easy. But having him say it? Be willing to take that risk for me? It meant a lot.

We talked until . . . well, until we weren't talking anymore. I suppose I fell asleep first. I dreamed of Rafe. I dreamed he was out there, in the forest, lost and hurt and calling me. Needing me. This time, though, I didn't bolt awake thinking it was real. Maybe I was just too tired. Or maybe, finally, I knew it wasn't real, couldn't be real, however much I ached to believe it.

Next thing I knew, I was waking to Kenjii licking my face and Corey saying, "Now this is when I really need a camera."

I'm sure that when I fell asleep, I'd been lying on my back, looking up at the sky as I talked to Daniel. But when I woke up, I was on my side, nestled with my back against him, his arm over me. I jumped up so fast I kicked him in the shins and he let out an "Oomph."

Corey's laugh rang out through the silent forest. "Oh, come on. You guys looked so cute."

"Cold," I muttered. "It got cold."

"Then let's hit the trail and warm up," Corey said.

EİGHTEEN

FTER ABOUT AN HOUR of walking, I started thinking maybe I'd cuddle up with Daniel again, just to
make Corey laugh. The morning had started on a
light note, but it darkened fast. The sky darkened too. We'd
escaped the threat of rain on our first night, but now the black
clouds gathering overhead said it had only been a temporary
reprieve.

The rain began as a light drizzle. Being part cat, I'm not
keen on rain, but I've always liked a light one, especially
on a hot summer's day, tramping through the woods or rock
climbing, enjoying the cool mist on my face, the sweet fresh
smell of it, the inevitable rainbow afterward. But this wasn't
a refreshing mist on a hot summer's day. It was an icy drizzle
that slid down the backs of our necks and plopped off the end
of branches and froze our ears and soaked our shoes.

"Can we stop?" Hayley asked.

"If I see a sheltered spot, we'll hole up for a while."

"Can we look for one? I have a blister—"

"We all have blisters," Sam said.

"We need to keep going," Daniel said. "We lost a lot of time yesterday."

"What? Are we on a schedule?" Hayley said. "Is there a bus waiting to pick us up somewhere?" She sighed, then said, "I hate complaining."

"So don't do it," Sam said.

Hayley glowered at her. "You think I like being the whiner? If Nicole was here, she'd be complaining just as much. We're tired and wet and miserable, but I'm stuck being the one who says it while everyone else just hopes I whine loud enough so we all get to stop and rest. Maya and Daniel can't complain. They need to set an example. Unless Corey's in enough pain that he snaps again, he's going to tough it out. And Sam? Well, she's not even human, so she doesn't count."

"Excuse me?" Sam said.

"Face it, you're not one of those bendo-things. You're a robot. A cyborg. Probably an evil one, programmed to murder us all in our sleep."

Corey snickered.

"Yeah?" Sam lifted a fist to Hayley. "You want to try that one again, blondie?"

Hayley looked at Daniel and me. "I rest my case."

"Hayley's right," I said. "About the complaining part.

We're not on a schedule and the harder we push, the more exhausted we'll get." I waved to the west. "The redwoods seem to thin over there. We might find a grove of ferns for some shelter."

We tramped over, and as we stepped from the thick trees, we all stopped and stared. Then Corey raced forward, arms raised.

"It's a road. Oh my God. A road!" He dropped to his knees by the roadside. "Oww."

Daniel helped him back to his feet.

"The knee is good," I said. "But the knee is not completely healed. Be careful."

"It's a road," Corey said, pointing.

"A dirt road," Hayley muttered.

"So? We've been slogging through the forest for two days. What do you want? A six-lane highway?"

"That'd be nice."

"Yeah, until you raced out, screaming for help, and got mowed down by a logging truck." He walked into the middle and turned, waving his arms. "It's a road!"

I patted his back. "It's a lovely road. Now, which way do we go?"

Corey looked one way, the brown ribbon extending into emptiness. He looked the other way, saw the same thing and his shoulders slumped.

"Damn."

❦   ❦   ❦

Yes, finding a road did not mean finding civilization. Not right away. But at least it was a two-lane road, which was better than stumbling over one of the many dirt tracks leading into the bush . . . and nowhere else.

And, like I said, on Vancouver Island, if you want people, your best bet is always to head south. So that's what we did.

The road wasn't as promising as we might have wanted. It was overgrown at the edges, and no hydro poles meant no nearby homes or cabins. But it smelled of diesel, and had tire tracks, so we knew it was still in use. At least no one was complaining anymore, and after a few minutes, the rain stopped.

We'd gone about five kilometers when we rounded a bend to see a tiny roadside store with a gas bar.

"Yes!" Corey said, pumping the air. "We are now, officially, rescued."

"You think?" Hayley said. "I'm not seeing any vehicles."

"Because it's out in the middle of freaking nowhere. They're probably lucky if they get three cars a day."

"No, I mean transportation for the person running the place."

Corey peered at the empty lot surrounding the small building. "Oh."

The shack had one gas pump out front, and a diesel one around the side. The lack of a vehicle meant that unless there was a house nearby, no one was manning the place.

"But it should have a phone," I said. "Or maps to show us

where we are. Also, there must be cottages nearby if there's a gas bar."

"Ha!" Corey said, spinning and pointing at Hayley. "Ha!"

He took off at a lope. We followed.

Corey stopped a few feet from the door. "Open weekends after Labor Day," he called. "What's today?"

"Not the weekend," I called back.

Corey walked to the barred window, then turned to us. "The window's filthy. I can't see anything."

"How about we try the door?" Sam said.

She was walking toward it when Hayley grabbed her arm and pointed to a window sign warning that the place was armed with security alarms and cameras.

"Um, yeah," Corey said. "Which will bring the local cops. If we're lucky."

"At this point, I'll take any ride out of here," I said. "Even handcuffed in the back of a police cruiser."

NINETEEN

T HE FRONT DOOR WAS unlocked. A bell jangled as Daniel and Corey walked in, Hayley and Sam following. I took Kenjii under a tree and told her to stay. As well trained as she was, I knew she was very hungry, and the smell of food might prove too much temptation.

"Hello?" Corey was calling as I went inside.

They'd stopped just inside the doorway and were looking around. It was your typical roadside store, crammed with nonperishable foods and items a cottager might need badly enough to pay twice the normal price. The place smelled of must and mildew, and the layer of dust on the cans suggested they'd been there a while. The dirty floor had a path worn down the middle, meaning it wasn't deserted—just not very busy.

Beside the door stood a cooler. It was unplugged and filled with pop cans and bottles. A handwritten sign advised those looking for milk to check aisle two, for the powdered and canned variety.

"No beer?" Corey said. "What kind of place is this?"

"The kind that knows better than to leave anything that'll make it a target for kids like you," I said.

Corey grabbed a Coke.

"Hey!" Hayley said.

"If they aren't here to man the shop . . ."

Daniel reached into Corey's back pocket. He plucked out his wallet, took out a still-damp twenty and put it on the counter. Corey grabbed for it, but Daniel gave a look that made Corey withdraw his hand.

"Fine," Corey said. "Drinks and snacks on me, apparently. Chow down, guys."

"I'm a little more interested in finding a phone," I said. "And figuring out if that open front door means someone's here."

"Nah," Corey said. "They were so eager to get out of this dump that they forgot to lock up Sunday night."

"Hmm."

I walked behind the counter. Tucked beside the cash register was a folded newspaper. Beside it rested a paper cup of coffee. I touched the cup.

"Cold?" Daniel said.

"Not hot."

He reached over, pulled off the lid, and stuck his finger in the coffee.

"Warmer than room temperature," he said. He flipped over the paper to check the date. "Today's."

"I don't see a bathroom," Corey said. "Maybe he's outside, taking a leak."

Kenjii let out a sharp bark.

"Sounds like someone found him."

He walked to the front door. When it didn't open, he put his shoulder into it and pushed.

"Um, try the handle," Hayley said.

"Um, there isn't one."

Corey was right. It was the kind you pushed open from the inside, in case your arms were loaded with supplies. He hit it harder. It didn't budge.

Daniel went over and they both heaved on it. The door groaned, but didn't open.

"Is anyone else getting concerned?" Hayley said.

My pounding heart said yes, but I struggled to stay calm. "Look for another exit." I walked toward the back. "Corey? See if you can get a window open."

"How about a side door?" Sam said. "There's one right here, behind—"

She swore and jumped away from the window.

"It's a trap," she said, backing into the middle of the room.

"What?" I walked behind the counter and found the door. Beside it was another filthy, barred window. Beyond that, I could see two human-size shapes.

I cleared a spot on the glass. "They might not be—"

I could make out Moreno and the woman I'd seen at the cabin. Behind them, a third person was trying to tie Kenjii to a tree. She'd been muzzled and was stumbling a little, as if she'd been tranquilized, but she still fought against the rope. Moreno went to help.

"Kenjii," I whispered.

A loud buzzing sound made us all jump. I found a radio tucked under the counter.

"Hello?"

"Maya. I should have known you'd be the one to pick up."

My hand gripped the radio tighter as I recognized the voice. "Who is this?"

"I think you know."

I moved to the front window. He was there. He lifted his free hand and smiled. I pulled back from the window.

"My name is Calvin Antone," he said. "But what's important isn't who I am, but what I am, to you."

Daniel moved closer. He could hear Antone. They all could. I thought of lifting the radio to my ear, but I knew that wouldn't help.

I walked back to the counter, taking shelter behind it.

"What are you doing to my dog?"

"We're taking good care of Kenjii. We just didn't want her to get hurt trying to protect you."

I twitched when he said her name. I didn't want him knowing that. He had no business with her or with any part of my life.

"Maya?"

"What?"

He sighed. "All right. We'll pretend you haven't already guessed. You're my daughter."

Daniel's eyes widened. I looked away quickly.

"Did you hear me?" Antone said.

I didn't answer.

"I'm your dad, Maya."

"No, Rick Delaney is my dad. If you're saying you're my biological father, then fine. You can be that. But my dad is Rick Delaney."

"I'm sure you feel that way—"

"No, it's a fact. He raised me and—"

"And he's done a great job. I'm grateful to him and your adoptive mother. But you've reached the end of what they can do for you. You're part of a world they know nothing about. You understand that, don't you?"

"Are you sure? I saw a subject list for Project Genesis. There's a Delaney on there. Elizabeth Delaney."

"A common enough surname. She's no relation to your adoptive parents. She was a half-demon—"

"Was?"

"She's dead, Maya."

I felt a pang of grief for this girl I hadn't known, one who shared my name.

He continued, "The Edison Group killed her. That's what they do when things go wrong. In the first wave of any experiment, there are bound to be problems. But to take such extreme measures? That's unforgivable, Maya, and I won't let that happen to you. To any of you." He paused. "Serena will be the only subject they kill in Project Phoenix. You have my word on that."

"The Edison Group didn't kill Serena," I said. "If they wanted to, they'd have managed an accident a lot more believable than a champion swimmer drowning in a still lake. I don't know what happened in Buffalo, but it's different here. You guys are the only ones killing people."

"We have not—"

"Rafe Martinez? Mayor Tillson?"

"Unfortunate accidents—"

"Caused by your team setting my forest on fire and kidnapping us."

A pause. "You're upset, Maya. Nicole told us you were close to Rafe. I'm very sorry, but we're here to help you now."

I snorted. "Right. That's why you locked us in here."

"I *am* here to help you. You're my child—"

"No, I'm a teenage girl who happens to share your DNA, which you donated to an experiment."

"Is that what they told you? I was supposed to be your *father*, Maya. Apparently, your mother didn't see it that way. She took you and your brother, and I've been trying to get you back ever since."

I flinched at the mention of my mother and twin brother,

but pushed it aside. "You don't work for the St. Clouds. They're the ones—"

"Who promised me I could be a parent to my children, then robbed me of that right after I found you again. Yes, I found you. I'm the one who tracked you down in Oregon. Then the St. Clouds set up a phony job interview for Rick Delaney and decided you were too attached to your adoptive parents. So they moved your whole family to Salmon Creek, while keeping me on the line, promising I could be part of your life as soon as you were ready to know the truth. It took me awhile, but I eventually figured out that was a lie. So I left."

"And took your story to a rival Cabal. Sold us out. Told them where to find us."

Silence. Then, "You've figured out a lot, Maya. You're a very smart girl." A small laugh. "I'd like to say that means you take after your father."

"No, I take after my parents. The Delaneys."

I turned off the radio, and looked at the others, who were staring at me.

"There isn't another exit, is there?" I said.

"Got a trapdoor over here." Corey waved us into the storage room. He pulled aside a filthy carpet. The trapdoor had been secured with a padlock, but he'd managed to pry the whole latch off.

"Does it lead anywhere?" Daniel said.

"No. It's just a hole where they stash the beer and smokes. Big enough to hide in, though."

Daniel shook his head and we walked back into the store, where the radio was buzzing again.

"If you don't answer that, he's going to come in here," Sam said. "They all are."

"And if she does answer, they'll come in anyway," Daniel said. "He was hoping she'd lead us out peacefully, but obviously that's not happening."

"I could fake it," I said.

"He'd know you were up to something."

They talked—Daniel, Corey, and Sam. I was having trouble concentrating. That damned buzzing radio didn't help. I went behind the counter to see if I could turn it off. As I picked it up, the newspaper fell to the floor. It flipped over and a headline caught my eye.

Bodies of Local Teens Recovered.

Before I could take a better look, Daniel said something about causing a distraction.

"That's probably our only hope," I said as I straightened. "The question is how to pull it off."

He told us his idea.

"No," I said when he finished. "Absolutely not. No one sacrifices themselves for this."

"We don't have time to argue," Daniel said. "I'll be fine—"

"But we won't," Sam said. "We need you to get us out of

here. It has to be someone else."

"And you're volunteering, right?" Corey said.

Sam opened her mouth, but nothing came out.

"Thought so." Corey turned to us. "I'll go. Play the hero for a change." A forced smile. "I hear chicks really go for that kind of thing."

"It should be me," I said. "That . . . guy. He wants me. I can distract—"

The crash of breaking glass had us all hitting the floor. Another crash as a second window smashed, glass tinkling. Shouts sounded outside.

I looked up to see brown liquid running down the wall under the broken window. Some kind of solidified gas? Sedative?

No—the window had been broken from the inside. A pop bottle lay on the sill, cola dripping down.

That had been Daniel's plan. Smash the windows. Then, after our captors raced around the front, thinking we were trying to escape, he'd run through the side door and pretend to be the last one out—that the rest of us had already made it to the woods while, really, we were hiding inside.

I leaped to my feet in time to see the side door swinging shut.

"Who—?" I began.

"Guys!" Hayley shouted outside. "Wait up! Please, don't leave me here."

Corey ran for the side door. Daniel caught him, hauling

him back. Corey took a swing at him. Daniel ducked and wrenched Corey's arm behind his back.

"She did this for us," Daniel hissed. "Don't blow it or she's given herself up for nothing. She'll be okay. We'll get her back."

Corey hesitated. Then he dropped his chin, and let Daniel steer him toward the trapdoor. Sam and I followed. I won't say I didn't glance over at that side door. I won't say I didn't feel like a heartless bitch, listening to them chase Hayley, knowing they would catch her and hold her captive, like Nicole. But Daniel was right. She'd made this sacrifice for us, and she hadn't done it hoping we'd all be taken captive with her.

TWENTY

DANIEL OPENED THE trapdoor leading into the crawl space, then prodded us inside, whispering "Move, move!" Sam and I burrowed past the boxes. Corey was right behind us. Then the front door opened, bell jangling.

Daniel jumped in, still holding the broken latch, and closed the trapdoor as one set of footsteps circled the shop. They stopped at the storage room door. Daniel tensed, ready to leap if the trapdoor opened.

"Clear!" Moreno yelled.

The steps crossed the store. The bell sounded again.

"Get in farther," Daniel whispered. "We need to hide better."

"Didn't you hear him?" Corey whispered. "We're clear."

"They'll look outside some more. Then they'll come back in."

The guys shifted the boxes, then we crawled in behind them. It was far from an ideal hiding spot. The crawl space wasn't even three feet deep. Dirt floor. I didn't want to think about what else was alive—or dead—down here. I twisted around and stretched out on my stomach. Sam huddled beside me, hugging her knees.

The guys wiggled backward to us, as they moved the boxes and cases of beer, stacking them so we were hidden.

How long should we wait? That was the question. Finally Sam asked it out loud

"Until we think it's safe," I whispered.

"Then twenty minutes more," Daniel said. "To be sure."

When it finally seemed as if anyone searching for us had to be gone, I told Corey to check his watch. He was just doing that when I heard the sound of the front doorbells.

Footsteps followed. Still only one set. Again they circled the shop.

"Definitely empty," Moreno said. "They've got to be out there."

A voice came through his radio. Then the door bells jangled again.

"They're trying to use the dog." It was Antone. "But she's not cooperating. She just lays down and growls at anyone who touches her."

Good girl.

"Well, there's no one in here," Moreno said. "What we

really need is the Enwright witch's sensing spell and a were-wolf tracker."

"Preaching to the choir, buddy. I've been hounding head office for two days now. They finally agreed to send the witch. No chance on a werewolf, though."

The door to the back room opened.

"What have we here?" Moreno murmured. A creak as he opened the trapdoor. Light filtered past the stacked boxes.

"Got something?" Antone called.

"Nah, just storage for the booze."

"Well, check it out."

Moreno chuckled. "Happy to, boss."

We held our breath as he pushed aside a beer case. I glanced over at Daniel. He had his eyes closed. Sweat shone on his forehead. His lips moved as he tried to mentally per-suade Moreno that he'd looked hard enough.

Let it work. Please let it work.

Moreno hesitated. Then he backed out and yelled. "Just boxes. You want a beer?"

I didn't hear what Antone said, but Moreno laughed and let the trapdoor fall shut. The bells over the door jangled a few minutes later. Daniel checked his watch. After twenty minutes, he helped me crawl forward, open the hatch, and listen.

"Nothing," I whispered.

"Give it another five minutes."

We did. Then I insisted on going first to check. I crept to one of the broken front windows, listened hard, then peered out.

The yard looked empty. I checked the side window. Same thing. I glanced back toward the storage room.

Hayley had made her sacrifice. Time for me to do the same.

I went out the side door. Looked around. Circled the building. Nothing. I took a deep breath and walked to the road, shoulders up, gaze forward, tensing for the first shout. Or the first shot.

When nothing happened, I looked around for Kenjii. Even whistled softly. They'd taken her. I pushed down a stab of panic. She'd be fine. If that man wanted to prove he was on my side, he'd take good care of my dog.

I looked both ways along the road. Empty.

When I went back into the store, Daniel was out of the crawl space.

"All clear," I said as I walked in.

"You shouldn't have gone outside."

"Yes, I should have. Better one gets caught than all of us. That's how it has to be from now on. As long as one gets home, we all have a chance."

He nodded. I gathered supplies from the store as he got the others. I took two incredibly overpriced backpacks, too. And, no, I didn't pay for them. Daniel didn't mention it, either.

It was one thing to worry about that when we thought we were nearly to safety, but another when it looked like we still had a very long journey ahead of us.

We hadn't talked about Hayley yet, or what we planned to do. For now, we just needed to put some distance between us and the store, in case they returned.

As we walked, I pulled out the newspaper I'd found.

"Getting caught up on current events?" Sam asked.

"No," Corey said. "She's doing her research for that essay we have due next week. You know Maya. Escaping a forest fire, helicopter crash, and crazed would-be kidnappers is no reason to ask for an extension."

"I'm sure she brought it for fire-starter, guys." Daniel glanced over. "Maya . . ."

My gaze was glued to the article as I read. When I tripped over a fallen branch, Daniel grabbed my arm and steered me to the side. Then he read the headline over my shoulder.

"Is that . . . ?"

I nodded. I tried to explain, but the words wouldn't come. I handed him the paper. He finished reading it.

"That's not . . . ?" he murmured when he finished. "How . . . ?"

"Okay, what gives?" Corey said. "Personally, I wouldn't care if the U.S. declared war on Canada. Doesn't seem relevant under the circumstances."

"This *is* relevant." I passed the paper to him and Sam. They read the first few lines.

"How can they . . . ?" Sam began. "That's not possible."

"Well, apparently, it is," I said. "They lost contact with our helicopter shortly after takeoff. Our flight disappeared. Search crews found the wreck last night."

"*South* of Vancouver Island?" Corey said. "Okay, my sense of location can be a little screwy, but that's not where we went down."

"It was found by a private search party," I said. "Hired by our parents' employer. Someone retrieved enough wreckage to move there and convince people that's where we went down. They recovered the bodies of the pilot and Mayor Tillson."

"I get that. But this?" Sam jabbed her finger at the middle of the article. "This is not possible."

Wreckage and two corpses wasn't all they found. They'd recovered Kenjii, too, apparently. That wasn't tough to fake— no one's going to test a dog. But the article said they'd also recovered DNA evidence that confirmed the death of the seven teenagers on board.

"But how the hell do you pull off something like that?" Sam said.

"They have our DNA," I said. "They must have made it seem like the crash was worse than it was, that there wasn't . . ."

"Much left of us," Daniel said. "Enough to provide DNA, but not enough to show our parents."

"Hold on," Corey said. "Isn't there one massive flaw in this logic? The search team belonged to the St. Clouds. *They* have our DNA. *They* could convince our parents we were dead. But *they* aren't the ones we're running from and they aren't the ones who found the wreck."

"They've cut a deal," I said.

"And cut us loose," Daniel murmured as he worked it out. "There are other kids in this experiment. Probably our whole class. This Nast Cabal discovered the experiment. The St. Clouds realized it. So they negotiated."

I nodded. "We 'die' and the Nasts get to keep us, if they can find us. The St. Clouds get the rest of the kids. They already had one project blow up on them. They weren't about to lose another."

"So they *negotiated*?" Corey said. "Using *us*?"

"Apparently that's all we are to them. Assets. Valuable ones, but not worth sacrificing the whole experiment for."

"So we can't go back to Salmon Creek," Sam said. "If we do, they'll just turn us over."

"The St. Clouds will. Our parents won't." I looked around. "Does anyone doubt that?"

Daniel said, carefully, "I'm not sure my dad wouldn't . . . let them have me."

"I don't believe that." I wasn't so sure, but I certainly

wasn't saying so. "But he won't be the one we'll approach. My parents would be best—I'm sure they knew nothing about this. Corey's mom is fine, too. And Mrs. Tillson isn't going to hand over Sam and Nicole to the people who killed her husband."

"Okay, so we still go back—" Corey began.

He stopped, wincing.

"Headache?" I said.

"Yeah, just hold—" He doubled over with a sharp intake of breath.

I grasped his arm. "Corey?"

"Bad one," he panted. "Okay, just—"

He let out a howl, his head dropping forward, his hands clutching it. Then he retched. Another heave, and a geyser of Coke sprayed the bushes.

I gripped his arm and tugged him until he was sitting, knees up, head between them, panting hard.

"Well, that's new," Corey muttered between gasps. "And I don't think I like it."

He winced again, face screwed up against the pain as he doubled over.

"Okay," I said. "Just breathe and keep your eyes shut. The sunlight's probably making it worse."

"That would help . . . if I wasn't seeing light even with them shut."

"What?"

"I'm getting flashes of—" A few panting breaths. "Light. Color. Could use a sound track."

"You're seeing things?"

He shook his head. "You get visions. I just get random—" Another curse as the pain hit again. "Flashes. Boring flashes."

Daniel knelt and held out a bottle. I thought it was pop, then saw the label.

"Beer?" I said.

"It helps. I knew his meds had dissolved, so I grabbed a few from the store."

Corey took it and twisted off the cap. A few gulps. Then a deep breath as he relaxed. Another long drink, then a sidelong glance at me.

"Yes, I'm self-medicating with booze and I know that's not smart. I wouldn't do it if I had the meds."

"So beer . . . helps?"

He shrugged. "Not as good as the meds. I've still got a killer headache. But it doesn't feel like an icepick driving into my skull."

I looked over at Daniel. His eyes were dark with worry. If these weren't just migraines—if they were linked to the experiments—we had no idea how to handle them. No idea if they were a normal part of Corey getting his powers or a sign that something was wrong.

Corey finished the bottle, then closed his eyes. "The

puking was new. And the pain was worse. The flashing lights are a recent symptom." He opened one eye. "See, I said I get all the cool powers. Raging migraines cured by booze. I really will be that guy in a bar—"

The sound of a revving engine made us all look up. We'd been walking parallel to the road. but deep enough in the bush not to be spotted by anyone driving past. This noise sounded like an ATV. We hid, and it passed, went a little farther, then stopped.

"Moreno to base. Moreno to base."

Someone answered.

Moreno gave his coordinates, then said, "Still no sign of the Morris girl. She can't have run far, though. I'll keep looking."

The ATV started up again.

"Hayley escaped," Corey said.

"You heard that?" I said.

"Um, yeah. We all did."

"Because we were supposed to," Daniel said. "He was talking too loud. He even turned off the ATV so his voice would carry better."

"Because he's talking into a radio," Corey said.

"I bet if we keep going, we'll hear him do the same thing a little farther down. It's another trap."

Corey looked at me.

"It . . . sounds like it," I said. "But if it's a good trap, then they really *did* let Hayley go. She's out here as bait."

"So you think you can outsmart them and rescue her?" Sam said. "No, the *smart* thing to do is keep going."

We argued about that, of course.

Finally I said, "I'm going to look for her. Just me."

"We can't—" Daniel began.

"I've got the super-powered hearing, and I can move quietly. I need to try."

TWENTY-ONE

As I MADE MY way through the forest, I'll admit I was also straining for a familiar bark or whine. I hadn't said a word about Kenjii since leaving the store. How could I without making it sound like I put her on the same level as Hayley.

I love animals, but I know they aren't people. I can't value them the same way. But that didn't mean I wasn't sick at heart over Kenjii. So as I walked through those woods, I was listening for her as much as I was listening for Hayley.

It was Hayley I heard, though. Stomping on dead leaves. Muttering under her breath. Kicking aside fallen branches.

Signs of a trap? Or just Hayley, pissed off because she'd escaped and there was no one around to rescue her?

A few days ago, I'd have gone with option two. Now, though, I couldn't see Hayley being so careless.

I shimmied up a tree and waited for her to pass my way. But once she got close enough for me to see her through the branches, she sat down to rest. When she didn't come closer, I started crawling along a branch, planning to cross to the next tree.

She started to look up, then caught herself, waited a moment, gave a loud sigh and slumped back against the trunk, giving her an excuse to look up.

I waited until she looked up, then bent to catch her gaze. She held mine and mouthed "trap," ending it with a yawn to fool anyone watching.

I looked around. I might still be able to rescue her. Whoever was watching couldn't be too close.

Hayley rose a couple of inches from the ground, rubbed her butt, and scowled, as if she'd sat on a root or a rock. She got up and made some noise, kicking the ground then shaking a young oak, dead leaves rustling. In other words, assuring her captors that she was trying to attract our attention. Then she walked beneath my tree and sat down again.

She picked up a stick and began idling poking around a patch of bare earth. Then she wrote "Don't be stupid." She erased it, doodled a bit, then wrote, "I'm fine."

I hesitated, but she was right. It was a trap and my chances of foiling it were slim to none. If I got caught, could I trust Daniel not to come after me? No. Could I trust Corey and Sam to make it to safety alone? No.

Finally, I shimmied back along the branch to the trunk. As

the needles rustled, Hayley nodded. Then she wrote, "Thanks for trying," rubbed it smooth, got up, and walked away.

Hayley had sacrificed her freedom so we could escape. She'd refused to let me try to rescue her. If someone told me a week ago that Hayley Morris would do this, I'd have said he was crazy. Or naive, because clearly she had an ulterior motive.

Had she changed? I didn't think so. The answer was simpler: I'd been wrong about her.

If I'd had a nemesis at school, Hayley was it. Always insulting me. Always challenging me. Always doing her best to run me down, while I'd stood firm and refused to stoop to her level.

Clearly, she was the aggressor and I was the victim. Only . . . well, it hadn't started out that way. Back in grade five, I'd caught her cheating. I hadn't tattled. Maybe, in retrospect, that would have been better, because what I did instead was make it very clear that I wanted nothing more to do with her.

When you accept a leadership role, you take on extra responsibility for your actions toward others. If you shun someone, the effect will trickle down through those who value your opinion. It wasn't as if Hayley was an outcast. She had her friends, and she was the queen of the "pretty girl" clique. In a bigger school, that would have been enough. In Salmon Creek, it wasn't.

I remembered what she said about flirting with Rafe to

make Corey jealous. I remembered, too, what Rafe had said. That Corey might make out with Hayley at parties, when he could claim he was just drunk and horny, but he'd never actually date her, because his friends—namely Daniel and me—didn't get along with her. I'd told myself Hayley had been using Corey, too—he was her backup when no summer boys were around. Now, knowing she'd wanted to make him jealous, I realized I'd been wrong.

I'd been wrong about a lot of things. Not just Hayley. I'd misjudged Rafe. Nicole, too. I'd been so sure of my judgments that I'd never questioned them even when the evidence suggested I was wrong.

I'd always thought of myself as an open-minded person. I had no patience with anyone who put down other kids because of their race, religion, or sexuality. But that's just one kind of open-mindedness. There's another kind, too, the kind that's willing to see people for who they really are and admit when you were wrong about them. That's the part I still need to work on.

I climbed down the tree and started making my way back to the others. I had to put aside my worries for now. Our pursuers could be anywhere. I needed to be careful.

When I was almost back, I heard branches snap as someone barreled through the woods.

I ducked behind a fallen tree. A dark shape sprang, then stopped short, just out of sight. A whine.

Kenjii.

I nudged aside branches until I could see her. She was still wearing the muzzle. A length of rope trailed behind her.

I closed my eyes to listen for the sound of anyone else. More twigs snapped as Kenjii caught my scent and raced around the fallen tree.

I grabbed her and held her close, whispering, "Shhh," as I kept looking and listening.

Kenjii nudged me, as if to say, *That's no welcome.*

I pulled the rope in. The end wasn't broken, as I'd hoped, but as I ran it through my fingers I saw red smears. I took a better look. Blood. Someone had been holding her and Kenjii had wrenched so hard she'd scraped the skin from his hands as she broke free.

I hugged her. "They couldn't hold you, huh? Good girl."

"Maya?"

I stood. It was Sam, coming through the trees. Daniel and Corey appeared behind her. Seeing the dog beside me, Daniel grinned.

"We got one escapee, at least," he said.

"Only one," I said as I tugged off the muzzle. "I found Hayley. She managed to communicate with me. It was a trap. There was no way . . ." I took a deep breath. "I wanted to try rescuing her anyway, but she said no."

"Too bad *dogs* can't talk," Sam said.

I glanced over at her.

"Um, we're all feeling bad about Hayley," Corey said. "Don't interrupt by wishing we could question the dog."

"That's not what I meant. Hayley could tell you it was a trap. He can't."

"Kenjii's a she," I said.

"Whatever. My point is that your dog has conveniently escaped, just like Hayley did. You don't think that's a trap?"

"If it is, then we've already been caught." I looked around. "Huh. I don't see the guys with guns yet."

"Because they've put a tracking device on her. Or in her."

I removed the rope. Then I took off her collar and handed it to Daniel to check while I ran my fingers over her, looking for tender spots.

"It's clean," Daniel said, handing me back the collar. "If she was still wearing the muzzle and rope, then they—"

"—wanted it to look like she really escaped," Sam said.

"There's blood on the rope," I said. "That means she pulled free from whoever had her."

"Or they're very detail-oriented."

"Oh, please," Corey said. "Seriously?"

I turned to Sam. "So what do you suggest?"

"Tie her to a tree and keep going."

I stared at her.

"I hope you're not serious," Daniel said.

"How about we tie *you* to a tree?" Corey said.

"It's a dog," Sam said. "I understand it's Maya's pet—"

"No, you don't understand," I said, barely able to get the words out. "I wouldn't tie any animal to a tree and leave it to die. *Any* animal. And certainly not my dog. She trusts me to

191 ⚘

look after her. I will not break that trust."

"I'm not saying we tie her and leave her for good. If she's tagged, they'll find her. If not, we can come back after—"

"After she's died of dehydration? Or been eaten by the first hungry cougar or bear that comes along and finds dinner staked out for it?"

Sam backed up and crossed her arms. "This isn't about doing what we *want*. It's doing what we *need* to survive. You think you're the only one who's had to make hard choices?"

"We just *made* a hard choice," Corey said. "We left Hayley—"

"There's a reason I don't have pets," Sam went on. "I found a kitten once. I took it from place to place as we ran . . . until the day we had to run without going back home. My parents said she'd find a way out of our apartment. I'm not sure of that. But there was nothing else to do. Hard life. Hard choices."

My parents would have made sure the cat got out, called a neighbor from a pay phone or something. As I looked at Sam, though, I knew she wouldn't agree. She'd been raised to avoid risk at all costs.

"Sam has a point," I said.

"What?" Corey said. "No way."

Daniel shot me a questioning look. Not questioning why I was going along with Sam, but wondering what alternative I had in mind, because he knew there was no way in hell I'd leave Kenjii behind.

"She could be tagged," I said. "And as we agreed earlier, not all of us need to get to safety. That means not all of us need to stay with Kenjii. I'll take her. You guys go another way."

Once again, our great escape devolved into chaos, which could be summarized as: "You can't do that." "Yes, I can." "I know you're upset—" "I'm not upset. We have a problem and I'm solving it." Expand. Mix. Repeat until one party wears down and surrenders. That party wasn't me.

Actually, I was surprised by how quickly Daniel gave in. Well, "quickly" being relative. But he did fold fast enough for me to suspect he didn't plan to actually let me go off alone. So I kept my ears tuned for signs I was being followed. But I didn't hear any. He'd realized this was the best solution for all.

I'd sent Daniel along the road, which seemed to be slowly veering inland. I stuck to a direct route south, through the woods. Soon I found an even narrower dirt road.

It was dusk when I came across a couple of cottages. They were little more than shacks. Both uninhabited. One was completely empty. The other had furniture. So I broke in and, no, I didn't feel guilty about that. Couldn't.

As I discovered, though, the only thing in that cabin was the furniture. No phone. No canned food. I had pop and energy bars from the store, though, so I decided to eat them at the table, which felt oddly comforting. I shared with Kenjii, as I'd done with all my rations.

By the time I finished eating, night had fallen. I considered spending it on the double bed. It was just a bare mattress—a stained and soiled one—but my muscles ached from sleeping on the cold ground, and I'd be better able to escape pursuers with a decent sleep. So I gingerly stretched out, using Kenjii as a pillow.

As everything got quiet, there was only one thing left to do. Think about what happened at the store today. Think about what that man said.

Calvin Antone. My father. I hated the sound of that. Even "biological father" wasn't much better. As for "bio father," I'd never used the term, even in my mind. Probably because I never thought about the man who'd fathered me.

I *did* think about the woman who'd given birth to me. I couldn't help it. She'd abandoned me. Now, I'd learned that I had a twin brother, and she'd kept him. It didn't matter if Rafe was right and she'd split us up for our own safety. She'd still chosen which child she wanted to keep, and there had to be a reason—maybe I cried more, maybe I fussed more, maybe she decided she'd rather have a son—but some thought process must have gone into it. She'd chosen him and rejected me.

I flipped onto my stomach and made a noise in my throat that sounded a lot like a growl.

I didn't want to feel anything toward my biological parents, positive or negative. I remember once my mom showed me an online forum for adopted kids. If I wouldn't share my angst with her and I wouldn't share it with a counselor, maybe I'd be comfortable with this. What she couldn't seem to understand was that I had no angst. On those forums I saw kids bitching about their adoptive parents and how much better their biological ones might have been, and I realized I had nothing in common with them.

I was sure there were others like me—who wouldn't trade their adoptive parents for anything—but those kids were doing fine, living their lives, just like me. They weren't complaining on Internet forums.

Now I had angst. Not only had my biological mother rejected me, but Rafe also said she had light hair and hazel eyes, even if she had to be at least part-Native because of the skin-walker blood. I'd grown up thinking I was one-hundred-percent Native, and finding out I wasn't threw me off balance.

Then I'd met my biological father and he wasn't just the sperm donor I'd imagined. Apparently, he was the parent who *hadn't* rejected me. He said he'd been searching for me since I'd been born. Then he found me, and he'd been there ever since, somewhere, watching me grow up.

Did I believe his story? I didn't want to. I wanted him to be lying, to be evil. Otherwise, he really had wanted me and when we finally got a chance to meet, he was on the side of the people chasing me. He was my father, and he was my enemy. He claimed to care for me, and he killed the guy I cared about. He wanted to give me a better life, and he seemed hell-bent on destroying the great one I already had.

So yes, I had angst.

More than angst, because when I thought about my biological parents, it forced me to think of the one thing that worried me more than anything else. The one thing I'd been struggling so hard not to think about. My mom and dad.

They thought I was dead. *Dead*. What were they going through? How were they coping? Were they safe?

Angst. Fear. Stark, gut-twisting terror. It didn't make for an easy sleep.

I tried to clear my head, but when I did, I realized how horrible this cabin was. Even Kenjii's dog smell wasn't enough to mask the stench of the mattress.

There was no place better to sleep inside. I left the cabin and walked until I was so exhausted that I didn't care how hard the ground was. Then I curled up with my dog and fell asleep.

TWENTY-TWO

MY DREAMS STARTED INNOCENTLY enough. I was at home, undressing for the night, then I collapsed into bed. I didn't stay there for long. The next thing I knew, I was in a medieval torture chamber, roped to the rack, being stretched until I screamed with . . . I wasn't sure how to describe it. Not pain. It was like stretching for a run, only it felt wrong, like I was overdoing it, my brain screeching for me to stop before I tore something, only I couldn't stop, because I wasn't in control. The ropes pulled tighter and tighter, until I was covered in sweat, gasping for breath.

I didn't know what my tormenters wanted from me, but apparently "screaming like a girl" wasn't it, because they ramped it up to a form of torture seen only in sci-fi movies—injecting bugs under my skin. I didn't actually feel the injections. But I felt the bugs. They crawled all over my body and burrowed into my flesh. That led to more screaming.

I lay there feeling my body being stretched beyond its limits, watching it writhe and contort as bugs skittered beneath my skin. And then, with no warning, the ropes were cut and the beetles vanished, and I was left panting with exertion and exhaustion, eyes squeezed shut until I dared to open them and—

I was lying on the ground. I caught a glimpse of one of Kenjii's paws and I remembered where I was. I blinked and yawned. Out of the corner of my eye I saw another of Kenjii's paws jerk, and I glanced over to realize it wasn't hers. It was the huge tawny paw of a cougar.

I leaped to my feet. Or I tried to, rolling awkwardly. I managed to get half up, then reached out to push to my feet and—

I screamed. Only it was no girlie scream this time—it was a snarling yelp. I looked down again at my hands, stretched out before me. Not hands. Paws. Cougar paws.

I gulped air. Even that didn't feel right and when I closed my mouth, a fang caught my lip.

I'd changed into a cougar. Transformed in my sleep.

As I swung my head, I caught sight of Kenjii. She was still fast asleep. I stared at her. If Kenjii wasn't leaping up with a cougar standing two meters away, then there couldn't be a cougar standing two meters away.

I was dreaming.

Oh.

I told myself I should be relieved, that I wasn't ready to deal with the shape-shifting, that I needed more information first, I needed to be prepared. Yet there was part of me that didn't want to be prepared. Didn't want to be so damned organized and informed all the time. The part that longed to just leap and experience.

Yet the transformation couldn't be that easy, could it? For the body to turn from human to animal must involve pain. Vast amounts of real pain, not just discomfort. That was only logical.

Damn logic. Why couldn't I have a little magic in my life, instead?

I sighed. It came out as a feline chuff, jowls quivering.

Oh, get over it already. You want magic, Maya? How about the ability to heal animals? The power to become one—painful or not.

That was magic.

I stretched, catlike, hindquarters up, front paws out. I stayed back from Kenjii, though. Part of me still hoped I wasn't dreaming, that she was just soundly asleep from her long day of adventure. After everything I'd been through, I was entitled to enjoy my fantasy while it lasted.

As I stretched, I flexed my paws and my claws shot out like switchblades. I relaxed and they retracted. In and out, in and out.

I took a closer look at my paws. They were as big as splayed human hands, oversize for climbing. If I looked closely at my flanks, I could see very faint spots, all but disappeared.

I pushed onto all fours and took a few steps. It wasn't as awkward as I'd feared. I knew how animals moved, and when I put that image into my brain, it was like an instruction set. My muscles obeyed and I walked. Forward. Back—

I tripped and landed on my rump. Okay, that explained why animals usually turn around instead of switching into reverse. Backing up on two legs is a lot easier than on four.

So what else was different? Everything I saw, for starters. The world came in shades of gray, like a high-quality black-and-white movie. My night vision seemed sharper, as did my hearing. The dark clearing where we'd fallen asleep looked twilit, and I could pick up the scuffle of a distant animal.

The most noticeable difference was the overwhelming number of smells. Musk and rot and a sharp, clean scent that I somehow recognized as water. I swallowed. Water.

I followed the scent until I found a stream, barely a trickle. I sat on my haunches and reached out a paw, ready to scoop some up to drink before realizing that really wasn't going to work.

I bent, stuck out my tongue, and licked the water. I knew I was supposed to lap, not lick, but that's not easy when you aren't accustomed to it. After slopping around and soaking my face, I managed to get a few mouthfuls.

When I had enough, I twisted to go and felt a weird ping on my cheek. It was like I'd brushed against something, but a more intense sensation. And my face was inches from the ferns bending over the stream. I tried again. Another ping, and I realized what it was. Whiskers. They were warning me I was close to hitting something. Like the backup sensors on my grandmother's car.

As I turned around, I felt another brushing sensation, this one not nearly as intense but even odder. My tail. It was off to the side and I couldn't really get a good look at it. So how could I move—?

My tail swung. Okay, that was easy. I took a closer look. It was thick and over half the length of my body. When I thought of moving it, it moved. Very convenient.

I crept forward, sniffing and listening and, occasionally, tasting. When I caught the faint smell of raw meat, my stomach rumbled. That part, I ignored. Definitely not something I cared to explore, and the mingled musk of a weasel or marten told me I'd be stealing dinner from someone else if I did.

The next scent on the breeze was also from a living being. And this one brought me to a skidding stop, paws outstretched. I lifted my head, nose twitching as I found the smell again, to be sure I wasn't mistaken.

Human.

Daniel and the others? My heart beat faster, tail swinging. Another sniff. No, these were scents I didn't recognize. Not consciously, at least. But as I stood there, nose raised to the wind, images flashed in my mind and told me I did know these people—I just hadn't realized I'd stored the scents.

Moreno. Antone. The woman. And the faint smell of a campfire.

As I sniffed the air, I started to seriously consider the possibility this was real. I'd dreamed of undressing. I must have done that, in my sleep, like I'd walked in my sleep two nights ago. As for the transformation, I'd seen Annie do it and it *had* seemed relatively painless. And why hadn't Kenjii woken? Because I'd moved away from her before I shape-shifted. She was too tired to hear me get up and I probably smelled the same as I always did. No cause for alarm.

This was real. I'd shape-shifted. I was a cougar. And Antone, Moreno, and the woman were close by.

Was Sam right, after all? Had they tagged Kenjii and were closing in? Time to check this out, while I still wore my handy disguise.

By the time I got to the camp, I knew they weren't track-ing my dog. If they had been, they wouldn't be staying so far away. I'd traveled at least a couple of kilometers to find them.

When I finally made it, I found two canvas tents and a pickup. From the looks of the small fire, they'd only recently pitched camp for the night.

Moreno, Antone, and the woman sat around the blaze. Moreno and the woman were drinking beer. Antone had a bottle of water beside him, and was crouched by the fire, poking a stick in. I caught the smell of roasting sausage. He pulled it out and put it into bun, then set the stick aside.

"Not going to make ours?" Moreno said.

"I'm sure you can manage."

"I burn everything. My people didn't cook over fire."

"All people cooked over fire at some point," Antone said.

"You know what I mean. Your family."

"My family lived in a suburb of Phoenix. I learned camp-fire cooking in Scouts, like most boys in America."

"Touchy, touchy," Moreno said. "I was just—"

"Being an ass?" the woman said.

Moreno muttered something, crushed his beer can, and threw it into the forest. The woman leaned over, took the stick, and started preparing a sausage. Antone walked into the forest, retrieved the can, and tossed it into the trash.

"Earth Mother be angry," Antone said as he came back to the fire. "Send big thundercloud."

Moreno made a face at him. As Antone sat again, I thought of what he'd said earlier, about losing my twin brother and me. Hunting for us. Finding me. Being strung along by promises from the St. Clouds.

Did I understand how he felt? I guess so. But I was only his child in blood. I'd been raised by others, and to think he could just take me away from them—then or now—was all kinds of wrong.

It didn't matter if he'd been given a raw deal. It didn't matter that as I watched him I saw hints of someone I might have liked. He was trying to take me captive and separate me from my family while endangering my friends along the way. He was the enemy. He had to be.

When Moreno went for a second beer, Antone said, "Enough. I don't mind you guys having one drink, but there's a reason I'm drinking water. We need to be alert here."

"Against what?" Moreno said. "Killer bunnies?"

"Don't dignify that with a response, Cal," the woman said.

A cough sounded from one of the tents, and they all glanced over.

"Penny, go see if she wants another sausage," Antone said. "I'd like to see her eating more."

"I have a Snickers bar in my bag," the woman—Penny—said. "I'll take her that. Kids always like candy."

"Not sure that applies to teenage girls, but you can give it a shot."

Teenage girls? Hayley? I inhaled. This close to the fire, though, all I could smell was smoke. I strained to see inside the tent as Penny pulled back the flap, but she didn't open it far enough.

I slid backward until it seemed safe to turn around. Then I circled the camp. I eyed a massive tree with branches stretching close to the tents. My claws extended and retracted, as if urging me to climb it. Tempting . . . The tents were in the middle of a large clearing, meaning there was no way I could get close from ground level. I saw a flap tied open on the tent roof. A vent that I could probably see down through.

Up it was then.

I'll say this much for cat form. It made shimmying up

a long evergreen trunk so much easier. I'd seen Marv—our local cougar—do it by taking a run at the tree and landing ten feet up it, but I wasn't quite ready for such athletics yet. So I started at the bottom, reached up, and unsheathed my claws. Four massive paws equipped with climbing spikes.

I was up the tree in no time. Getting out on the branch was a little tougher. I had to creep along while using my tail for balance. It was the tail part that threw me. I was sure I'd get the hang of it, but for now, I was just glad I had sixteen claws digging into the tree to keep me from sliding off every time I wobbled.

Halfway along the branch I smelled who was in that tent. And when I did, a tiny growl rumbled up.

Nicole.

Penny emerged. "No to the sausage and no to the candy bar. I'd say she's understandably upset, but it seems more like a hissy fit. She didn't want to come back out here. She was quite comfy in Vancouver, with her soft bed, hot baths, and room service."

"All the more incentive for her to lure her friends out so she can get back there," Antone said. "Hayley obviously wasn't going to do it."

They talked for another minute, enough for me to confirm what had happened. Kenjii had escaped and Hayley hadn't done her job, so they'd swapped her out for Nicole.

As I thought of Nicole, my ears flattened and my chest vibrated with another growl. I swallowed it. Was Nicole really responsible for Serena's death? What if Sam was mistaken? Wasn't that exactly the sort of thinking I'd berated myself for earlier—jumping to conclusions?

I continued creeping along the branch until I could look down through the mesh skylight and see her, sitting on a sleeping bag. She wasn't bound—there was no way out except past her captors. A lantern provided illumination and a pile of magazines provided entertainment. She was reading one, leafing through the glossy pages.

I told myself that was her way of dealing with stress, but still . . . ? Reading fashion tips? If it was me, I'd be plotting my escape, no matter how unlikely it seemed, just to feel that I was taking control of my fate.

I shimmied a little closer and the branch creaked. Nicole looked up. She saw me, and her mouth opened to let out a shriek. I froze. I was stuck out on a branch, with no easy way to back up and escape. She didn't scream, though. For a minute, we just stared at each other. Then she lifted the lantern and squinted, her gaze sliding along my side.

"Maya," she whispered.

I followed her gaze to my flank. There was my birthmark, black fur forming a paw print.

"It is you, isn't it?" She stood. "They told me what you are."

She smiled up at me and I saw the same old Nicole, sweet and shy, yet all I could think was, *You killed Serena.* I looked into her eyes and it wiped away that last piece of doubt.

"You came to rescue me," she said, keeping her voice so low I could barely hear it.

When I just stared at her, she said it again.

"You *are* here to rescue me, right?"

I thought about how easy it would be to drop from my perch, slash through that tent, and take her down. I imagined my fangs clamped around her throat, and felt a kernel of horror in my gut, but it was only a kernel.

"Stop that," she hissed, yanking her gaze away. "Go get the others. You outnumber these guys. Together you can save me."

I didn't move.

She looked at me again, and the sweet and shy Nicole disappeared. Her eyes blazed.

"The others aren't here, are they?" she said. "You have no intention of rescuing me. Why would you? I'm competition for your precious Daniel. You don't want him, but you don't want anyone else to have him either. You're a selfish bitch, Maya Delaney. A slut, too, fooling around with every guy in sight, right under his nose."

As Nicole raged, the hair on my neck prickled, because in her eyes, I saw madness. Obsession and madness.

"Everything comes so easy for you, doesn't it, Maya? School, boys, friends, sports. Even your precious animals. You can't just take care of them like any normal person. You have to be some kind of animal whisperer. Magical healer. So damned special. Like Serena, captain of the swim team and the best singer on the freaking island, and how much does she practice? Sings in the shower. Paddles around the lake. Do you know how hard I work? It's never enough. You two get the trophies and the solos and the As and the boys."

You're crazy, I thought. *Did they do this to you with their experiments? Or is this just you?*

I started inching back.

"You're just going to leave me here?" she said. "Well, you know what, Maya? I could use a little company."

She screamed, a long drawn-out shriek of feigned terror.

TWENTY-THREE

M ORENO WAS THE FIRST to see me, and he let out a curse as loud as Nicole's shriek.

He pulled a gun from his hip. An automatic pistol.

Antone knocked it from his hand and pointed his flashlight at my flank.

"It's Maya," he said.

He started toward me. I was inching back, the branch too thin for me to turn around.

"It could be Annie," Penny whispered, her gaze fixed on me. "Come looking for her brother."

Antone shook his head. "That's Maya." He met my gaze. "I know it is."

He kept walking until he was directly under my branch.

"This is your first time, isn't it?" he said, his voice soft.

"You're scared and you're confused—"

I let out a snarl that reverberated through the quiet forest.

Antone chuckled. "Or maybe not. I should have guessed you'd hit the ground running." He smiled. "Or hit the trees climbing. But you're trapped now. I know that's not fair. You came to rescue your friend and—"

"She didn't come to rescue me," Nicole spat as she stormed out of the tent. "She came to taunt me. She's a spoiled brat—"

"Get her out of here," Antone said, eyes never leaving mine. "Maya, you know you're trapped, and I'm sure you want to put up a fight, but that's not going to help anyone."

I hunkered down, measuring the distance between us.

"Cal . . ." Penny said. "Back away. She's getting ready—"

"She won't." His gaze fixed on mine. "She might want to, but she won't."

I dug my claws deeper into the branch, testing my purchase. My tail rose and flicked from side to side as I adjusted my balance. I crouched. An easy leap. He wouldn't get out of the way. He was too confident that I wouldn't hurt him.

My hindquarters twitched. My rear legs tensed. I sheathed my front claws. I let out one last snarl. Then I leaped.

He realized then that he was wrong. That I felt no tie to him. Felt no sympathy for him. That I would rip his throat out if that protected my friends.

At the last second, I twisted. Penny fired the tranquilizer

gun, and I felt the darts whiz past. I heard Antone's shout. Heard Penny curse as she realized she'd missed. Heard Nicole shout for them to shoot me before I killed them all.

I wasn't about to kill anyone. That wouldn't save me. Wouldn't save the others. I didn't know if I could have or not. Only that it would be a life wasted, so the point was moot.

When I twisted, I flung myself at the tent roof. I hit it and the tent went down. I heard them swearing then—their quarry was in the midst of a mass of billowing canvas, impossible to shoot.

Before the tent could collapse completely, I grabbed a mouthful of canvas and ran into the forest, wrenching it along with me. It was too heavy to drag very far, but I didn't need it to go far—just to the first trees where it caught, wedged between them like a sail. I let go and tore off into the forest.

Behind me, I heard an ATV roar to life. But I already had a huge lead.

Cougars are decent sprinters, but they aren't long-distance runners. Soon I was exhausted and had to slow to a steady lope. By then, though, my pursuers were long gone, having headed north—the way I started running—while I'd looped south.

I found Kenjii easily, as if I could instinctively retrace my steps. When I got back to the clearing, I collapsed into sleep.

I dreamed of the rack and the bugs again. Then I dreamed of Serena at the lake. Only this time, I was right beside her, paddling around, laughing and goofing off. Then I saw Nicole, at the side, almost hidden in the bushes overhanging the lake. She slipped into the water.

I grabbed Serena's arm and started dragging her toward shore. "We have to get out."

"Oh, no." Her hand wrapped around my wrist. "I just got you in."

She tugged me out farther, then flipped onto her back and floated. Beneath the crystal-clear water, I could see Nicole swimming, coming closer with each stroke.

"It's Nicole," I said, pointing.

Serena grinned. "Good. I invited her, but you know how she is. All work and no play. I don't see why she has to practice so much. I don't."

Nicole grabbed Serena by the leg. She let out a giggling shriek as she was pulled under. I dove and managed to grab her under the arms and pull her up. She came up sputtering and scowling.

"What was that for?" she said, pushing wet hair from her face.

"It's Nicole," I said, grabbing her arm again. "She's trying to drown you."

Serena laughed. "Nicole wouldn't hurt me. She's my friend. She's just—"

She went under again as Nicole dragged her down. I swam after them, but this time they were moving too fast. I could see Serena's face. Her eyes glittering as she tried not to laugh. Then, as she went deeper, worry crept in, and she reached for me, pulling against Nicole. She started to kick, mouth opening in a scream. They hit the bottom, and a cloud of dirt billowed up.

I hit something, too, an invisible barrier. I clawed at it, screaming as Serena fought and writhed and kicked at Nicole. Then she tried to get to me, her fingers stretching up, higher and higher and then, an inch away, they stopped.

I battered at the invisible barrier. Nicole crouched there, holding Serena down. She looked at me and she smiled.

I shot up from sleep, a scream still in my throat. Hands gripped my wrists.

"Maya! It's me!"

Daniel. Dragging me to shore. Not knowing that Serena was out there, drowning.

"Serena!" I shouted. "Let me go and get her. Please get her."

Arms went around me. "She's gone, Maya."

"No, she's—" I looked over his shoulder as he hugged me and I saw the forest. Heard Kenjii whimper. Felt her tongue lick the tears from my cheek and thought, *This isn't right.* I backed away and took a better look around. No lake. Just a gray forest, sun rising to the east.

"I was dreaming," I said. "Again."

"Can't say I blame you." Daniel eased back as I moved away to sit on the ground. "Been having a few anxiety dreams myself."

I looked at him and the events of the last day slowly returned.

"You shouldn't be here," I said. "I'm still dreaming, aren't I?"

"That depends. Am I better looking?"

I gave a soft laugh and shook my head.

"Do I at least *smell* better than I did yesterday?"

"No. Sorry." I rubbed my eyes and yawned. "Where are the others?"

"Sleeping a couple hundred meters that way." He pointed. "I figured that was far enough from you."

"I thought I told you we should separate."

"And you expected me to listen? The point was that we shouldn't be close enough together that the bad guys could swoop in and nab us all. Gotta admit, though, when you looked like you were going to sleep in that cabin, even Sam was tempted to join you. We would have, too, if you hadn't come out and set off again."

I stretched. "Well, Kenjii isn't tagged. I—" I stopped and blinked harder, then murmured. "Or was *that* a dream . . . ?"

"What?"

"I shape-shifted in my sleep. But if you were nearby all night and I'm dressed . . ."

"Your T-shirt's on backward. Your socks and shoes are

off. Your jeans aren't zipped. And I'm pretty sure those aren't Kenjii's."

He pointed to two large cougar tracks in a patch of dew-damp earth.

"But how . . . ?"

"I stayed downwind so Kenjii couldn't smell us. She probably didn't wake because she was exhausted. As for the clothes, I guess you do more than shape-shift in your sleep. Which is convenient."

"So I really did . . . ?" I looked at the tracks again. "Wow."

"And you're going to tell me all about it, right?"

I zipped my jeans and pulled on my discarded socks and shoes. "Later. Right now, I need to tell you what I heard."

I gave him the amended version. Very amended, because I couldn't tell him about seeing Nicole or he might want to return for her. I was still determined that he'd never find out that Nicole went after Serena. And he'd certainly never find out *why*. No one deserves that kind of burden. Especially Daniel.

I told him I'd found the camp and overheard that Kenjii had escaped and Hayley had failed to trap us, so they'd shipped her off and were looking for other ways to find us. That was all he needed to know for now.

It was still morning when we found a paved road. Actual vehicles traveling that road would be even better, but apparently, too much to hope for.

We walked about fifteen minutes before we heard an oncoming car. Corey stepped into the middle of the road. A pickup whipped around the curve. Corey waved his arms. The guy in the pickup laid on his horn and veered past, sending Corey stumbling as his bad knee gave way.

Daniel and I helped him up.

"Oww . . . ," he said.

"There'd have been a bigger *oww* if he hadn't swerved," I said. "That would not look good on your obituary. Survived a helicopter crash, armed kidnappers, and three days in the woods, only to get mowed down by a passing redneck."

"From now on, we'll flag down cars from the shoulder." Daniel looked at Corey, who was rubbing his sore butt. "Or maybe the ditch."

The next vehicle didn't come for a long time. It was a car full of guys not much older than us.

"Quick, girls," Corey said. "Give them some incentive. Take off your—" He glanced at Sam. "Maya, take off your shirt."

Sam clubbed him in the arm, hard enough to make him yelp.

We waved and yelled. They waved back and kept going. Idiots.

"Eventually someone's going to pick us up," I said. "We've spent three days hiking through the forest, and we look like it. Someone's going to stop."

☙ ☙ ☙

Finally, we found someone who had stopped. It wasn't for us, but only because he hadn't made it that far. We rounded a bend to see a gray-haired guy getting out of his van, having pulled to the side to take a piss. He was still about fifty meters away. We picked up speed and yelled, but he was already heading into the woods.

"Must have a shy bladder," Corey said.

True. With these back roads, most guys settled for walking around their vehicle for privacy. Some didn't even do that.

"He left the van running," Corey said.

"No," Daniel said.

"Yes, we shouldn't take his ride," Corey said. "But we're exhausted, out of food, nearly out of water, and that van is our best chance. Do you really want to just trust he'll help us?"

"No, I want to make sure he will. I'll try using my powers. If that fails, we'll have to resort to . . . other incentives." Daniel flexed his arms. "We can't take his ride, though. We don't know how far he might need to walk to the nearest town. You two hang back," he said to Corey and Sam. "Maya, make Kenjii stay with them."

"Excuse me?" Corey said. "Sam and I aren't going to scare—"

"Four teenagers and a dog will scare any old guy," Daniel said. "So will two guys. So will . . ." He glanced at Sam.

"Thanks," she said.

"You know what I mean. Maya's friendly. And she can keep her cool."

"I'm not sure that's any less insulting," Sam muttered. But she waved us ahead.

Corey took Kenjii's collar and led her into the ditch, where they hid behind bushes.

"Hello!" I called as we approached, far enough away that I hoped I wouldn't startle the man. He still came stumbling out, zipping up his pants.

"I'm sorry," I said. "But we're from Nanaimo. We were on a school hike yesterday and we got lost. I'm sure they're looking for us. It was probably in the paper . . . ?"

"Don't read the paper." The man inched toward his vehicle, gaze locked on Daniel. "You kids stay away from my van."

"We're not going to steal it, sir." Daniel moved forward carefully, his voice taking on his persuasive tone. "We just need help. Like my friend said—"

"Town's that way." He pointed south. "About twenty kilometers."

"Which is a very long hike, sir." Daniel met the old man's gaze as he kept walking forward. "We're really tired and we don't have any food or water. If we could just ride in the back—"

The man pulled a switchblade from his pocket. "Don't come any closer, boy. Not you either, girlie. I got robbed on this road once. Not going to happen again."

"Please, sir," Daniel said. "We aren't—"

The man darted to the driver's side and leaped in as Daniel raced around the van. The man slammed it into gear. The van lurched forward. I grabbed Daniel and yanked him out of the way as the van swerved onto the road.

Corey came out from behind the bushes as we walked back. "Next time, we consider my plan?"

"I think so," Daniel mumbled.

"At least he told us there's a town along this road," I said. "Same way we're heading."

"How far?" Corey asked.

"He didn't say," I lied. "But it can't be too far."

Daniel glanced at me, then nodded.

TWENTY-FOUR

TWENTY KILOMETERS IS INDEED "too far" when you're ready to drop already.

"I should have listened to Corey," Daniel said. "I was so sure I could convince that guy. It's worked until now."

"Not on Moreno," I said.

"Sure it did."

"At the store, yes, but we couldn't get him talking earlier. Obviously it's not going to be a foolproof power or you'd have the ability to make anyone do anything. My guess is that they have to want to already. The woman at the tattoo studio wanted to get rid of us. Moreno wanted to skip searching a filthy crawlspace. That old guy *really* didn't want to help us."

"In other words, don't rely on special powers."

"Same way I'm not going to let you run in front of a moving van even if I have healing abilities."

"Okay, so—"

Corey—who'd been walking ahead with Sam—let out a whistle. He gestured to a tractor trailer, pulling out of what looked like a parking lot.

We jogged up to Corey and Sam.

"Please don't be closed for the season," Corey murmured as we picked up speed. "Please don't be staffed by witches and demons, lying in wait for us. Please, please, please, just give us a break."

As we approached, we saw the sign. REDWOOD MOTEL AND RESTAURANT. There were three vehicles in the lot—two cars off to the far side and a pickup with a topper in front of the restaurant doors.

"This is good," Corey said. "Tell me this is good."

"People. Phones. Food." I grinned over at him. "Yep, this is good."

Daniel caught Corey's arm. "We should let the girls handle this."

"Huh?" Corey said. "We just need to make a phone call, right? Hell, I'll give them my other twenty to cover it."

"I just . . . I think we should hang back. We're in rough shape. That guy with the van was worried about me, not Maya."

Corey sighed. "Fine. For once, you've earned the right to paranoia. Go get 'em, girls." He passed me the twenty. "Just in case."

I told Sam we should go through the side door and slip

into the bathroom to clean up before we talked to anyone. The side door actually led into the motel office, but no one was at the desk. A sign referred customers to the restaurant for service. A glass door separated the two. Through it, I could see the bathrooms at the rear. I was waiting for the server—a blond woman about my mom's age—to turn her back when I caught sight of a newspaper on the motel office counter. One look at the lower headline and I realized I could use it, which meant cleaning up wasn't the right move.

I picked up the newspaper and walked into the restaurant. The server looked up, as did the sole patron—a guy about thirty-five.

"Can I . . . help you?" the server said, gaze traveling over our dirty clothes.

"I hope so." I set the paper on the table she was resetting and pointed to the headline: MISSING ISLAND TEENS DEAD. "That's us."

The woman glanced at the paper, then at us. Her lips tightened. "That isn't funny, girls."

"I'm not joking."

"Those poor kids are dead and—"

"No, they're not. Someone made a mistake. I'm Maya Delaney. This is Samantha Russo. Our helicopter went down off the northeastern coast. We've been walking through the woods for three days." I gestured at my clothes. "As you can see."

"You can't be—"

"That's our names right there," I said, pointing at the list in the paper.

"Prove it."

"Our helicopter crashed in the ocean, lady," Sam said. She pulled sodden rectangles from her pocket and dropped them on the table. "That's my ID."

I opened the paper to an inner page where the piece continued. There were photos of two missing kids. Rafe and Nicole.

"How the hell did they get Rafe's picture?" Sam muttered.

"Those aren't us," I said.

"Convenient," the server muttered.

It wasn't convenient. It was intentional. Submit photos of the kids they knew weren't wandering around the forest.

There was a class picture at the bottom of the article. It was tiny and blurred, although my copy at home was perfect.

"We're in this one." I pointed to the class shot. "That's me, and that's Sam over there."

"I think that's Bryan," Sam said.

"Is it?" I squinted. "Maybe . . ."

It was impossible to tell, really. I wouldn't even be sure which one was me if I didn't recognize my tie-dyed shirt.

"Okay," I said. "Our pictures might not be recognizable, but come on. Why would we lie about it?"

"Same reason my own kids lie," the server said. "To get attention."

"Seriously?" Sam said. "We're going to hatch this elaborate scheme, and launch it in your crappy little—?"

I stepped on Sam's foot.

"We're dirty," I said. "We're exhausted. Look outside. We didn't come in a car. So how did we get here? Where did we come from?"

"Nanaimo, I'll bet." She said it the same way people in Nanaimo would say Vancouver, with a sneer that said nothing good came from the big city. "Maybe Victoria." She peered at us. "Probably Victoria. Only rich kids can afford to mess up nice clothes like that. Private school, I'll bet. You talk like you come from a private school."

"We do." I jabbed my finger at the paper. "Salmon Creek School. Privately owned by the St. Cloud Corporation. Our teacher's name is Mrs. Morris. She's the mother of Hayley, one of the girls they said died. There are thirteen kids in our class, which covers grades eleven and twelve. We're in eleven. Look, do you have a computer? I can show you Maya Delaney's Facebook page. Which has *my* photo on it. I'll have to use my password to access it because all my details are set to private. That should prove it's mine."

"You kids these days are too smart for your own good," the server said. "I'm sure you've got Facebook pages set up for this scheme."

"What scheme?" Sam said, her voice rising. "What possible motivation could we have to do this?"

"Attention." The server crossed her arms. "I bet you've

got friends out there taping us. Make fun of the locals. Post the videos on YouTunes."

"YouTube," Sam muttered.

"See?" She shook her head. "Spoiled brats. You aren't even thinking about these poor kids and how their parents must be feeling."

"Yes." I met her gaze. "I am thinking about how *my parents* are feeling. They think they just lost their only child. I need them to know that I'm alive."

I glanced at the lone customer. He looked away quickly and focused on his lunch.

I turned back to the server. "If I can just use your phone—"

"Why? To call your friends to come and get you? Better get walking, girl. It's a long way to town."

She kicked us out after that. There was nothing we could do, nothing we could say. She knew the story—those kids had died in a crash on the other end of the island. DNA said it was the missing kids and everyone who watched *CSI* knew DNA never lied.

"It's official," Sam said as we walked out. "We're screwed. The universe is conspiring to destroy us."

"If it was, I think it could have managed that a few times by now."

"Ah, but that's the trick. You cheat death, it keeps trying. Didn't you see that movie?"

"All of them, actually. Serena loved—" A brief pause. "She loved horror movies."

"Did she? I'd have thought her more the romance type."

"Girls?"

I glanced back to see the man from the restaurant. I slowed to let him catch up.

He was a little older than I'd first thought. Maybe forty. Sandy brown hair. Short beard. Golf shirt. Trousers. Loafers. He looked like a schoolteacher.

"I'm sorry about what happened in there," he said. "I don't know anything about that helicopter crash—I'm on vacation with my family, and haven't been reading the papers. But I've got a girl about your age, and I can't imagine her going to all this trouble to pull a prank. Even if she did . . ." He shrugged. "Kids do silly things sometimes. No excuse to strand them in the middle of a forest."

I noticed Daniel and Corey circling around by the trees and subtly motioned for them to wait.

"Thanks," I said. "We really just need to call our parents. If I could borrow your cell phone, that would be great." I pulled out the twenty. "I know it might be an expensive call, but this should cover it."

"No, no." He waved the money away. "You make that call and you take as long as you like." He reached into his pocket and came out empty. "Huh. My phone must have fallen out in the truck. Just a sec."

He walked to the pickup. We waited. A couple of minutes

later, he came back shaking his head.

"Phone not there?" I called.

"No. It's the damnedest thing because my wife made sure I brought it. I hope it didn't fall out when I was getting gas."

"Can you do us a favor then?" I said. "Talk to the server and get her to let us use hers? I can pay, like I said."

He shook his head. "I already tried putting in a good word for you. She's having none of it. I'll have to give you girls a lift into town."

On Vancouver Island, hitchhiking is considered a perfectly feasible way to travel, prohibited only on the highway, where you could get hit. In Salmon Creek, though, we got stranger-danger classes from kindergarten. Ours were probably a little different from most—we were taught that anyone in Salmon Creek could be trusted; it was the rest of the world we needed to watch out for.

Some kids did start hitching rides into town when they hit that awkward "old enough to hang out in Nanaimo but not old enough to drive there" stage. If I'd tried it, I'm not sure who would have killed me first—my parents or Daniel.

I didn't trust this guy. I didn't like his story about the cell phone. I didn't like his excuse for not helping us with the server. Even if I totally believed him, I wouldn't have gotten in the truck. So why was I considering it?

Because he *had* a truck. And we needed it, and if he did turn out to be a creep, even Daniel wouldn't argue about abandoning him by the roadside.

"I'm . . . not sure. Can we . . . ?" I glanced at Sam. "Can I talk to you?"

I pulled Sam aside and told her what I had in mind. As I did, I motioned for Daniel and Corey to move through the woods, closer to us. Then we went back to the man.

"Okay," I said. "We'd really appreciate a lift. My friend here has to, uh, go to the bathroom before we leave. She's been holding it a long time. I know they won't let her use the one inside, so she's going to use the woods."

Sam had already taken off, loping toward where Daniel and Corey were hiding with Kenjii. There, she'd tell them the plan—we'd get into the truck, and make sure the guy paused at the exit, so they could jump into the back.

While Sam was gone, I asked the man about his vacation, to keep him occupied. Sam talked to the guys, then gave them time to make their way over near the exit.

When she came back, we climbed into the truck. I sat between the guy and Sam. As I settled in, I reached for the radio, then said, "Is this okay?"

He smiled. "Sure. You might not like my station, but you can change it."

I left it on his—country music—and cranked it up loud enough to hide any noise the guys and Kenjii were about to make.

The pickup pulled to the roadway. There was a stop sign, but around here, most people just roll up, glance around, and pull out, and that's exactly what he was going to do until I said, "Sam! Your ID. Do you have it?"

He stopped. She checked her pockets and I checked mine, bouncing in our seats, hoping to cover any other movement as the guys got in the truck bed.

"I think you left it inside," the man said. "It wouldn't be any good anyway."

"I guess you're right." Sam sighed, as if resigned to the loss.

He pulled out onto the road and turned north.

"Um, isn't the town south?" I said.

"Southwest, actually. This is quicker."

He pulled onto the first side road—little more than a rutted trail.

"Are you sure you should take this?" I said. "Your truck looks really new."

He laughed. "That's what trucks are for, hon. No sense buying a four-by-four if you don't plan to go off-road. Just hold tight. We'll be there before you know it."

He had no idea where this road led. That was obvious as he drove along, leaning forward, straining to see. Was he looking for a place to pull over?

I swallowed a bubble of panic. I knew this might be what he had in mind. The guys were in the back. Everything was okay.

He turned off onto another path.

"Um, I don't think this is a road," I said.

"Sure it is. It comes out at—"

The truck lurched a couple of times . . . as he surreptitiously tapped the brakes.

"Uh-oh," he said. "Come on. Please don't—"

A sudden stop had us all hitting our seat belts.

"What happened?" I said.

He shook his head and cranked the engine, making it whine. He pretended to hit the gas, muttering, "Come on, come on." Then he swore when nothing happened.

"Can you fix it?" Sam asked.

"I can try. Got my tools in the back."

"Great!" we said in unison.

He got out. We did the same. I stood beside Sam and she grinned at me. The man reached for the back door on the truck topper. As I braced for the cry of surprise, I couldn't help grinning myself. We were about to have transportation. And this time, I wouldn't feel bad about taking it.

Only there was no cry of surprise. No scrabbling of claws. No shout from Daniel or Corey. The back was empty. The guys hadn't made it in.

"Run!" I whispered.

I dove into the forest. That was instinct for me—avoid open areas, take refuge in dense woods. I heard Sam's running feet. But there was no crashing of undergrowth behind me. I looked over my shoulder to see her racing along the open trail.

A shot fired. A rifle shot. Grow up in the forest, and you

recognize that sound the way an inner-city kid recognizes pistol fire.

"Stop or I shoot again," the man said. His voice had changed. Not calm and jocular now.

I looked around frantically.

"I said *stop*!"

A second shot. A yelp.

Sam dropped out of sight.

Oh God, he'd shot Sam.

TWENTY-FİVE

I FOUGHT THE URGE to run to Sam and instead picked my way through the trees, heading in her direction.

"Don't worry," I heard the man say to Sam. "I just winged you. Now you wait right there while I go find that pretty little Indian friend of yours."

He jogged down the trail, passing Sam where she lay. Good. Keep going. Please keep going.

I crept through the trees until I was alongside Sam. I could still see the man. He stood a few meters away, peering down the empty stretch of trail.

Sam tried to wave for me to get the truck. I shook my head and motioned that he had the keys. Then I mouthed, "Where are you hurt?" She pointed to the side of her leg. I could see it now, blood darkening her calf. A long way from the femoral artery. Good, but she wasn't racing out of here anytime soon.

"No way your friend got to the road that fast," he said. "So where is she . . . ?"

He scanned the forest. I stood perfectly still, and his gaze passed over me.

I'd screwed up. Really screwed up. It'd been too complicated a plan. Too easy for something to go wrong. I'd looked at this man—clean-cut and quiet—and at worst I'd seen a garden-variety pervert who'd take us into the woods, maybe try to feel us up and hope we might like it. Not a dangerous predator. Just a middle-age guy with a creepy fantasy.

The gun changed everything. The gun meant I had, yet again, been too confident in my assessment and, this time, wagered lives on it.

The man walked back to Sam, who still crouched on the ground, hand pressed to her wounded leg.

"Where did your friend go?" he asked.

"I don't know."

"I asked you once. I won't ask you"—he kicked her—"*again.*"

I had to grip the tree to keep from running at him. Heat raged through me, and I thought it was fury until I saw my arms pulsing.

Oh, yes. God, yes, please!

The man pulled his foot back to kick Sam again.

"I didn't see!" she yelled. "You shot me, remember? She was in front of me and then you fired and I fell, and I'm guessing she didn't stick around."

"You're a little smart-ass, aren't you?"

"No, I'm just smart enough to know that *she's* smart enough to hide after you shot me. And I'd think *you'd* be smart enough to know that if I had seen where she went, I'd point you in the opposite direction."

Keep talking, Sam. Please keep talking.

I crouched and closed my eyes and focused. I imagined myself changing into a cougar as I got down on all fours and tried to move my arms and legs into what seemed like the proper position.

I felt the fever ripping through me and saw my skin bubbling, muscles underneath contorting, but no matter what I did, nothing changed. *I* didn't change.

"Just go look for her," Sam was saying.

"You'd like that, wouldn't you, girl? Give you a chance to get away."

"Tie me up then. You've got rope, don't you? All you guys have rope."

"All you guys?" The man kicked her again. I gripped a tree and squeezed my eyes shut and prayed for my body to change. "You think this is something out of a movie? You don't get it, do you?"

"Oh, I get it. Your mommy was mean to you, so now you hate women. Can't face ones your own age, so you chase teenage girls."

The man let out a snarl of rage and kicked Sam so hard she started choking.

"Does that make you feel better?" she sputtered when she got her breath back.

What the hell are you doing? I wanted to shout. *Now is not the time to cop an attitude. You're pissing off a psycho with a gun—*

The man grabbed Sam and heaved her up, and it was then that I realized he wasn't holding the gun anymore. It lay beside him, tossed down in his fury.

I crawled toward the rifle. The man held Sam up and swung her against a tree. He pulled back his fist and hit her in the stomach.

I sprinted for the weapon. He heard me coming and dropped Sam. As he spun, I hit the ground, skidding until I snatched the rifle. Then I rolled out of the way and leaped to my feet.

When I pointed the gun at him, he laughed. "Do you even have a clue how to fire that?"

I lined up the sight on a tree fifty meters away, and I pulled the trigger. Splinters flew from the trunk. The man paled and grabbed for Sam, but she'd already staggered out of reach.

"You won't shoot me," he said.

"No?" I aimed at his chest. "Whatever you had in mind for us, I think it deserves a bullet or two."

"Does it? I think you girls deserve whatever you get. You know better than to get in the car with a stranger. If you do it, then that tells me you want something."

"The only thing we wanted was help. Now toss me your keys."

He grumbled and spat insults, but after a moment, he reached into his pocket and pulled them out. Then he pitched them at me, hard and fast, and lunged, hoping to startle me so he could get the gun.

I saw the keys coming. He was already charging, though, and I knew I had to shoot.

Shoot him in the chest. Kill him because that would guarantee our safety. I felt the impulse. Same as I had with Nicole at the tent. Same as I had with Antone.

I fired. The bullet hit him below the shoulder. He fell, his mouth working, eyes wide with shock.

"It might not be fatal," I said. "Depends on how long it takes you to find your cell phone."

I emptied the rifle's magazine. Then I laid down the gun.

"I'd suggest you tell the police it was a hunting accident. Otherwise I'll have to tell them the truth."

I helped Sam to the truck. As she got in, she winced, then glowered at the man lying on the ground.

"If I could kick him without falling on my ass, I would," she said.

"Hopefully, he's hurting worse than you are. See if you can find a license or registration in the glove box. The cops are going to get an anonymous tip about this guy."

Sam grinned as I started the truck. "You can be seriously awesome sometimes, Maya." She paused. "And I mean that in a totally non-girl-crush kind of way."

"You don't have to clarify that."

"Yeah, usually I do." She exhaled in pain and leaned back. "Let's get the guys, get me fixed up, and get out of here."

I might not have my learner's permit yet, but I could drive. Dad had taught me a couple of years ago so I could take the Jeep back to Mom after dropping him off across the park.

We didn't get far before we saw three figures running toward us.

Daniel and Kenjii were in the lead. I don't know who looked more worried—or more relieved when I pulled over.

"Thank God," Daniel panted. "We couldn't get the damned latch open."

Corey jogged up. "Guy sent Daniel flying when he pulled away. We tried waving and yelling, just to get him to stop, but he didn't hear us. Luckily, we saw where he turned. Took us awhile to get here, though."

"I screwed up," I said. "I'm sorry."

"You got the truck," Corey said. "Seems like it worked to me."

"Yes, please make her stop," Sam called from the truck. "She's been apologizing since we got away and it's really getting on my nerves."

"Sam was shot," I said, lowering my voice. "I really screwed—"

"Make her stop!" Sam yelled. "I got shot a little. He got shot worse. We now have a truck. Mission accomplished. It was your plan, Maya, but we all agreed to it. Stopping to whine is only going to get us nabbed by the cops when that bastard calls 911."

"I wasn't whining," I said.

"Close enough."

Daniel took the driver's seat. Corey and I got in the back with Kenjii. I directed Daniel to take the next side road, where it would be safer for us to stop so I could get out and take a better look at Sam's injuries.

The bullet had gone clean through her calf muscle, missing the bone. The bleeding had stopped and I could remove the tourniquet. I cleaned the wound as best I could, then bound it with bandages from the glove box first aid kit. I wanted to find a town and a drugstore, clean and dress it properly, but Sam refused. We were only a couple of hours from Salmon Creek. Plenty of supplies there.

So we went home. God, it felt good to say that. After three days of hell, home was so close it was almost surreal.

Except we couldn't actually just drive into town, because there was a very good chance the Nasts had Salmon Creek staked out. Or the St. Clouds could also be there. That meant we had to get to someone's house without cruising down Main Street. So we took the long way in, circling around the north and coming in from the west.

I wanted to go home. To my park. To my parents. Maybe I was being selfish, but I thought they'd be our safest point of contact. The others agreed, but there was no way to drive into the park without going down Main Street. Any other route was a few kilometers' hike and Sam couldn't do that. I wasn't sure any of us could.

The next best bet was Corey's mom. She was the sheriff, and had raised Corey and his brother, Travis, alone after his dad died. His father had worked in the lab, though. Had he been the one who'd signed on to the experiment? Had Corey's mother been left in the dark, like Daniel's dad? We didn't know, but I trusted her enough to go there. The others did, too, which, considering my recent track record with character judgment, was more reassuring.

Corey lived in what we jokingly called "the burbs," which meant that his house was on the outskirts of town. The forest edged the property, so we could park elsewhere, then sneak up.

"Guess Mom's taking the day off," Corey said as we drew close enough to see the sheriff's SUV in the drive.

"Considering she thinks you're dead, I'd imagine she's taking a lot of days off," I said.

He paused at that, as if it was the first time he'd really thought it through. Everyone believed we were dead. His mother and his brother, Travis, would be in there, grieving . . .

"Let's get inside," he said.

We went through the backyard. The house looked fine, as

did the ones around it. The fire had obviously been stopped or diverted before it reached town.

Travis was allergic to dogs, so I put Kenjii in the garage with a bucket of water filled at the tap. In the meantime, Corey tried the back door, but it was locked. He didn't want to knock, so he retrieved the house key and opened the door.

When I followed him in, the smells of the house wrapped around me. My arms started to tremble and at first I thought it was the change starting again, but then I realized it was relief.

We were safe. Finally safe.

I followed Corey into the living room. When I looked at the sofa, I wanted to throw myself on it. Sprawl across the cushions and turn on the TV. Curl up and watch the flickering images until I fell into a deep sleep.

I've never actually done such a thing in my life. Sure, I watch TV. But we don't have one at my house and I'd never felt the lack, because I don't like being cooped up inside.

Now, after three days in the forest, that human part of me was sick of trees and streams and forest paths. It wanted a sofa and a TV and a shower. God, it really wanted a shower.

"Mom?" Corey called. He cut himself short and swore. "I probably shouldn't do that. Scare the crap out of her." He took a step toward the kitchen, then paused. "Or maybe I *should* yell. Warn her before her dead son appears from nowhere." He glanced at us. "Arghh! I'm overanalyzing. When this is over, I need a long break from you guys."

"And we'll need one from you," Sam said.

"Just relax," I said. "Call her. Find her. It doesn't matter. You're about to give her the best heart attack of her life."

He grinned. "Right."

He took off, jogging through the house, calling for his mom. Sam started to follow, then saw we weren't and realized this was a moment we should leave to Corey.

I collapsed onto the sofa with a sigh. Daniel plunked down beside me, then twisted to stretch out, legs going over mine.

"Oh my God," I said, shoving his feet off my lap. "Do you know how bad those smell?"

He tried to stick them in my face. I grabbed him around the ankles and tickled the bottom of his feet. He let out a shriek.

"Well, you're still ticklish," I said. "And you still giggle like a girl."

He tried to grab me, but I held his feet tight. Sam slid from the recliner and limped into the next room.

"Our immaturity is scaring her off," I said. "Sorry, Sam. Come back and we'll act our age."

"No, I'm just grabbing some food. You two carry on. You've earned a maturity time-out."

I let go of Daniel's feet and he pulled them off my lap.

"We're home," I said. "Well, not our home but . . ." I leaned back into the cushions and let out a happy sigh. "Close enough for now."

"Feels good, doesn't it?"

"Unbelievably good."

I opened my eyes and glanced at him.

"Thank you. For keeping me on my feet and getting us back here."

"Um, pretty sure you did at least half of the 'getting us back here' part. And I needed some help staying afloat, too." He paused. "Well, not as much as you, but that's because I'm a guy and we're naturally tougher."

I threw a pillow at him.

"She's not here," Corey called as he thundered down from the second floor.

TWENTY-SIX

"MOM ISN'T HERE," COREY said. "Neither is Travis. So much for my grand resurrection." He slumped onto the sofa. "We'll have to wait for them. Which is a little anticlimactic."

We decided to clean up and eat. Start looking and feeling human again.

"There's not much in the way of food," Sam said. She'd come out of the kitchen with a Coke and a spoon heaped with peanut butter.

"What?" Corey said. "Mom knows better than to let our cupboards get empty or I'll dig up her stash of fancy chocolate bars."

"The fridge is practically bare," Sam said. "Grocery shopping is apparently the last thing on your mom's mind.

I'm sure there's more in the cupboards. I just stopped at the peanut butter."

We went into the kitchen. Corey headed straight to a cupboard and pulled out cereal and cookies.

"Pop's in the fridge," Sam said.

Daniel got that. As he stood there, door open, he glanced at me. I was looking past him at a loaf of bread, uncovered and rock hard, on the counter. Beside it was a pitcher. The smell of sour milk hit me as I moved closer.

Corey's mom wasn't here. She hadn't been here since the fire.

Daniel shook his head at me. *Don't say anything yet.*

I accepted a Coke from him and cookies from Corey. Then I took a bowl of cereal out to Kenjii. Not ideal, but no worse than the granola bars I'd been feeding her.

As we headed back into the living room, I noticed the phone on the counter.

Daniel followed my gaze and laughed. "Um, yeah. We're holed up, waiting to notify someone that we're back . . . and there's a phone. We've been in the woods way too long."

He picked it up. Sam leaped forward and grabbed it from him.

"It could be bugged," she mouthed.

Corey opened his mouth to argue, but she motioned for him to wait until she hung up. As she lowered the phone, she stopped. She looked at it. Lifted it to her ear. Frowned.

"It's dead," she said.

Corey took the phone from her. He jabbed a few buttons. Then he strode into the study and picked up another phone.

"Dead?" I said.

He nodded.

"Must be from the fire," Sam said. "I'm surprised they even have electricity."

Corey said nothing. He was staring at the empty desk. All the wires for a laptop dangled over the edge. He turned and tapped an empty shelf behind him.

"My laptop should be here." He gestured at the empty desk. "It was when I left." He turned to Daniel. "Okay, obviously between the fire and the crash, Mom hasn't come home. But she didn't take my laptop. She told me to pack it. I didn't."

"Why?" Sam said.

"Because my homework's on it," he said, in a tone that implied this was a stupid question. "Laptop perishes in the fire? I get a free pass on every assignment."

"Which I'm sure she knew you'd try, so she took it. I'm supposed to be the paranoid one, guys, and I—"

Corey was already gone, heading for the stairs again. He took them two at a time. Then he pitched forward, hands clutching his head as he let out something between a moan and a strangled cry.

Daniel raced upstairs to help him to his feet . . . and Corey promptly puked on him.

"You were done with that shirt, right?" Corey mumbled as we half carried him into his room. He started to say something else, and heaved again, this time twisting enough to vomit on the floor instead.

Sidestepping the puddle, we got Corey onto his bed. He went into fetal position, hands over his head, moaning.

"Where are your pills?" Daniel said.

"Bathroom."

"We'll find them," I said, and started to go.

Corey grabbed my sleeve. "Stay."

"Good idea," Sam said. "My bedside manner sucks. I'll help Daniel."

They left. I knelt beside Corey's bed, holding his hands as he groaned and writhed, his face shiny with sweat.

"Bad?" I whispered.

"Oh yeah." He opened one eye. "Don't tell Daniel. You know how he gets. But they're a lot worse." He licked his lips and looked over my shoulder, making sure Daniel wasn't there. "It's like a flash of light splitting my skull. Then more flashes. This time—"

His face screwed up in pain and he curled up, panting. "Seeing stuff. Crazy stuff."

"Like what?"

"Can't tell. Just—" Another jolt of pain. "Stuff. Images. Don't make sense."

He took a few deep breaths, then let go of my hand and pushed up on his elbows. Another look toward the door.

"He can't hear you. What do you see?"

"You know how when you dream, stuff from your day

comes back, only it's all mixed up? That's what it's like. I see things and sometimes I recognize them, but they're . . ." He searched for the words. "In the wrong place. Out of context. That's it. Out of context."

"Like what?"

He hesitated, then shook his head. "Nothing imp—"

"Like *what*, Corey?"

"Rafe." He said the name quickly, as if getting it out before he could decide not to. "I saw Rafe and I saw you. Only it's . . . not any place I've seen you two together."

"Someplace you don't recognize."

"No, it's your place." He waved at the window. "You, me, Rafe, Daniel, and your dog out behind your house. It's like seeing a memory that never happened. Which is why I think it's my brain spitting out garbage. But if I tell Daniel . . ."

"He'll worry it's a neurological problem."

"Neuro . . . ? Right. Brain. You could just say brain, you know."

"Neurological covers more than just the brain. It—"

He held up his hand. "If there's one bonus to this disaster, it's not having to go to school for a while. Don't spoil that for me. Please."

I smiled. He opened his mouth, then winced again. When he opened his eyes, he looked over my shoulder and let out a sigh of relief.

"Finally. Drugs." He put out his hand. "Give 'em."

"They aren't there," Daniel said. "We searched the

medicine cabinet, the drawers, everywhere. There's . . . a lot of stuff missing. I think your mom is planning to be gone a while."

"Probably didn't want to leave pills lying around," Sam said. "No need to give anyone a reason to break in."

"Let's hope they didn't take the alcohol, too," I said as I stood.

Corey shook his head. "I think I'm okay—" Another wave of agony doubled him over, retching.

"I'll grab a beer from—" Daniel began.

"No, I'm okay. Really. Just get dressed before you scare the girls." He waved at Daniel, bare-chested after taking off his soiled shirt. "Help yourself to my closet."

"You wear a medium. I don't."

"That's just because I like my shirts fitting better."

"Tighter," I said.

"And, again, I don't," Daniel said. "I'll wash this one."

Corey made a face at him and waved him off. Once Daniel was gone, he collapsed, panting, as if he'd been holding back.

"If a drink will fix this—" I began.

"No."

"You're refusing a drink?" Sam said. "From what I hear, that's a first."

He flipped her off. Not good-humoredly either. She grumbled and hobbled from the room.

"There are more pills downstairs," Corey said. "I . . . have a stash."

When I lifted my brows, he said, "Yeah, the headaches have been getting worse for a while. I didn't want my mom to know. That's how I found out booze helps. Only I'd rather not, so I've been hiding pills, saying they're gone so I can get more."

"That was—"

"Dumb, I know. I should have told someone, which is why I'm telling you now."

"If they aren't there, can I grab you a beer?"

"I . . ." He glanced at the door, again looking for Daniel. "Last resort, okay? Yeah, I know, I drink at parties. But that's different. Drinking to feel better is . . ." He looked up at me. "We've both seen what that does with Daniel's dad. Maybe it's a different kind of 'drinking to feel better,' but I don't want to go there unless I have to."

"Okay, let me look for the pills."

I found the medication. When I came back upstairs Daniel was waiting. I motioned that I'd give the pills and water to Corey and come back. When I returned, he waved me into Corey's mom's bedroom.

"We need to talk about Corey," I said as I walked in and closed the door. "I'm really worried about these headaches."

"I know. So am I. But there's something I need to tell you

first. I was looking in here in case she had backup pills. The drawers are empty. Same as the closet. Same as the bathroom. They didn't just leave for a few days—"

"Hey!" Corey yelled.

We hurried in to find him standing at his dresser. "Where's my stuff?"

"Your clothes?" I said.

"No, they're here. I was trying to find a clean shirt for Daniel and noticed my stuff is gone." He waved at the empty dresser top. "Trophies. Photos. My St. Christopher's medal."

"Mementos," I murmured.

Corey was right—all his mementos were gone. So his mom must have decided she couldn't stay in Salmon Creek. When Serena died, her parents had left town—too many memories. A check of Travis's room confirmed it. They'd taken their clothes, everything of value, and everything easily transported, leaving behind perishables and furniture.

"What about my clothes?" Corey said.

"Those are hand-me-downs Travis wouldn't want, all things considered," I said. "Your mom just took things that were important to you. Things to remember you by."

"But it's only been three days," Corey said. "Mom isn't like that. Hell, she spent four months talking about buying a new sofa and another two shopping for it before deciding to stick with the one we had."

"Okay," I said. "Well, maybe . . ." I paused, hoping someone else would fill in the blank, but they just looked at me, expectant. "We should look outside. Hayley's place is right across the road and Brendan's house is around the corner. I think we can trust Hayley's parents and Dr. Hajek."

Brendan's mother was the local veterinarian, who'd helped me with countless injured animals. I trusted her.

But who didn't I trust?

Earlier, I'd been prepared to trust no one. But now that I was back in Salmon Creek, that changed. I thought of all the people I'd grown up with—the kids, their parents, the teachers and doctors and shopkeepers. My gut trusted them all, which was crazy, because they all drew a paycheck from the St. Clouds. Even my parents.

Not everyone could be innocent. Most probably weren't.

So who could we trust?

I stood there, frozen in doubt as Corey and Daniel watched me.

"M-maybe not Dr. Hajek," I stammered. "I mean, I know her but . . . Maybe just the Morrises. Or . . ."

"We don't know who we can trust," Corey said. "I think my mom's innocent. You're sure your parents are. Maybe we're both right. Maybe we're both wrong. But I do know if my mom was involved, she didn't do it to make money or get a nice house or anything like that. You said Rafe's mom joined the experiment because she thought she was doing something good for her kids. Fixing something. Giving them better lives. I'm going to bet that's what they all thought. Whatever they did, they're still on our side. These people

251

chasing us? They're not. Bottom line."

I hugged him.

"See?" he said to Daniel over my shoulder. "I told you chicks love it when you get mushy."

I socked him in the arm. "Okay. We venture out, then. Head over to the Morrises' and hope someone's there."

TWENTY-SEVEN

I'D SUGGESTED TAKING A look out the front, then have one of us zip across the street. With only four houses in the court, there wasn't much chance of us being spotted.

They elected the girl with the super-hearing as scout. The others would stand watch and Daniel would whistle if they saw anyone.

I stepped out the front door. The court was eerily quiet. I paused in the shadows of the porch and listened. The harsh jeer of a Steller's jay shattered the silence. Then I picked up the *rat-a-tat-tat* of a woodpecker. Otherwise . . . nothing. Just the wind whistling softly, branches creaking.

I rubbed the back of my neck and made a face. So what if it was quiet? We didn't live in the city. Salmon Creek had just lost its mayor and seven teens. It was a town in mourning.

I looked across at Hayley's house. The windows were

dark. I scanned the other houses in the court. All the windows were dark.

It was afternoon. The sun was shining. No need for lights.

Something moved in the Morrises' second-story window. I jumped. Then I saw a flash of orange. Hayley's cat had jumped onto the ledge.

I let out a sigh of relief, then dashed across the road.

I went in through the side garage door, which Corey said was always open. Ms. Morris's car was parked inside. I hurried to the house door and knocked.

No one answered. I knocked again, then tried the knob. The door was locked. Not surprisingly, Corey also knew where they kept the key.

I unlocked the door, slipped inside, and called, "Hello?" Silence.

"It's, uh, Maya," I said. "Maya Delaney." Like they'd need a last name.

No one answered.

I walked down the hall. The house was as silent as the court outside. Dark and still. A sour smell permeated the hall, and when I peeked into the dining room, there was a glass of milk left on the table, beside a folded newspaper. I took another step and a squeak stopped me short. A mouse sat on the table, hunched over a partially eaten cookie. It squeaked at me again, then scampered away.

I backed out of the dining room and hurried to the stairs. As soon as I got to the bottom, I smelled cat urine. I raced up the steps. The door to Hayley's room was open. Her cat still perched on the windowsill, and he hissed and spat when he saw me.

Fear and panic hit me like a fist to the gut. The cat's fear and panic.

The room went dark. Then it flashed to life, and I was on the floor, racing from room to room, fear coursing through me, looking for someone, anyone. But every room was empty and all I could smell was smoke, drifting through the open windows. Smoke everywhere and my people gone.

I surfaced from the cat's memories. He was still on the windowsill, hissing.

"It's okay," I said. "Everything's okay."

Before I could try to calm him, he sprang. I leaped out of the way. He tore off down the stairs. I got to the kitchen just in time to see a cat door swinging closed behind him. I ran to the door and yanked it open. An orange blur flew into the underbrush and was gone.

I stood there, heart racing as I stared after the cat. I could still feel his terror. When it finally subsided, I stepped back inside, closed the door, and leaned against it.

They were gone. The Morrises had evacuated and hadn't come back. Hayley's cat must have been outside at the time and they couldn't find him. No one had been home since.

Okay, so the families who had lost kids hadn't returned after the evacuation. I guess that made sense. It had only been three days. There would be funerals to plan.

Funerals to plan. Oh God, my parents. Had they already held the service? Picked out a tombstone to mark an empty grave?

I couldn't think about that. They'd know the truth soon enough. We just needed to speak to someone who *had* come back.

I ran back to Corey's.

"They're gone, aren't they?" Sam said as I came in. She was standing by the front window with Corey. Daniel had met me at the door and ushered me inside.

I nodded. "It doesn't look as if they've been back since the fire. I guess they're staying somewhere else for a while."

"I don't think it's for a while," Sam said. "We just saw two moving trucks."

The trucks—one behind the other—had driven along the street past the end of the court. Corey, Daniel, and I went out to check the other houses in the court. I looked in on Kenjii first, but left her in the garage for now. We jogged over to the Morrises' house, then through the woods to another court behind it. The Hajeks' house was there. All the windows were dark. We cut across the backyard to the deck and peered through the patio doors.

As still and silent as the Morrises' house. There was no need for a key here—they'd left the patio doors unlocked.

We stepped into the kitchen. A hush fell around us and we found ourselves creeping forward, as if one squeaky shoe might disturb resting spirits. That's what it felt like, too. Stepping into a mausoleum. Dust motes floated past. The stillness enveloped us as we walked into the living room. We stopped and stared.

Every piece of furniture was gone, only bright, clean squares on the carpet where they'd been, like a blueprint for an unfinished room. We backed into the kitchen and went through to the dining room. Empty. Bare wires hung from the ceiling, where a chandelier had been.

"Okay," Corey whispered. "I'm officially creeped out."

Daniel and I didn't say a word. As if by mutual agreement, we all went outside and crossed to the next house. The Tafts were an older couple whose kids went off to college years ago. I only saw them at town parties, where they always brought homemade fudge. They gave out caramel apples for Halloween, and Serena and I used to sneak back for seconds, as if they wouldn't recognize us. They never said anything, though, just played along and gave us another. Sometimes two.

The Tafts worked at the lab. Both of them. That meant they must have worked on the experiment. But I couldn't reconcile that with the nice couple who made fudge and gave out caramel apples.

There was no car in the drive. No lights on in the house. That same hush seemed to seep from the very walls as we snuck up to the glass French doors. We peered into the living room. Empty.

Corey was flying off the porch before we knew it. We went after him, and caught up as he stepped from the forest onto the north end of the road that turned into Main Street.

Daniel grabbed his arm, but Corey shook him off, hissing, "There's no one here."

"But there might be—"

Corey spun on him. "There's no one here. Don't you get it? No one is *here*."

When Daniel tried to take his arm again, Corey shoved him, hard, and strode to the top of Main Street. We joined him and the three of us stood there, looking down the road.

It was completely empty. Not a car, not a person, not even a bird perched on the wires.

Not just empty. Desolate.

The wind whistled down the street, making the awnings over the shops flap and groan. A paper whipped against my feet and I grabbed it. A spelling test from one of the primary students, big block printing and bright happy-face stars. I looked at the name. Stacey. One of the grade two students. I'd coached her in track last year.

"Everyone's gone," Corey whispered. "They just . . . left."

A sudden snarl made us jump. A dog tumbled out from between two buildings. Another leaped on it, snapping and snarling. Wild dogs. They'd always been in the woods—dogs gone feral—but Dad kept them out of the park and the town. More dangerous than a bear or a cougar, he said, because they weren't wary of humans.

The dogs stopped fighting and plunged back into the alley. They came out again, growling. One had something in its mouth and the other was trying to snatch it away. Something with long white fur.

There were no animals here with long white fur. No wild ones, that is.

Oh God.

I thought of the Moores' Pomeranian. Merrie Grant's white angora rabbit. Mrs. Tillson's Persian cat. I stared at the shapeless piece of white fur being pulled between the dogs. Bloody white fur.

Daniel grabbed my shoulder and turned me around.

A snarl, louder now, and I glanced over to see the dogs watching us. Two more came running from between the buildings.

"Holy hell," Corey whispered.

"Can we go now?" Daniel said.

Corey nodded and turned to run, but Daniel stopped him.

"Slowly," I said. "Don't turn your back on them. Canines are all about dominance. You run, they'll chase. Back away slowly. Stay together."

We did that. One of the dogs started toward us. Another took a tentative step.

"And if they attack anyway?" Corey whispered.

"*Then* we run."

The two dogs took a few more steps our way. Then the smallest one dove for the bloody bundle of fur, snatched it up, and raced off. The other three tore after it. We breathed sighs of relief and hightailed it back to Corey's house.

After we told Sam what we'd found, Daniel said, "They're clearing out the town."

"That doesn't make sense," she said.

"Doesn't it?" I said. "The Nasts know about the experiment, so Salmon Creek isn't a secret anymore. Between the fire and the crash, the St. Clouds have an excuse for pulling up stakes."

"So now what?" Corey said. "No one's here. We have no idea where anyone went. We're just as screwed as we were this morning."

I shook my head. "We have food, water, and transportation. That's a lot more than we had this morning. All we need is a way to track down our parents. We might find that at my place—we have shortwave radios."

It was just the excuse I'd been waiting for. With every step we'd taken, I ached to go home, but there was still the risk of getting there, and I hadn't dared without a good reason.

"We might not need to go all that way," Sam said. "If we can get to my place, my cell phone's there."

"You have a cell phone?" Corey said.

"Every teen has a cell phone. Or so my aunt and"—her voice caught—"uncle thought. I told them I didn't have anyone to call, but I think they figured that would change if I had one. It's in my room."

Daniel's hand went to the small of my back as he leaned down. "We'll get the phone, then we're going to your place. I promise."

I nodded. We got Kenjii and headed out.

TWENTY-EIGHT

GAIN, WE SNUCK IN the rear. That's the advantage of living in a forest—every yard in Salmon Creek backs up to it.

The Tillson place was only half empty. The St. Clouds must have been working in stages, first taking what people wanted most—personal items—then coming back to remove the rest and clean up.

The movers were still working on the upstairs, apparently. It really didn't look much different from what I remembered from visits with Nicole. I suppose that's because the only person whose personal belongings had to be taken was Mrs. Tillson.

I thought about that. I guess I hadn't realized it before. Mrs. Tillson thought her entire family was gone. Her husband dead, only child killed in the same crash, along with the niece she'd been raising.

"She took my stuff," Sam said.

"Hmm?" I turned.

"My stuff's gone."

"Well, yeah," Corey said. "She didn't expect you'd want it."

"No, I mean . . ."

Sam shook her head and looked away, and I understood what she meant. Mrs. Tillson had removed mementos of Sam, just as she had her own daughter's. I could see in Sam's face that it meant a lot.

She found her phone hidden under her bed, turned off. "I'm going to call her. Sorry, guys, you can go next—"

"Yes, you go first. We'll . . ." I motioned the guys out. "I'll get washed up."

The guys had already cleaned up. Or done the best they could with a quick wash and teeth brushing at Corey's. There hadn't been any spare toothbrushes, so I'd done mine with my finger and tried not to look in the mirror. One glance had told me that no amount of touch-ups was going to help. I needed a twenty-minute shower.

"And this clothing is getting burned," I said as I raked a comb through my tangled hair.

"There's a fireplace downstairs," Corey said. "I'll take it for you right now."

I gave him a look. "Once I have something to wear."

"Grab a shirt from Nic's room," Daniel said. "She won't

mind. It might be a little small but . . ."

"That's fine," Corey said with a grin. "I won't mind either."

It was good to see him grinning, even if there was a hint of desperation in his goofing around. We were all on the edge of panic, trying not to think about what happened in Salmon Creek, what happened to our parents, where we'd go from here.

Still, there was no way I was wearing anything of Nicole's. I'd sooner put on Sam's stuff, even if black really wasn't my color.

I was about to ask Sam if I could borrow something when she came out, phone in hand. Her expression said she hadn't talked to her aunt.

"There's a signal, isn't there?" I said. "They can't block the whole town."

"No, I've got a signal but . . ." She looked up. "Her cell number's been disconnected. I tried a few times."

I took the phone and called my mother. Then my dad. Both times rang through to a message saying the number was no longer in service. I tried a third number plucked from memory—a guy I dated last summer, I think. Someone answered. I hung up.

"The phone works," I said. "But my parents' numbers are disconnected, too."

"Cutting off contact," Daniel said.

I glanced at him.

"Who pays for their cell service? The St. Clouds, right?"

I nodded. "They're on the corporate plan, like every-one—"

Everyone else in town was on the same plan, even if they didn't work for the St. Clouds directly. That was one of the benefits of Salmon Creek life. Free cell service for all. Cell service that could be discontinued or monitored at any time.

"So why did they leave ours—" he stopped. Then he snatched the phone away from me. "We can't use that."

"What?"

"They didn't disable our phones. They must think we could still have them. If we do, and they dry out after the crash . . ."

"We could use them and they could track us." I dropped the phone onto the bed. "We need to get out of here."

Sam picked up the phone and turned it off. "We didn't talk to anyone. It'll be fine."

Daniel hesitated, then said, "We have to get to Maya's place and check the shortwave radios."

Sam's leg wasn't up to the walk. I'd suggested retrieving the truck and trying to zip into the park without being noticed. Daniel said it was too risky. He asked Corey to stay behind with Sam, but clearly Sam wasn't comfortable with that. I suggested Daniel stay. She refused. I didn't like leaving her behind, but that's what she wanted, and she wasn't budging.

The moment I stepped into the park, my eyes filled with

tears. It looked exactly as I'd left it. As we walked along the trail, other than the smell, there was no sign that there had been a fire. It had been veering south when we'd last seen it, but I'd barely dared hope that meant my park had been spared. I knew the animals in my rehabilitation shed were all safe—Mom had transported them to a facility in Victoria when the fire hit—but I was worried about every other creature out there, too.

When we reached the house, I stopped. The Jeep was gone. The windows were dark.

"They aren't here," I said, barely able to get the words past the lump in my throat.

"Let's go in," Daniel said. "Make sure."

The front door wasn't even locked. I stepped inside. The air was heavy and empty. Just empty.

Even Kenjii hung back, as if it was the home of strangers. She gingerly walked through and looked around, sniffing, then stood at the back door and whined.

"I'll get her some food and water," Daniel said.

Corey stayed with him. I went straight to my dad's office. His computer was gone. So were his shortwave radios.

I headed upstairs. Nothing had been touched. My parents' clothing was still there. My stuff was still there. A few drawers were open, in the bedroom and the bathroom, from when Dad must have packed our evacuation bags.

I stood in my parents' room, looking at their hastily made bed, an empty duffel bag taken from the closet, then dumped on the floor, rejected. There was something else on the bed. Picture frames. Three empty ones.

In an evacuation, we weren't supposed to take anything but an overnight bag. Most people would grab other stuff, though. A laptop. Jewelry. Whatever was important to them. My dad had taken their wedding photo and two baby pictures of me.

My eyes burned again. I hurried into the bathroom and turned on the tap. The pipes spit and hissed. Nothing came out.

"Hydro's off," Daniel said as he stepped into the open doorway. "For you guys, no electricity means no water. I found jugs under the sink for Kenjii. Do you want me to bring one up?"

I shook my head.

He moved closer. "We'll find them, Maya. It's just a matter of getting to your grandmother."

"Only we can't do that, can we?" I said. "The St. Clouds and the Nasts will be prepared for that. I need to let her and my parents keep thinking I'm dead until I can . . ."

I took a deep breath. "I don't even know how to finish that sentence. Everything was about getting back here and telling my parents. But they aren't here. I don't know where they are. I have no damned idea what to do next." I looked up at him. "Do you?"

"I . . . I have some thoughts." He cleared his throat. "We'll come up with a plan."

I brushed past him and headed for the stairs.

"Maya."

I turned. He stood there, looking as lost and confused as I felt.

"I'm sorry," I mumbled. "You're right. We'll come up with something. I just . . ." I looked through my bedroom door and out the huge windows at the forest. "I need to go outside for a minute. Just . . . for a minute."

Corey was still in the kitchen when I got downstairs. I brushed past him. Kenjii tried to follow as I slid out the back door. I closed it with a whispered apology.

I ran into the forest. I planned to keep going, get in deep enough to relax and refocus and, yes, maybe feel sorry for myself for a few minutes before I faced the others again. As I was running, though, tears filled my eyes and I nearly flipped over a downed tree.

I swiped at my eyes and I looked at the tree, and I remembered the last time I'd seen it. Remembered who'd sat on it.

Rafe.

Fresh tears. I tried to blink them back, but it was no use. I looked at this place, this tree, and I saw Rafe. Heard his laugh. Felt his kiss. Even smelled him. I closed my eyes and the feeling was so vivid I swore I could just reach out and . . .

But I couldn't. I wouldn't ever again, and as I sat there crying, I didn't think about what I'd felt for him and what might have been. I thought about *him*. The person, not the guy in my life.

I thought about everything he'd told me about his past,

and I wished he'd told me more. I thought of what he'd said to me about his dreams for the future, what he wanted in life, and I realized how little of that I knew. He wanted to fix Annie. Beyond that? I had no idea. Was there a future he'd wanted? One he'd imagined? Or had he just concentrated on the present and getting through it?

Only he hadn't gotten through it. He hadn't fixed Annie. He'd come to Salmon Creek to find me for answers, and I'd gotten him killed. No future. Not for Rafe. Just . . . gone.

I looked down at the leather band on my wrist—his bracelet—and thought, *I don't deserve this.* I was ready to pull it off, climb a tree, and leave it there, in his memory. Then I stopped.

I didn't deserve his bracelet, but maybe I still could earn it. Find Annie, if she was still alive. Help her. Finish what he started.

I took a deep breath and touched the bracelet's cat's-eye stone. *I'm going to fix this. I know I can't*—my breath caught—*can't fix it all, but I'll do what I can.* I promise.

I squeezed my eyes shut and I sent out the promise again, fingers on the stone. I sensed him close by. Felt him, smelled him—

"I knew I'd find you here," a voice said behind me. "Sooner or later."

My heart stopped and I knew I was hearing wrong, that it must be Daniel, come to find me, but my mind was still fixed on—

"Rafe," I whispered.

I turned. He was walking out of the forest and he was grinning and . . . and there was no "and" because that was all I could think.

My eyes shut. I didn't want them to. I didn't care if it was an illusion, I wanted to see him one more time before the vision disappeared and I was left with that last horrible memory of him falling from the helicopter.

"I know I'm looking a little rough," he said. "But I didn't think it was that bad."

His voice came closer. "Open your eyes, Maya," he whispered. "It's me."

TWENTY-NINE

I OPENED MY EYES and when I did, he was right there, and all I could see was his eyes, those amazing amber eyes that I could fall into and—

I stumbled back. "You're not real."

"Mmm, actually, I am. Not a ghost." He brushed his hand over the tops of the tall grasses, making them sway. "Not a zombie either, or I'd smell even worse by now. Not a ghost, not a zombie, just a freaking *insanely* lucky guy."

"I saw you fall."

"The fall isn't the problem. It's the sudden stop at the end. Avoid that and . . ." He waved his hands down his body. "Apparently, you can survive."

"That's not . . . You can't . . ."

"Did I mention the insanely lucky part? Great thing about this island? Really big trees. Gotta love those redwoods, especially when they break your fall. Still it was a helluva hit and I've got the war wounds to show for it."

He held out his bare arms, covered in healing scratches. There were more on his face. I looked at him then, my first good look, as hope started to flutter in my chest.

Except for the scratches and a purpled bruise on his chin, he looked exactly as I remembered. Blue jeans, tank top, faded denim jacket, boots. Black hair curling over his collar. Brown eyes flecked with gold. Crooked smile threatening to burst into a grin.

"Got impaled, too." He lifted his shirt and turned around to show me what looked like a scabbed-over stab wound in his side. "Dislocated my shoulder. Passed out from the pain. When I woke up, the shoulder was fixed—one of the benefits of being a shape-shifter I guess—and the rest was healing. I was unconscious for a while, apparently."

"I . . . I still—"

"Can't believe it?" Rafe shrugged. "I'm guessing a regular person wouldn't have survived. But we're part cat so maybe falls aren't so bad. I think I lost one of my nine lives though." He twisted to look at the stab wound. "Maybe two."

I threw my arms around his neck and kissed him, and when I did, I knew he was real—the heat of him, the smell of him, the feel of him, the taste of him so incredibly real that it surpassed anything my memory could conjure up. He wrapped his arms around me and kissed me back, and it was like every other amazing kiss he'd given me, multiplied ten-fold. I kissed him until I couldn't breathe, and then I kissed him a little more, until I had to pull back, gasping.

"I have *got* to die more often," he said. And he grinned, that incredible blaze of a grin that made me kiss him again.

When we finally pulled apart, he brushed his palm over my still-damp cheeks.

"Your parents are okay, Maya," he murmured. "They've just left. The whole town left."

"I know. That's not . . ." I stepped back, out of his arms, and looked over at the fallen tree. "I came out here and I saw that, and I remembered us . . . You . . ."

He looked startled and . . . something else I couldn't quite put my finger on, but definitely startled, like he hadn't ever thought I'd be crying over him.

"I dreamed you were alive," I said. "You were calling me and you needed help, and I wanted to go but . . ." I swallowed. "It didn't make sense. I told myself you couldn't be, so I didn't, and I'm sorry if—"

"You wouldn't have found me, Maya. If I called you, it was only in my dreams, when I was out cold. I never expected you to come after me. I should be dead." He tugged me into his arms. "I'm just really, really glad I'm not."

He kissed me, and it wasn't like the other ones, all fire and emotion. This one was achingly sweet and when we separated, the look in his eyes was . . . almost sad.

"I—I don't know where Annie is," I said. "I'm sorry. I—"

"Don't be." Another quick kiss, then he put his arm

around my waist and started leading me back toward the house. "We'll figure all that out later. Right now—"

The sliding back door to the house squealed. Daniel stepped onto the deck. Rafe and I were still in the woods, but we could see him, through the trees, and he could see us. He stopped dead. Kenjii raced past him. She barreled down the steps toward us, and gave me a passing lick before jumping on Rafe. He pushed her down, laughing.

"See, I am real," he said.

"Hmm, still not sure," I said. "Dogs are supposed to be able to see ghosts, you know."

"Maybe, but I'm sure that guy can't." As we stepped from the woods, he waved at Daniel, who'd come down to the bottom of the steps and was frozen again. "Though he does look as if he's seeing one." He raised his voice so Daniel could hear. "Yes, it's me. Not a ghost or a zombie or a long-lost twin brother."

"Rafe . . . ?" Daniel started walking slowly across the yard.

"In the flesh. Battered and bruised flesh, but apparently it takes more than a fall from a helicopter to get rid of me."

"Wow. I can't believe it, but obviously . . ." He looked Rafe up and down and shook his head. "Wow."

"Holy hell." Now Corey stood on the back deck, staring.

He came over and we had to go through the whole thing again. Yes, it was Rafe. Not a ghost. Not a zombie. Not a long-lost twin brother. As ludicrous as all those ideas sounded, though, they seemed more likely than the truth—that a guy fell from a helicopter and survived.

"You sure about the twin thing?" Corey said when Rafe had finished.

"Yes, I don't have a long-lost twin brother."

"I do," I said. "Or so I've heard."

Rafe grinned at me. "Yes, but I'm not him."

"Which is good."

"Very good." He squeezed my hand.

"We'll . . . be inside," Daniel said.

"Uh-uh," Corey said. "Romantic reunions are officially on hold, even for guys who've returned from the dead. We're neck-deep in crap here and we need to dig our way out. Or at least come up with a plan." He looked from me to Daniel. "Ideas?"

"I . . . have a couple," Daniel said. "I just need . . . time to think them through."

"Sure," Rafe said. "While you do that, can I tell you mine? I've been here almost a day. Plenty of time to think as I waited for you guys to show up."

"We should head back to Sam," I said. "She's at her place."

Corey nodded. "And I want to know how in hell you not only survived the fall, but made it back here before us."

Rafe seemed a little surprised at how quickly Daniel and Corey bought his "miracle heal" story, until I explained that they knew about the skin-walker thing. I told him briefly about benandanti and our theories of Salmon Creek, so he wouldn't think I'd just randomly confessed to having supernatural powers. Then he gave his story.

How did Rafe make it back so fast? Same way we did. He stole a ride. A motorcycle. In his case, though, he skipped all the steps between. No tortuous trek through the woods—he'd landed relatively close to a town. No attempts to get help, because Rafe wasn't like us. His life experience was closer to Sam's. His mom had sheltered him as best she could from the ugliness of life on the run, but he hadn't grown up in a world where you could stroll into town, ask strangers for help, and expect to get it.

Annie used to have a motorcycle, he said, and she'd taught him to ride it. He also knew how to hot-wire one. I wasn't asking how. Like I said, his life experience wasn't ours.

"And you knew we were alive?" I said as we approached the outskirts of town.

"I knew *you* were alive."

That made me feel . . . I don't know. There was a flutter of happiness at the thought, but some guilt, too, because I'd had the same experience. I'd known that he was alive. Yet I hadn't trusted it.

"Are you going to even ask who else survived?" Corey said. Did I imagine the touch of sarcasm in his voice?

"Well, obviously you guys and Samantha," Rafe said. "I'm guessing . . ." He shrugged. "I'm guessing, um, no one else made it. Not exactly the subject anyone wants me discussing, I'm sure."

"Hayley and Nicole were kidnapped," I said.

I told him the story as we cut over to the Tillson house.

"So you'll want to try to get them back," Rafe said as we crossed the back lawn.

"Um, yeah," Corey said. "Sorry to throw a wrench in this supposed plan of yours—"

Rafe sighed. "Look, Corey, I know you don't like me. Daniel doesn't either, but he's being nice about it for Maya's sake."

"I'm not—" Daniel protested.

"It's okay. I didn't go out of my way to make friends in Salmon Creek. I know that. I acted like an ass, and as Maya may have told you, I had a reason, one that probably still makes me an ass. I'm glad to hear Hayley's okay. Of everyone in Salmon Creek, I treated her the worst, so I'm hoping I get the chance to apologize. I'm glad Samantha is okay, even if we don't get along. As for Nicole? I know her about as well as I know you and Daniel. Which is about one step up from 'not at all.' Of course, I'm glad you're okay. I know you'll want to get your friends back. I'm absolutely fine with that. But if you expect me to be as worried about them as you are, that's not going to happen."

"No one expects you to care about Nic and Hayley as much as we do," Daniel said. "But I am glad to see you're okay."

"For Maya's sake. I know." He waved off Daniel's denials. "I don't expect more. And, chances are, I'll turn out to be an ass after all."

He said it jokingly, but he broke eye contact, and didn't look my way either, just nudged me toward the house. I wondered if it did kind of hurt him, getting a cool reception from the guys.

That reception didn't improve once we got in the house. Rafe was happy to see Sam was okay. Whether you like a person or not, you don't wish them a horrible death. Sam, though . . . Well, I'd spent long enough with her now to realize she was lacking certain filters most of us have.

"So, I guess you'll be moving on, then?" she said. "Got things to do? Places to be?"

Daniel winced. Corey lifted his brows. Rafe only sputtered a laugh.

"Well, at least you didn't say you're sorry to see me alive," he said.

"You know what I mean," Sam said.

"Um, no," I said. "We don't. Rafe just survived a fall from a helicopter and trekked back here to meet us—"

"Meet *you*," Sam said. "And what I meant was that he'll be leaving to look for his sister. Right?"

"I am looking for Annie," Rafe said. "But I can do that with you guys, especially if she's been captured by the same people who have Nicole and Hayley. Maya tells me you have a cell phone. It probably wasn't a good idea to use it, but since no one swooped down while you were waiting here—"

"Which is why I insisted on waiting here." Sam lifted her chin. "If the Nasts were tracking the phone, they'd have come here and found me alone. But no one showed up. Now, Maya, if you can stop gaping at Rafe for a few minutes, we really should come up with a plan."

I glared at her. "I spent three days thinking I'd watched him fall to his death."

"Leave her alone, Sam," Daniel murmured. "This isn't the time."

"I'm just saying it's not the time for *that* either. We need to focus and having Maya moon over Rafe is making everyone uncomfortable."

Rafe grinned. "Doesn't bother me."

"Because your ego really needs the encouragement."

Rafe's grin hardened. "You don't know anything about me or my ego, Samantha. I'm going to ask you to give the attitude a rest for a while. Maya tells me you and Daniel are benandanti, and I remember my mom mentioning them. You guys have a sixth sense for evil. Clearly, I'm not triggering Daniel's radar or he wouldn't let me in the same room as Maya. Am I tripping yours?"

Her mouth opened and I could tell she wanted to say he was, but she closed it again, so hard her teeth clicked. After a moment, she said, "You think you're better than everyone else. You think the rules don't apply to you. You breeze into town, working your charm on all the girls, then walk away when you realize they aren't the skin-walker you're looking for. You find her"— Sam pointed at me—"and you use her, too, but apparently, she's forgiven you. Maya's smart and she's sensible, so maybe I'm trying to figure out why the hell she's with you when there are great guys like . . ." She stumbled, as if searching for a name. "Like Brendan. You've got some kind of hold over her, and I don't like it."

Rafe leaned over and whispered. "It's a love spell I picked up from a witch over in Nanaimo. But don't tell Maya."

"You think you're funny."

"No, I think you have your own issue with me and I think I know what it is. But it has nothing to do with me personally, so I'm going to try not to take it personally. And, while I might be enjoying this—" He lifted his hand, which was still clasping mine. "I know it's as temporary as a love spell. Give it a few hours and she'll hate me again."

"Hate's a strong word," I said.

"Strong emotion is better than indifference." He grinned at me, then looked at the others. "Now, if we can stop bickering for a few minutes, I'll tell you my plan." His gaze moved to Sam. "Which I'm sure Maya and Daniel will change, if they don't outright reject it, and I'm fine with that."

"What did you have in mind?" Daniel said.

THIRTY

R AFE'S PLAN WAS SIMPLE: get us to the mainland. His mom had given him the names of some people there. Supernaturals who had worked on the experiment and then left it. One was a woman in Vancouver.

Rafe hadn't made contact with any of them earlier because his mother had told him to reach out to them only as a last resort. This was, Rafe figured, a last resort.

Sam wanted to leave right away. Rafe thought we should get a good night's rest. Daniel agreed, and Corey seconded Daniel. As the three of us long-time residents pointed out, getting off the island at night wasn't easy.

Next the guys were heading out to find a house we could hole up in—someplace the Cabals wouldn't expect to find us. Sam's leg wasn't up to scouting, and Rafe thought I should stay with her, take a break, get a hot shower, and put on the fresh clothes I'd brought from home. That may have been his nice way of saying I really needed that shower.

As the guys headed downstairs, I called Daniel back. Rafe hesitated even when I waved him on, but after a moment, he went with Corey.

I led Daniel to the master bedroom and closed the door behind us.

"What's up?" I whispered.

"Hmm?"

"You've barely said a word since Rafe showed up. You don't trust him."

"What? No. Of course I trust him. The guy fell out of a helicopter so we wouldn't."

"But something's bugging you. Is it his story?"

"No. It's a miracle he survived, but like you said, he's part cat. They always land on their feet." He smiled, but it was strained.

"Then you don't buy the part about how he got back here."

"I do. He said he left the motorcycle behind the Blender. Easy enough to check. If he was lying, he'd say he ditched it in the woods somewhere."

"Uh-huh. You've thought this through, I see. Which means it's bugging you."

Daniel put his hands on my upper arms and leaned down to look me in the eye. "Nothing's bugging me, Maya. Well, except the fact that our town is empty, and we have no idea where anyone is or how to find them."

I dropped my gaze. "Right. Sorry. You're quiet because you have other things on your mind. I'm worried, too. I know it doesn't seem like it, because Rafe's back and obviously I'm happy about that, so maybe I'm not as focused as I should be. I'll snap out of it."

He gave me a quick hug. "Don't. Something in this whole mess has gone right for you. You're allowed to be happy." He met my gaze. "Okay?"

I nodded.

"Go have a shower and try to relax," he said. "You're going to need your energy, and I'm going to need my co-captain."

I was in the Tillsons' bathroom, still dressed, starting the shower, when I heard a faint click, and I wheeled to see Rafe coming in, holding a card he'd used to pop the lock. His free hand covered his eyes.

"Excuse—" I began.

"Oh, sorry. Didn't know you were in here," he said, his hand still over his eyes as he frantically motioned, apparently trying to stop me from stating the obvious—that he'd *broken* in and knew full well I was here.

I pulled his hand from his eyes, and mouthed, "What the hell?"

"Play along," he mouthed back. "Please."

There was no teasing glimmer in his eyes. They pleaded with me so desperately that I felt a chill in my gut.

I went to turn off the water. He grabbed my arm and shook his head. Then he moved me closer to the shower, leaned in and whispered, "Ask me to join you."

"What?"

He clapped a hand over my mouth and whispered, "Trust me. Please."

I remembered Sam saying she'd stayed behind to make sure her phone call didn't bring someone running. What if it had? What if they'd come while we were gone and cut a deal with her? Or snuck in and planted bugs, and were just waiting for the right time to nab us?

I cleared my throat. "Better not stick around or I might ask you to join me."

Rafe chuckled. "If I thought you were serious, I'd take you up on that. I was just coming in to do a better job washing up. There wasn't any water at your place and my cuts and scrapes are filthy. Guess it'll have to wait."

He waved for me to continue. When I arched my brows, he motioned to us, then to the shower. He wanted us in the shower, where no one could hear our conversation. Which was a little extreme. And extremely awkward. He'd given me a lead-in, though, so I used it.

"No, you really should get them cleaned," I said. "And I should take a look at them. I suppose we can accomplish both if you keep your shorts on . . . and keep your hands to yourself."

He grinned. "Fine by me."

I turned my back and took off my jeans and socks. When I'd finished, he was climbing into the shower. While the view was very nice, my gaze went to his shoulder, to the paw-print birthmark there, a mirror image of the one on my hip.

I hadn't told him about my first shift to cat form. Now, suddenly, I wanted to. Really wanted to. I wanted to share that with him, see his reaction, tease him about beating him to it and hear his laugh—

He turned and waved me into the shower with him. He backed up to give me room, but it was a shower stall—not much room to be had. The hot water beat down, soaking through my shirt. I leaned back into it, forgetting Rafe as I luxuriated in the feeling of hot, clean water.

When I opened my eyes, he was watching me. Really watching me. I looked at the water pounding off his lean chest, trickling down to his soaked boxers, and . . . and I wasn't thinking it'd be nice to lean over and give him a chaste kiss. Really wasn't.

I was sure this would be a scene I'd lock away to replay when I was alone, but for now, I couldn't cross that space between us. He'd brought me here to tell me something, and even if he hadn't, I wouldn't cross it, because that would lead to places I wasn't ready to go.

You don't make out half naked in a shower with a guy if you aren't planning on going somewhere with it. Actually, you shouldn't *be* half naked in a shower with a guy if you aren't planning on going somewhere with it. But under the current circumstances, normal rules didn't apply.

I eased forward and leaned up to his ear. "Is this what you wanted?"

He chuckled. "Mmm, I'd better not answer that." His gaze traveled down me, then zipped back to my face. "Sorry."

"Focus, Rafe."

"I am. Just on the wrong thing." He leaned in to kiss me, but pulled back sharply, his face twisted in a look of pain, like he'd just been jabbed in the back.

"Are you okay?"

"No. Not really." His look then was so wistful I felt that chill again. Then he leaned down to my ear and whispered. "It's a trap."

"Sam?" I whispered. "You think they came while we were—"

"No. Not Sam."

"Then . . ."

I looked up into his face and saw the pain there, his eyes dark. Then I looked out the shower door at his clothing, dropped in the far corner of the bathroom.

If he'd just wanted to talk to me in private, he could have gotten me aside easily. Just let me come with them to look at houses. Talk to me in one of them. Or in the forest. But he'd been the one who'd wanted me to stay behind. Who'd suggested I take a shower.

I looked at his clothes again and whispered, "They're bugged."

He didn't reply, but I saw the answer in his eyes. I backed toward the door. He caught me and slapped his hand over my mouth, then leaned down to my ear. Water trickled from his hair onto my shoulder.

"I won't let them take you, Maya," he whispered. "I swear I won't. I'd never do that."

He pulled me back under the spray and spoke against my ear. "They grabbed me when I got to town. It's the St. Clouds. They have Annie. Either I help them or they won't help her. I . . . I had to, Maya."

His eyes pleaded with me to believe him. I did. Annie meant everything to him. If they had her, he'd go along with any plan to save her. But that didn't mean I didn't feel like I'd been betrayed. By someone I'd finally trusted.

"I know this means it's over," he whispered. "I got a second chance, and I blew it, and I . . ." He swallowed and turned his head, his expression hidden behind the curtain of water. "I'd give anything not to do that. I would, Maya. I know you don't believe me, but it's true."

When I pushed past the pain of betrayal, I did believe him. Because he'd let go of my hand as we dangled from that helicopter. Because he'd been ready to die to save me. And because even if he wasn't looking me in the face, I could hear the pain in his voice.

"It's going to be okay," he said. "I wouldn't let anything happen to you. I have a plan and you'll be safe."

"And the others?"

"Them, too." He looked at me again, still close enough to whisper through the pounding water, close enough for me to feel the heat of his breath. "I know that's just as important to you, and I swear everyone will be okay. For now, though, you need to go along with the plan. It's the only way we'll get out of this place. And you can't tell the others."

"What?"

He gripped my arms and pulled me even closer, gaze locked on mine. "They need to act like everything's okay, so you can't tell them. Not even Daniel."

I backed up, freeing myself.

"That's the deal-breaker, isn't it?" he murmured. "Daniel."

"I trust—"

"I know you do. But I don't, and not because I think he's untrustworthy, but because I don't know him well enough to be sure he won't screw up. The only person I trust is you."

Then trust me when I say you can trust him. But that was asking too much, because if the situation was reversed, I'd say it was unfair. I trusted him. But would I put my family's life at risk if he gave his word that someone else could also be trusted? No.

"If things go wrong, I have to tell him," I said. "If he's in danger, I have to warn him."

Rafe hesitated, then nodded.

"There's no woman in Vancouver is there?" I said as I

pushed back my wet hair. The water was cooling now. "No contacts your mom gave you."

"No, that's a story they fed me. But we're going to follow it, because getting you guys to Vancouver is the best chance you have."

You guys. Not us. Best chance *you* have. Not we.

"When we get to Vancouver, you'll pretend to suddenly realize it's a trap," he said. "You'll turn on me and you'll run, and leave me behind."

"But they'll—"

"They'll catch me. I know. It's the only way. They'll think I did my best, so Annie will be safe. I wish—" He looked away, then leaned toward my ear again so I couldn't see his face. "There's no other way. Annie needs me. And you . . . you don't. Not like that. You can look after yourself and . . ." He straightened and gave me a crooked smile. "By then you'll be happy to be rid of me, I'm sure."

I leaned forward and whispered, "No, I won't."

Then I kissed him. Just a kiss, my hands still at my sides. When I pulled back, he looked stunned. Then he rubbed his mouth and said, "I know that just means you understand. At least, I hope you do."

"I do."

I understand that you had an impossible choice to make. I understand that I couldn't be that choice. It had to be both of us—Annie and me—safe, and what you wanted didn't matter. Just like when you let go of my hands in the helicopter.

I said the same words he'd said to me before he'd let go.

"It's okay."

A twisted smile. "No, not really. But it'll be okay soon. Or as close as it can get."

THIRTY-ONE

R AFE LEFT THEN. GOT out, dried off, dressed, and slipped away before anyone caught him. I washed in the now-cool water. Or I think I did. I couldn't remember doing it, though the walls were flecked with suds when I got out.

I'd forgiven Rafe for what he'd done. I suppose that surprised me a little. But he really didn't have a choice. I couldn't hold that against him.

Back when he'd told me why he'd come to Salmon Creek, I hadn't forgiven him nearly as quickly. There had to be a better way to find the other skin-walker, I reasoned, one that didn't hurt the feelings of every girl in town. But a lot had changed since then. A lot had changed in me, and even if I still thought *I'd* have found another way, I understood that he'd done his best, that he regretted any hurt he'd caused.

This time, I wasn't even sure there was another way.

That didn't mean I was okay with it. Okay with his decision, yes, as painful as it was. What I wasn't okay with was the overall situation. We were sitting in a trap. The St. Clouds—and maybe even the Nasts by now—were out there, watching us and listening. And there wasn't a damned thing I could do about it because Rafe was right—we needed to get to Vancouver, where we could lose ourselves in a metropolis. Until then, we had to act like nothing was wrong. No, *I* had to act like nothing was wrong. The others couldn't know.

But Daniel . . . Daniel wasn't just "the others." Not telling him felt like a betrayal. It *was* a betrayal. I'd told Rafe that I wouldn't, but the more I thought about it, the less certain I was I could keep that promise.

We gathered food and supplies from the other houses. As for money, I'd cleared out the emergency stash my parents had forgotten, and even if I knew they'd want me to have it, it still kind of felt like stealing. The others did the same, taking money from anyplace they knew their parents hid it. We all had bank cards, too—all except Rafe. We agreed to take out the maximum just before we got on the ferry.

Would our accounts be blocked? We didn't know. If not, would the banks alert our families? Would our parents think some ghoul had taken the cards from the crash wreckage? Or would they realize how unlikely that would be—not only finding our cards but our PINs—and would that make them consider the possibility we were still alive? I hoped so. God, I hoped so.

We decided to stay at Principal Barnes's house. He had a ten-year-old son and a daughter in the grade below us, so there were three bedrooms, plus a sofa bed. Daniel wanted the sofa bed, so he could sleep on the main level, in case anyone broke in. I'd get Kenjii to stay with him, as backup.

Sam and I took the kids' rooms. Both had just single beds, and I'd suggested Sam and I could share the master room instead, but Rafe said no. Give that to Corey and he'd use the futon in the covered back patio and guard the back door.

Did he need to sneak out and report in? Maybe. We'd barely spoken since the shower. Or, I guess, I'd barely spoken to him. I couldn't stop thinking about his clothes being bugged.

I was heading to bed when Daniel appeared. "Is everything okay?" he whispered when we were inside my room with the door closed.

"Sure."

His look called me a liar. "You and Rafe. Something's up."

I hesitated and the urge to tell him everything was so strong, I had to clamp my jaw shut.

"No," I said quickly. "Everything's fine. I just . . . It's a little much right now. I thought he was dead, and he isn't, and . . . I'm feeling a lot of things." Which was the truth.

"Okay. I just wanted to make sure there wasn't a problem."

There is. There's a huge problem. And I should tell you. If anything goes wrong and you get hurt, I'll never forgive myself.

"No problem," I said. "I'm just confused and exhausted and worried about my parents, and really hoping we'll get somewhere tomorrow."

"We will."

I lay in bed and stared at the wall. Rafe had put me in an impossible position. If I didn't tell Daniel, what did that make me? The kind of girl who fell head-over-heels for a guy and forgot her friends? Who'd put her new boyfriend ahead of those who'd been in her life for years?

Where did my loyalty lie? Part of me wanted to say "with Rafe." He'd been willing to die for me. Now he was giving up his freedom for me.

But where did my loyalty really lie? There was no question. With the guy who'd been by my side since I was five. Who'd watched my back since I was five. Who'd suffered with me through Serena's death and Rafe's supposed death and everything else. The guy whose own loyalty I never questioned.

I had to tell Daniel.

I waited until everyone was asleep, then crept downstairs. Through the living room doorway, I could see Daniel on the sofa bed, Kenjii lying across his feet. She lifted her head, but I put out my hand, telling her to stay, and she lowered it again.

I walked to the covered porch. Rafe was on the futon, still dressed, no blankets or pillow, sleeping with his head on his arm. It was chilly, with the cold night air seeming to blast through the window glass. I found a blanket folded by the wood-burning stove.

I went back to Rafe, unfolded the blanket, and crawled in beside him.

He woke as I was pulling the blanket up over us.

"Maya?"

I put my fingers to my lips and lay down. When I opened my mouth, he put his hand over it and waved at himself, reminding me that he was still wired. Then he leaned to my ear again, his voice so low I'd never have heard it without skin-walker hearing.

"I have to sleep with my clothes on. But I know why you're here. Daniel."

"I—"

He covered my mouth again and whispered in my ear. "You need to tell him. I was hoping you wouldn't . . ."

He trailed off, but stayed by my ear, so I couldn't see his expression. I knew what I'd see if I did, though. Disappointment. Hurt.

"I'm so sorry," I whispered.

He hugged me. A tight hug. Fierce. Then his lips went to

my ear again. "Don't be."

I tried to look away, but he caught my chin and kissed me and it was such a sweet kiss, and I felt so guilty, like I'd betrayed him, and my throat seized up and tears trickled down my cheeks, onto his.

He pulled back and looked surprised, then wiped the tears away with his thumbs, holding my face in his hand.

"It's all good, Maya," he whispered. "I mean that. I see how you and Daniel are, and I want you to trust me that much, but I know I have to earn it and I've done a crappy job so far. Still you trusted me enough to tell me first. That's a start. A big start."

He bent down and his kiss was so full of longing that tears pricked my eyes again. When another one rolled down my cheek, he wiped it away.

"No more of that," he said.

"I'm just—"

"I know." His lips moved to my ear. "So am I."

I put my arms around his neck and hugged him, face buried in his neck, and he hugged me back, making no move to kiss me again, just holding me. Then he put his lips against my ear and whispered, "I'll find a way to get back to you, Maya. I promise." I knew he *couldn't* promise, neither of us could promise, but in that moment, I let myself believe it, and I curled up against him, closed my eyes, and fell into the first deep and dreamless sleep I'd had in a week.

᭜   ᭜   ᭜

Rafe woke me in the morning.

"Sorry," he whispered. "But I can hear Kenjii moving around, and if Daniel comes in and finds you here, it won't matter that we're both fully dressed. I'll get my ass kicked."

I shook my head. "He wouldn't. What I do with you is my business."

"Mmm, still pretty sure there'd be ass-kicking if he found you in my bed."

I snuck out. Time to talk to Daniel. Except he wasn't on the couch. I stood in the doorway, staring at the empty spot.

"Hey, you're up," Daniel said behind me.

I turned to see him in the kitchen doorway, a box of cereal in his hand.

"No milk, but they do have Froot Loops. I know you love Froot Loops."

"Thanks." I took a step toward him. "But first I need to—"

Corey came bounding down the stairs. "Did I hear the breakfast bell?"

"Food's all gone," Sam called from the kitchen.

Daniel backed up, disappearing from view. I hesitated.

"What's up?" Corey said.

"Nothing. Just . . . the Froot Loops are mine."

"Not if I get them first."

After breakfast, Rafe distracted the others while I led Daniel into the garage.

"It's about Rafe, isn't it?" he said as we settled on the garage steps.

I nodded. "I have to talk to you and you're not going to like it."

He exhaled. "Yeah, I already know what it's about."

"You do?"

"I'm being a jerk to him. He tried to talk to me about wrestling at breakfast, and I blew him off. We all keep complaining that we don't know him, but when he tries to get to know us, we shut him down. I'm sorry."

"That's not—"

"I have nothing against the guy. I don't know why I keep . . ." He rolled his shoulders and rubbed the back of one as he made a face.

"Bad sleep?"

"Yeah. But we're *all* stressed and worried and tired, and that's no excuse for being a jerk to Rafe."

I stretched my legs, then took a deep breath and said, "Actually, I might know what's setting you off with Rafe. That's what I wanted to talk about."

He didn't answer, and when I glanced over, he looked shocked. Shocked and . . . something else. Before I could get a better look, he turned away.

"I don't have a problem with Rafe, Maya."

"Well, I do," Sam said as she opened the door.

Daniel clambered to his feet.

"You *do* have a problem with Rafe, Daniel," Sam said. "We all do."

"This is a private discussion," Daniel said.

"Not if it's about Rafael. Everyone's pussyfooting around and I'm tired of it. The guy is an asshole and—"

She followed our gaze and turned to see Rafe standing behind her, arms crossed.

"What?" she said. "You don't think I'd say this to your face? I will. You're a self-centered jerk, Rafe Martinez. You've got everyone convinced that you sacrificed yourself for Maya and Daniel, but that's crap. You didn't let go. You slipped. Maya wanted to believe there was more to it, so she convinced Daniel—"

"She didn't convince me of anything," Daniel said, his voice low. "I was there, too, Sam. He let go."

"So? He's not actually dead, is he?"

Rafe sputtered a laugh. She glowered at him, then at Corey, who'd joined them, grinning as he heard. Even Daniel had to wipe away a smile.

"What?" she said. "He isn't."

"The, uh, fact that he survived his heroic sacrifice really shouldn't be held against him," Daniel said. "Look, I'm fine with Rafe—"

"No, you're not. Heroic sacrifice or not, he's still a jerk. He waltzed into Salmon Creek and stole Maya."

"*Stole?*" I said.

"It's not your fault. You two are both skin-walkers. It's animal magnetism. You can't help yourself." She glared at Corey, who was cracking up behind Rafe. "Stop that. You know it's true. Maya's too smart to fall for an arrogant, self-centered—"

"Enough," Daniel said.

Sam sighed. "I know you're trying to be fair, Daniel, but you need to stand up for yourself, not let this smirking bad boy wannabe waltz in and—"

"Enough!" Daniel's roar made everyone stumble back. He climbed the steps and stopped in front of Sam. "I don't know what your problem is, Sam, but you've now insulted everyone here except Corey."

"Oh, she already zinged me," Corey said. "I started rubbing my temples and she suggested I don't really get headaches. It just hurts me to think."

"It was a joke," Sam said, flinching under Daniel's scowl.

"Inside," he said. "Everyone. We need to leave. Now."

"But—" I began.

Only Rafe heard me. He tapped Daniel as he passed. "I think Maya still needs to talk to you."

Daniel turned.

"I do," I said. "It'll only take a minute."

"We'll talk on the way," he said. "We really need to get going, and if Corey's getting a headache—"

"It's not bad," Corey interjected. "I'll be—"

"You won't be fine. We need to look after that first. Now,

everyone, grab your stuff and let's go."

After they'd gone by, Rafe came back to me, still standing on the garage steps.

"When we reach the highway, say you need a pit stop," he whispered, lips at my ear. "I'll distract the others and you can take him aside."

"Thanks. I know you'd rather I didn't tell—"

"I've gotten used to the idea. And you want to tell him, which is more important."

Corey shouted, "Come on, you two," and I hurried in to make sure he took his pills before we left.

THIRTY-TWO

WE TOOK THE TRUCK. Corey's mom's SUV would have been more comfortable, but also extremely recognizable with the police logo. Not that it mattered, since we were already being tracked, but I could hardly say that.

Daniel drove. I rode shotgun. I'd tried to get Sam to take that spot, so her leg would be more comfortable. She'd refused. We opened the window into the topper, though, so we could talk, and left the curtains open.

We took the worst of the back roads. Again, that wasn't necessary. Again, I couldn't say so.

Daniel was driving along an empty dirt road when a service truck pulled out in front of us. He eased off the gas.

"It's okay," I said. "It looks legit."

"So did the fire-and-rescue—"

The truck swerved suddenly, swinging around until it blocked the road.

"Reverse!" Corey yelled.

Daniel had already put the truck into reverse and it was spinning backward. Then he hit the brakes hard enough to send everyone flying.

I looked in the side mirror to see two vans blocking the road behind us.

"They've boxed us in," I said.

Rafe was on his knees, peering out the rear window on the topper. When he turned, I could see genuine shock in his eyes.

"They didn't trust you," I murmured.

"What?" Daniel said.

"Nothing, just— Is that a lane? There! Go down there!"

He did, but as he turned into the lane, I realized it was a driveway.

"Doesn't matter," Daniel said, hitting the gas. "I'll get us as far as I can."

As he rocketed along the lane, I scanned the surrounding forest for any opening big enough to drive through. There wasn't one. Just narrow tracks, ending at a cottage, trees hemming in all sides.

"We're going to have to run," Daniel said. "Everyone out! Into the woods! Split up!"

As we scrambled out, I yelled, "Sam! She can't run."

Daniel swore and raced around to the rear. Corey and

Rafe were helping Sam down.

"Go," she said.

"Corey and I can carry you," Daniel said. "Just grab on—"

"Then three of us will get caught instead of one. Go."

She pushed Daniel. When he hesitated, she shoved him hard enough to knock him off his feet.

"You know it's the right thing," she said as he scrambled up. "They won't hurt me. Without you, I'm the only benandanti they have."

We didn't know that, of course. But she was right that we'd never escape carrying her.

"We'll come back for you," Daniel said.

"After you have backup, please. No offense, but you guys aren't up to fighting these people."

Daniel nodded. "But we will come back."

"I know." She hugged him. It was an awkward, one-armed embrace that caught him off guard. She pushed him away before he could say anything. Then she turned to me. "Look after him. Don't let him do anything stupid."

"I will."

When I looked for Rafe, he wasn't there. Then I saw him jogging back from the woods.

"Debugged," he said to me.

Daniel gave us a look, but I couldn't explain then.

We ran into the forest just as the service truck was on us. Kenjii brought up the rear, herding us. When a man shouted, she wheeled and snarled. Then she charged.

"Kenjii, no!"

The shot hit her square in the chest and she reared up, toppling over backward and hitting the ground, and if Daniel and Rafe hadn't both been holding me back, nothing would have stopped me from going to her. But they held me and all I could do was fight and scream at them to let me go, until Daniel said,

"It's a dart, Maya." He pointed at her, struggling to rise. "Just a tranquilizer dart."

That stopped my heart from pounding, but it didn't mean I wanted to abandon her. They had to drag me away, Corey helping, until I heard someone say, "Load the dog in the back with the girl," and I knew there was nothing I could do.

So I ran, stumbling at first, still seeing Kenjii lying in the dirt, struggling to rise. Daniel kept me upright and kept me moving.

"They aren't following us," Corey said. "*Why* aren't they following us?"

"They know it won't be hard to find four kids tearing through the woods," Rafe said. "Daniel's right. We need to split up. Better than that, we need a target. One person to make more noise than all the others put together. That'd be me." A wry smile my way. "I'm good at causing trouble."

"It'll work better if there are two targets," Corey said. "Rafe and I go separate ways. We make noise. You two keep going. We hope that splitting their attention means no one gets caught."

"I'll do it," Daniel said.

Corey thumped him on the back. "I know you would, but you and Maya are our best chances of getting help. Don't worry—I don't plan to get captured. We'll meet you guys . . ."

"At the ferry," I said. "They won't expect us to follow the same plan."

"But how would they know what we had planned?" Corey said.

"They must have planted bugs," I said quickly. "Maybe in the house or in the truck. We'll meet at the ferry. They won't expect that."

Before they left, I took Rafe aside. "Will you be coming back?" I whispered.

"They double-crossed me. I don't know what that means for Annie." His eyes darkened, but he shook it off. "I can't trust them. Better I come with you, and try to rescue her."

"Good. I mean—"

"I know what you mean." He turned to leave, then came back with a folded note. He shoved it in my pocket. "Just something I was going to give you before I left."

He jogged away. Then Daniel and I took off. We moved as quickly as we could, making the least amount of noise possible.

"They know everything," I said finally. "The St. Clouds. They—"

"—had Rafe bugged. He told you."

I glanced back, but his face was expressionless. Intentionally expressionless.

"The St. Clouds caught him coming into Salmon Creek," I said. "They have Annie. They used her to get him to trap us. But that's not what happened here. He was supposed to get us to Vancouver so they could grab us there. Once we arrived, I was going to turn on him, say I knew he was working with them. We'd take off. They'd think he'd done the best he could. That was the plan."

I looked back again. Daniel's face still wasn't giving anything away, but he nodded, as if he understood.

"Obviously they figured out what he was doing," I said. "Or they fed him a false plan, so they could make sure he didn't double-cross them." I stopped and turned around. "I'm sorry, Daniel. I tried to tell you."

He paused, then swore. "Back at the house."

"I should have tried harder. I'm sorry."

"You did try hard. I was too distracted to listen. It wouldn't have changed anything anyway. We have to keep going." He turned me to the west. "We'll head toward that ridge. Find a place to hole up."

As we raced toward the ridge, I heard a cry. Then a shout. Rafe? Corey? There was no way of knowing. When a second shout rang out, I told myself they hadn't both been captured, but I wasn't sure I believed that.

Daniel and I kept running. We could see the ridge now. Safety. Just get—

Something whizzed past me.

"Dan—!" I whirled, shouting a warning, only to see him stagger backward, a dart embedded in his shoulder. Another zinged past my arm. Daniel yanked me to the ground. We crawled into thick bushes.

I tugged the dart from his shoulder. He blinked hard, eyes unfocused. He shook his head to clear it.

"I'm fine," he said. "Just a little woozy. Must not have gone in deep enough."

I scanned the ridge, and I caught a flicker of light reflecting off metal.

"Sharpshooter," I whispered. "But you can't do that with tranq darts."

"These people can resurrect extinct supernatural races, Maya," Daniel whispered. "I think their technology goes a little beyond the norm."

"Right. Okay." I took a deep breath. "Follow me."

I started crawling through the brush. I'd gone only a few steps when I realized Daniel wasn't behind me. I turned to see him on his stomach, blinking hard.

"Nope," he said. "It went in deep enough."

I scrambled back to him.

"Go on, Maya," he said.

"No."

Ignoring his arguments, I tried to lift him, arm over my

shoulders. When that failed, I tried dragging him from the bushes, pleading with him to help me, to just get himself a little ways away from where he'd fallen, *please* just a little ways. But he was almost unconscious, fighting just to keep his head up.

"Go on, Maya," he said, words slurring. "Remember what we said. Only one has to get away."

"Then it'll have to be Rafe or Corey. I'm not leaving—"

"They got Rafe and Corey. You know they did. Go."

I shook my head. "I won't."

"One of us has to get away." He managed to look up at me, his eyes so unfocused I knew he couldn't see anything. "Please, Maya. Go."

He dropped then, a dead weight, falling on his side. I could hear a team coming.

"I'm sorry," I whispered. "I'll make it up to you." I bent and kissed Daniel's cheek. Then I left.

THIRTY-THREE

O NLY I DIDN'T LEAVE. Not the way he wanted. I couldn't.
I hunkered down nearby as two strangers
retrieved Daniel. They said nothing, just loaded him
onto a stretcher and carried him away. Two others continued
the hunt for me. I waited until they had passed, then hurried
after the stretcher.

They took Daniel back to the cabin. I prayed this meant
they'd set up camp there, so that would be where they'd hold
the captives. Of course that would be too easy. I arrived to
see them loading Daniel into the back of the van. They were
talking to someone inside.

"—find the Delaney girl," a man said.

I recognized the voice that answered. Dr. Inglis, head of
the laboratory in Salmon Creek.

"Once Maya's in the forest, she's gone," she said. "She's

as at home there as any wild animal. Our only hope was to catch her with one of the others." She sighed. "We'll give it a few minutes. Then we're pulling out. The helicopter is waiting back in town. I'd like to get these kids on it before they wake up. That gun doesn't carry a big enough dose to keep these guys out long and Bryant took the rest."

I peered out at the setup. Just the one van. Had they already taken Sam and Kenjii?

I had to make sure that van didn't leave. Give Daniel time to wake up. If I could put a hole in one of the tires, maybe two, that would stop them. I just needed—

My arms ached. I rubbed one absently, and felt the muscles knot. When I looked down, they were moving under my skin.

Not now. Please not now.

I took a deep breath. Nothing to worry about. This had happened before and it didn't go anyplace. The only time I had shape-shifted, I'd been asleep. Just ignore it and focus—

My legs gave way, like someone yanked them from under me. I crashed to the ground.

"What was that?" the man said.

"Deer, probably," Dr. Inglis said. "But go check it out."

I tried to get up, but my legs wouldn't obey. The muscles kept spasming and seizing, and it was all I could do to keep from gasping. Still, I managed to pull myself deeper into the undergrowth.

"Nothing," the man said.

I collapsed, body convulsing, the world going dark as my mind slid toward unconsciousness.

No, please no. Not now. Please not now.

I panted for air, my body wracked with sudden fever. I tugged at my shirt.

Right. I had to get my clothing off. If I was going to shape-shift, I had to get everything off, and it gave me something to focus on, to stay conscious.

Undressing wasn't easy. The signals from my brain seemed to short out on the way to my hands and my body kept jerking. When I finally fumbled most of my clothes off, I blacked out.

I came to, stretching, body aching. When I reached out a hand and saw a paw instead, I leaped onto all fours and peered through the trees, heart pounding, certain I'd see an empty driveway.

The van was still there. I lowered myself to my belly and crept through the undergrowth.

"—really have to get going," Dr. Inglis was saying. "I don't want those boys waking up."

"Let me check in with the team one more time."

I reached the tree line and looked out. How was I going to rescue anyone now? I couldn't open the van door. I couldn't slash the van's tires—

I stopped and lifted a paw. My claws shot out. I let out a soft chuff.

That made it easy.

I started forward, gaze fixed on the rear tire, farthest from where Dr. Inglis and the man stood—

I stopped. So I slash the tires and then what? Fight them all? Including the team out in the woods?

Time to reconsider.

I retreated to a tree, dug in my claws, and started to climb. I got about five feet off the ground before realizing I was forgetting something.

I headed back into the woods to get what I needed, then I came out and climbed the tree. There was a branch a few feet from the top of the van, but I went higher, so I'd be hidden. I stretched out on the limb to wait.

"They're still looking," the man said as he signed off the radio.

"The boys are going to wake up any second—"

"I know. I told them we're leaving. They can keep looking for the skin-walker girl."

"Her name is Maya," Dr. Inglis said.

The man shrugged. As they got into the van, I crouched on the branch, tail behind me like a tightrope walker's pole. When my balance was right, I leaped, aiming for the limb overhanging the van, but I wasn't that agile yet. I caught the branch, slipped, and struck the roof with a bang as the van started backing up.

The driver hit the brakes. I flattened myself on the roof.

The man rolled down the driver's window and peered into the side mirror. Dr. Inglis did the same on the passenger's side.

"Looks like you hit a fallen branch," Dr. Inglis said. "Just back over it."

The van continued down the lane. Then it turned left, heading back to town. Another turn, onto a dirt road so narrow that evergreen branches steepled over it and I had to flatten out again to avoid getting poked in the eye.

I waited until we'd left the other road behind. Then I lifted my big front paw and brought it down on the roof with a thump. When the van didn't slow, I did it again, twice in succession, pounding hard.

The driver eased off the gas. Dr. Inglis's window was still cracked open, and her voice came through it.

"It's the boys waking up," she said. "Hit the gas, not the brakes."

The driver did, the van sailing over the rutted road, me clinging to the top.

I thought of another way to get their attention. But could I do it? I wasn't even sure I knew how.

I closed my eyes, focused all my energy deep in my gut and then—

I let out a scream. A true cougar scream, the nails-down-a-chalkboard wail that sends campers fleeing their tents in the middle of the night.

The driver hit the brakes. And I went sailing along the

roof, my claws scraping uselessly across the metal, the clothing I'd retrieved fluttering around me, blocking my vision as I tumbled over the front of the van and hit the hard-packed dirt.

I lifted my head, dazed, and found myself staring into the grille. The driver slammed the van into reverse and the vehicle jumped back, ready to make a fast getaway.

"No!" Dr. Inglis shouted. "It could be Maya."

The van stopped. It idled there as they argued inside. I heard the word *gun* but that was all I caught because as they talked, I was creeping past the van.

When I reached the back, I started to run. Dr. Inglis shouted. The doors opened as they leaped out.

I didn't go far before I swerved, then ran full tilt at the van, back legs propelling me so fast the road sped by in a blur. Then I launched myself.

I didn't think I could make it. Leaping hurdles was one thing. But jumping high enough to land on a van roof?

I actually went too high and landed so hard the whole van quaked under me. I planted my paws, lowered my head, looked at the driver, and let out a snarl that sent him stumbling backward. Silver flashed in his hand, but as he raised it, I saw it was just the keys. His other hand was empty.

"Don't startle her," Dr. Inglis said.

"Don't startle—?" he squeaked. "That—that's a mountain lion."

"She has the birthmark. It's Maya."

"I don't care. It's a goddamned mountain lion."

"I know. Isn't she beautiful? A young cougar in perfect physical condition. Did you see that leap? She must have been riding on the roof earlier. She climbed the tree to get on it. Do you know what that means?"

"Do I *care* what that—?"

"She planned this. There's no loss of cognitive function. She's an intelligent young woman in the body of one of the world's finest predators. This is what we've been working toward. This is everything we've dreamed—"

I pounced. I hit the driver in the chest and he went down, keys sailing from his hand and landing in the weeds alongside the road. He punched me in the nose. As a human, that would sting. As a cat, it was like a pile-drive straight to the brain.

I fell back. He started to scramble away. I managed to recover in time to grab his leg and pulled him up short. His hands dug into the dirt as he struggled to get free. Then he lifted a handful of that dirt and tried to throw it in my eyes. I chomped down on his foot. He let out a scream as loud as a cougar's. Blood filled my mouth, rich and coppery and hot.

A gun fired. I let go and wheeled to see Dr. Inglis holding a rifle.

"Please, Maya," she said. "These aren't tranquilizer darts. We don't have any with us. I don't want to shoot you. Can you understand me?"

I snarled at her.

"Everything's gone wrong," she said. "I told them we needed to tell you all the truth sooner. I said the early symptoms had begun and you'd figure it out, but the St. Clouds wanted to fly in themselves to be there when we broke the news. They hesitated and others took advantage. Others who don't care about you the way we do."

I glanced back at the man on the ground, clutching his bleeding foot. I snarled again.

"He's not one of us," she said. "He's St. Cloud security. A nobody. The people who count are the people from the lab, from Salmon Creek. We care about you and we are going to make sure your lives change as little as possible, and only for the better."

I looked at her. She seemed sincere, which meant she didn't know about the deal the St. Clouds made with the Nasts—giving us away. Or maybe she thought it was a ploy, one they wouldn't go through with. I knew better. These were businessmen. She was a scientist, which made her as much of a nobody as the man I'd bitten.

"We'll make sure you're taken care of," she continued. "Make sure you get back to a normal life. All of you. Just like Salmon Creek, only someplace else. They've already found a new location. But you have to show them that you won't fight them. That they don't need men like him." She waved at the security guy. "You need to come with me, Maya. Stop fighting and trust us. I don't want to hurt you."

She didn't. I could see that in her eyes. And I could see

it in the way the gun now dangled at her side. I tilted my head and studied her. Then I started lowering myself to the ground.

"Good. Thank you, Maya. We'll—"

I pounced.

THÍRTY-FOUR

D R. INGLIS STAGGERED BACK, gun still clutched in her hand. It fired. The shot went wild. I hit her and we went down. Her head struck a half-buried rock. Hit it hard. Her eyes widened, and she collapsed, unconscious.

I nudged her. Even opened my mouth and wrapped my jaws around her throat and dented her skin with my fangs. When she didn't move, I let go. I picked up the gun in my mouth and moved it into the long grass, out of her reach.

I turned to see the man inching back toward the other side of the road. Looking for something else tossed into the weeds. The keys.

He was on his stomach. I walked over, caught him by the collar and dragged him off the road. As I did, I could smell the blood, could see it stretching in a trail behind us. He struggled feebly at first, then stopped, and when I dropped him and looked into his face—his skin pale, pupils dilated, breathing shallow—I knew he was going into shock.

I looked at his foot. It was covered in blood. How hard had I bitten him? Harder than I meant to.

And what would he have done to me? Worse. That's how I had to think of it.

As I was wondering how I'd get the van open without hands, my paws started to throb, as if telling me hands were coming soon.

The shift back was easier. Probably because I passed out faster. When I came to, Dr. Inglis was still unconscious on the road. I scooped up the keys. As for my clothing, all I could see right away was my T-shirt and panties. Good enough for now.

I was still tugging my shirt down as I opened the back doors of the van. A thump sounded from within. Then, before I could even see inside, Corey said, "Don't! It's Maya."

I flung open the door to see Corey holding Daniel by the back of the shirt. In one hand, Daniel held what looked like a shard of metal. He let out a relieved sigh and dropped it.

"How'd you know it was me?" I said.

Corey shrugged. "Good guess." His gaze shunted to the side, and I knew it wasn't a guess at all.

No time to ask.

I looked in the van. I couldn't see anyone else, but I looked anyway.

"Rafe's not here," Daniel murmured. "They must have

taken him with Sam and Kenjii."

"So you rescued us on your own?" Corey said.

"Yes," I said. "You were saved by a girl. Horrible, isn't it?"

He slid out and looked down at my bare legs. "Not just a girl, but a half-naked one. Now that's hot. If I'm still unconscious, don't wake me, okay?"

I rolled my eyes and waved them out, then went to find the rest of my clothing.

The guys had been bound, but only loosely, Dr. Inglis apparently not wanting them to get injured on the ride. While I'd been fighting, they'd gotten free.

We used the ropes to tie up Dr. Inglis and the security guy, who had also passed out. We made their bindings light—we wanted to delay their return to town, not leave them in the woods to die.

I wrapped the man's foot, but that was the best I could do. We took their radios and left.

As we climbed into the van, all three of us in the front, I told Daniel they'd taken the others to the helipad. I expected him to say we couldn't go there, couldn't try to save them, but he just nodded and said, "Then that's where we're going," and started the van.

We parked at the ruins of a cottage that had been abandoned years ago, then we slipped through the forest to the far end of town, to the helipad on top of the laboratory.

I knew we were too late when I heard the *whoop-whoop* of the helicopter preparing for liftoff. We ran behind the town hall.

There was a fire escape around back. As kids we used to dare each other to climb it and spy on Corey's mom, always hoping to see some big arrest in progress. There wasn't even a jail cell in the tiny police station. But we'd always hoped anyway.

Now I swung onto that ladder and climbed. Hiding behind the roof peak, I peered out to see the helicopter lift from the pad. I could make out figures inside. At least three heads, plus the pilot.

Someone with dark hair was sitting beside the rear window.

The figure turned. It was Rafe. He shielded his eyes and he seemed to be looking straight at me. I raised my hand. He raised his.

His lips moved, but there was no way I could tell what he was saying. Then another figure leaped across his lap, long black hair swinging.

Annie. She waved frantically, grinning, then disappeared, pulled away by Rafe, quieting her.

I pushed to my feet as the helicopter rose. Rafe reappeared. He flashed four fingers, then a thumbs-up, and I knew that meant everything was all right, or as all right as it could be, that he was okay and Annie was okay, and so were Sam and Kenji.

Then, with one last lurch, the helicopter lifted off.

We took Mrs. Tillson's car. We didn't dare use the van, in case it had a GPS. Maybe the car did, too. Not much we could do about it.

We still had our money, but our bags were lost. Again, nothing we could do.

Daniel headed for Nanaimo. I stared out the window, lost in thought.

"What did he give you?" Daniel asked.

I glanced over at him. "Hmmm?"

"Rafe. He put a paper in your pocket before he left. Was it anything important?"

I'd forgotten all about it. I jammed my hand into both my pockets, certain the note had fallen out. It hadn't—the paper was just folded into a small square and shoved deep.

It was actually printouts. Two pages. Watermarked CONFIDENTIAL.

"Rafe must have grabbed them when he was taken captive the first time," I said. Daniel had told Corey about this earlier on the drive. "They're memos about an escape."

Corey leaned over to read them. "Not our escape, though. Does that say Buffalo?"

Daniel looked over sharply. "Buffalo?"

I nodded. "It's about the experiment that went wrong. Project Genesis. Details of what happened."

"And what happened?" Corey said.

I had to finish reading the first page before I could answer. Then I explained. As we'd guessed, Project Genesis was another experiment with genetically modified supernaturals. Only these ones seemed to be normal types. Well, "normal" in the sense that we'd heard about them before. Witches, sorcerers, half-demons, werewolves, and something called necromancers.

"I've seen them in video games," Corey said. "They control the dead."

"Zombies?" I said.

"Right."

As supernatural types went, that seemed weird, and I suspected there was more to it. According to the notes, some of the kids had problems. So they locked them up in a group home. The kids figured out why they were there and escaped. And apparently came back and destroyed the laboratory, killing Dr. Davidoff and several others.

"Why can't we do that?" Corey said.

"Because we don't know where to find anyone," I said. "Even if we did, we aren't ready for that. They had help. A father and an aunt who'd been in on the experiments."

"So what happened?" Corey asked. "And what does this have to do with us?"

I read the second page. Then I told him.

We ditched the car in one of the big shopping plazas in Nanaimo's north end. From there, we'd hop a city bus to the ferry. Before that, though, I found a pay phone. I put in my money and dialed my grandmother's number in Skidegate.

It rang four times. I knew the machine was going to pick up, and as I waited, I considered what I'd say. I had to make sure she knew it was me, not some ghoul pretending to be her dead granddaughter. I couldn't give any information about where I was. I just wanted to get a message to my parents that I was okay. I imagined what would happen then. I imagined them confronting the St. Clouds, demanding to know where I was, accusing them of lying and threatening to call the authorities.

I imagined how the St. Clouds would react to that.

My grandmother's voice invited me to leave a message. I closed my eyes and listened to her. As I hung up, I whispered "I love you." Then I went back to the guys.

We splurged in the gift shop, buying hoodies. Then we split up to buy the ferry tickets, and didn't reunite until the boat left the harbor.

We stood on the back deck, watching our island fade into the mist. When it disappeared, I took out the notes from Rafe again and reread the second page—details on the subjects who'd escaped. Rafe had added notes at the bottom, about a real contact his mother had given him.

He might know more, he'd written. *Find him. Then find them.*

"Find them," I whispered, shaking my head. "How do we find them if the St. Clouds can't?"

Daniel put his arm around my shoulders as we leaned over the railing, cold mist spattering our faces, our island long vanished. "We try."

I leaned against him and nodded. *Try.* That was all we could do. And we would.

TURN THE PAGE
FOR A
SNEAK PEEK

The **DARKNESS RISING**
series will conclude in a stunning
finale for Maya and her friends—

the Rising

ONE

I WAS RUNNING THROUGH the forest. Running on all fours, huge tawny paws touching down so lightly they seemed to skim the ground. Yet somehow my pursuers were catching up. The pounding of their boots was so close I swore my tail switched against them as I ran.

I couldn't keep this up. Cougars are sprinters, not distance runners. I had to get into the brush, up a tree, someplace, anyplace where I could hunker down, invisible, until they passed, and then—

A dart hit my shoulder. I reared back, snarling, clawing—

"Maya!"

Hands gripped my front legs. No, not legs. Arms. I saw hands wrapped around my wrists, a familiar face in front of mine—wavy blond hair in need of a brush, blue eyes underscored with dark circles, wide mouth tight with worry and exhaustion.

"Daniel . . . ?"

He released my wrists.

Corey's voice sounded to my left. "Um, guys? Causing a bit of a scene here."

I looked around to see strangers staring. A man in a button-down shirt was making his way over, gaze fixed on us. Behind him was a counter stacked with books. In front of me was a computer, while Corey was seated at another beside me.

A library. We were in a library.

The man walked over. "Is there a problem here?" He was looking at me and I wasn't sure why, until he shot a glare at Daniel and I realized how it must have looked, him holding my wrists as I struggled.

"No," I said. "We were just . . . goofing around."

Not the right thing to say in a library. Even Corey—the king of goofing around—winced.

"I'm sorry," Daniel said. "It won't happen again."

As he spoke, he held the librarian's gaze and kept his voice low, calm. Using his powers of persuasion. With Daniel, it really is a power. I don't think the librarian needed it, though. He seemed content to leave us be. But the incident had caught the attention of people around us and, under the circumstances, we really couldn't afford to make ourselves memorable. So we left. Quickly.

"Well," Corey said as we tramped down the front steps. "It's not the first time we've had to leave a library. But it is the first time I wasn't responsible."

"I was having a vision," I said. "I can't control those."

"Uh, no, Maya. Unless you snore during your visions, you were asleep."

"I don't snore." I looked at Daniel. "Tell him I don't snore."

Daniel feigned great interest in the fountain. Corey didn't ask how Daniel would know if I snored. Daniel and I had been best friends since kindergarten. Though our parents had decided sleepovers required separate rooms years ago, we'd spent the last few days sleeping side-by-side as we trekked through the wilds of Vancouver Island. Not a voluntary hiking trip, either. A helicopter crash had stranded us with Corey and three other friends. That helicopter had been supposedly rescuing us from a forest fire that threatened our town, but it'd actually been kidnapping us. Now, less than a week later, we were in the city of Vancouver, only the three of us left, the others captured by the people we were still fleeing.

"You were exhausted," Daniel finally said. "Corey and I slept on the ferry. You didn't. I would have let you keep sleeping . . . but the snoring *was* getting kinda loud."

I aimed a kick at him. He grabbed my foot and held it, making me dance and curse. A passing security guard shot us a warning look.

3 ⚘

"Holy hell," Corey said. "It's a sad day when I'm the responsible one. Speaking of responsibility, I'm going to take the reins of leadership and suggest food. It's nearly eight. Maya, use that cat nose and lead us to dinner."

Yes, my dream hadn't been pure fantasy. I was a shapeshifter. I'd discovered my secret identity about a week ago. Not surprisingly, it marked the point where life went to hell—for all of us.

I wasn't the only supernatural kid in our tiny town. In fact, Salmon Creek seemed to have been built as a petri dish to resurrect extinct supernatural types. Project Phoenix. I was a skin-walker, like Rafe and Annie, a brother and sister who'd come to Salmon Creek looking for answers. Daniel was a benandanti—a demon-hunter. As for Corey, we were pretty sure he had powers, too, but we didn't know what they were yet.

And as for the people chasing us, it was two groups, actually. The St. Clouds—who'd founded our town and Project Phoenix—and the Nasts, a rival supernatural corporation that thought we seemed like valuable commodities. Our friends were now divided between the groups, and we were on the run, trying to find someone to help us get them back. We wanted something else back, too: our parents. They'd been told we'd died in that helicopter crash. I'd been trying very hard not to think about that, what they were going through. I just kept telling myself it would all be fixed soon. It had to be.

We ate dinner in a chain restaurant. It wasn't one we knew, and we'd stood inside the door for five minutes, going over the menu, feeling like country mice in the city. That's nothing new. We grew up in a town of two hundred people. Put us in a metropolis of two million, and it didn't matter that we were private-school educated and wearing the same labels as every other kid—we still felt like hicks.

"This is what we need, guys," Daniel said after we ordered. "A huge city where we can just blend in and lie low for a few days."

"I know," Corey said. "But I feel . . ." He looked around at the other tables and scowled. "It's the St. Clouds' fault. All those years of stranger-danger classes, teaching us that no one outside Salmon Creek can be trusted. They did that on purpose."

"I know," I murmured.

"Teaching us to be afraid of the outside world so we'd never leave, when the real danger wasn't out here at all. It was right there. With everyone who was supposed to be looking out for us. Everyone we were taught to trust. Our teachers. Our doctors. Even some of our own parents might have been in on it. Hell, I'm not even sure my mom wasn't . . ."

He trailed off. I didn't rush to tell him I'm sure she hadn't been a willing participant. We'd already been through this. There were no guarantees.

In Corey's face, bitter and angry, I could find no trace of the guy I'd grown up with, the one who was always grinning, always up to something, never thinking any further ahead than the next party.

I cleared my throat. "So, what did you guys find out while I was sleeping on the job?"

We'd gone to the library to research a name that Rafe's mother had given him to contact as a last resort. We had no idea if this guy could—or would—help us, but it was our only shot.

"Cyril Mitchell is an unusual enough name. I narrowed it down to the most likely guy—the others were too young. I have a phone number, but that's it." Daniel unfolded two notes from his pocket. Scrap paper from the library. He ran his finger down his notes and let out a deep breath. If Corey looked bitter, Daniel looked defeated, and it was just as painful to see.

"It's okay," I said. "We call the number. We talk to whoever answers. That's all we can do."

One of the toughest parts about making that call was picking a pay phone. Not only are they rare these days, but we wanted one a fair distance from where we'd spend the night. Sure, the risk that someone was tapping this guy's phone—or that he was working for the people chasing us—was slight. But right now we only trusted one another.

We caught the SkyTrain and found a pay phone. Then I prepared to call the man we hoped was the right Cyril Mitchell.

While Rafe had been captured the first time, he'd found information about another experiment: Project Genesis. The kids who'd been guinea pigs in that one had supposedly escaped, along with their parents. Rafe was sure Mitchell would know more. If we could find those subjects, maybe they could help us.

I pumped five dollars in coins into the pay phone and dialed.

When a woman answered, I asked to speak to Cyril Mitchell.

"Sorry, wrong number," she said.

I read her back the number I'd dialed.

"That's right, but there's no one named Cyril here."

Before she could hang up, I said, "I really need to get in touch with Mr. Mitchell and this is the only number I have."

"I'm sorry. I can't help you."

My mind whirred, trying to think of something else to say before she hung up. But she stayed on the line. As if she was waiting.

"Do you know any way to get in touch with Mr. Mitchell?" I asked finally.

"No."

So why aren't you hanging up?

If Mitchell knew about Project Genesis and Project Phoenix, both top-secret supernatural experiments, maybe he was on the run, too. Maybe this woman was waiting for something—a name, a code word.

But if he's on the run, why would Daniel be able to find his number so easily?

Maybe it wasn't the right Cyril Mitchell. Or maybe it was and she could tell I was young and I was scared, and didn't want to hang up on me.

I took deep breaths and clenched the receiver.

This was our only lead. Our *only* lead. I couldn't let it slip away.

"I'm going to leave a message," I said. "Just in case." I chose my words carefully. "My name is Maya Delaney. I'm a Phoenix from Salmon Creek, British Columbia."

I paused. It took at least three seconds for her to say, "I'm sorry, but you really do have the wrong number." Which told me she'd been listening, maybe even writing it down.

"Just take the message. Please. Maya Delaney. Phoenix. Salmon Creek. He can contact me at . . ." I read off the email account Corey had set up at the library. "Do you need me to repeat any of that?"

A long pause. Then, "He can't help you, Maya."

My heart thudded. This *was* Mitchell's number. "Can I speak to him? Please?"

"Not without a—" She stopped herself. "He died six months ago. I'm his daughter."

I took a deep breath. Tried not to panic. "Okay. Can you help? Or can you give us the name of someone who can? Please?"

"No." A pause. "I'm sorry."

She hung up.

TWO

W E SPENT AN HOUR trying to call back. We even used different pay phones. She wasn't answering and she'd turned off the voice mail.

We took refuge in a half-constructed condo building. There were plenty of them around. Vancouver had been booming a few years ago, insanely priced condos popping up everywhere, eyes fixed on the Olympics. Then the economic crisis hit and developers fled.

We hadn't said much since our last attempt to call Mitchell's daughter. There was nothing to say except "What now?" and no one dared ask that. When the silence got too heavy, I snuck off to the highest level with a solid floor—seven floors up. I perched on the edge, letting my legs hang over as I stared toward the distant ocean. Toward my island.

I ran my fingers over the worn leather bracelet on my wrist, over the cat's eye stone. Rafe's bracelet, the one he'd given me.

A few minutes later I heard footsteps. Daniel.

He didn't come over and I didn't turn, in case he was just checking on me. I heard him settle behind me. Then silence, broken only by the soft sound of his breathing.

"You going to stay back there?"

His sneakers scuffed the floor as he rose. "I didn't want to disturb you."

I held my hand up behind me, and his fingers closed around mine. I clasped his hand, feeling the heat of it chase away the October chill. He sat beside me, his legs dangling, too.

"We need to find these other subjects," I said. "Project Genesis."

"I know, but . . . At the library, I searched on all kinds of words from those pages Rafe gave us. There's nothing. It's a dead end."

Silence thudded down again. I stared out at the city and tried to rouse myself. We had to move. We had to do something. The thoughts would skitter through my brain, only to be swallowed by a yawning black pit. Move where? Do what? Our only lead was gone and I felt lost. Too beat down to even look up for a spot of light.

"I think we should go to Skidegate and try to contact your grandma," Daniel said.

I looked at him. I wanted to shout for joy and throw my arms around his neck and thank him for giving me exactly what I wanted—contact with my family. But I only had to look at him, his eyes anxious, his face drawn, holding himself still as he awaited my response, and I knew this wasn't about choosing the right path. It was about making me happy. Or making one of us happy. Lifting the dark cloud for one so we could all breathe a little easier. He knew I wanted this more than anything. So he was giving it to me, caution be damned.

"I . . . don't think that would be safe," I said slowly.

"We could make it safe. We'd go over to the Queen Charlotte Islands and make contact with one of her friends, ask them to take her a note. She's a smart lady. If she knows what's going on, she'll find a way to meet us without being followed."

"You've thought this through."

"I've gone over all the options. There's my brothers, but they're too far away and I'm not sure how much help they'd be." His two older brothers were at university in Toronto and Montreal—clear across the country. "Corey's grandparents are in Alberta, but he said they wouldn't understand—they'd call his mom right away."

We couldn't let that happen—if our parents found out we were alive—and we weren't there to warn them—they'd confront the Cabals, not knowing how dangerous they were.

Daniel continued, "I've never met Corey's grandparents,

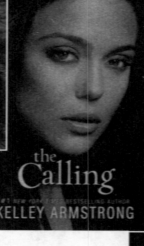